Travel A

M. John Harrison, one of Britain's ⸺
most compelling and imaginative in this acclaimed new ⸺
short stories. Worlds that are bigger inside than outside, love and the loss
of love, characters who destroy themselves by wanting to be more than
they are, the undercutting effect of desire, dreams of escape – all are
explored in fourteen richly textured tales loosely bound together by the
theme of travelling to get somewhere, whether spiritually or physically.

'Harrison's fascination with the metaphysical haunts his stories . . .
Harrison remains a pre-eminent wizard of words, his tricks are simply
more subtle than before.'   *Scotsman*

'Each story reads like a reflection of a parallel universe briefly glimpsed
and remembered. Harrison's prose is unfailingly exquisite and the tales
collected here are wonderfully crafted and a pleasure to read. His work
is often gritty and disturbing, but so too is it poetic and witty. Highly
recommended.'   *Enigma*

'Harrison quietly revels in emptiness, muted memories of loss, scenes of
chill rain and solitude. The collection features a number of pieces that
reclaim the alien and strange from the everyday with a satisfying
absence of cliché as they explore recurring themes of loss, hard-earned
wisdom and the shifting nature of reality. There's genius here – a magic
all his own.'   *Locus*

'There is so much going on in one of Harrison's paragraphs that the
idea of palimpsest occurs. It really is as if there are stories scribbled over
the rubbed-out tales underneath. There are layers and layers and layers.
He's quite remarkable. M. John Harrison is an astonishing writer, and
Travel Arrangements is a deft and dextrous collection.'   *Interzone*

M. John Harrison

Born in Warwickshire in 1945, M. John Harrison was employed as a groom, a teacher and a clerk until the publication of his first piece of fiction in 1966. His novel *In Viriconium* was nominated for the *Guardian* Fiction Prize in 1982 and *Climbers* won the Boardman Tasker Memorial Award in 1989. His most recent novels are *The Course of the Heart* and *Signs of Life*. His short stories have appeared in magazines as diverse as *Omni* and *Harper's*, and he has reviewed fiction and non-fiction for the *Spectator* and the *Times Literary Supplement*. He now lives in west London. *Travel Arrangements* is his fourth collection of short stories.

'Like all good literature, Harrison's stories are worth reading again and again: the more you read, the more you understand.'   IAIN BANKS

'M. John Harrison is a blazing original. His books are fictions of elegant delirium, dark and transcendent by turns . . . A great imaginer and an extraordinary writer.'   CLIVE BARKER

'A cross between John Fowles and Iris Murdoch.'

Independent on Sunday

'M. John Harrison scries the world with a sharp, unforgiving eye.'

PAUL MCAULEY, *Interzone*

'Grittier than Carey and wittier than McEwan.'

Times Literary Supplement

'If you've never discovered M. John Harrison, now's your chance. Far too long the most underrated writer of his generation, he's one of the best we've got.'   *Time Out*

M. JOHN HARRISON

Travel Arrangements

Short Stories

Flamingo
An Imprint of HarperCollins*Publishers*

Flamingo
An Imprint of HarperCollins*Publishers*
77–85 Fulham Palace Road,
Hammersmith, London W6 8JB

www.**fire**and**water**.com

Published by Flamingo 2001
9 8 7 6 5 4 3 2 1

First published in Great Britain by
Victor Gollancz 2000

Author photograph © Nick Royle

ISBN 0 00 654603 X

Printed and bound in Great Britain by
Omnia Books Limited, Glasgow

To Malcolm Edwards

Acknowledgements

Thanks to the editors who encouraged me to write these stories, especially Ellen Datlow, Lindsay Duguid, Nick Royle, David Pringle and Gordon Van Gelder.

'Old Women', *Womens Journal*, 1983
'Small Heirlooms', *Other Edens*, ed. Holdstock & Kilworth, 1987
'The Gift', *Other Edens 2*, ed. Holdstock & Kilworth, 1988
'The Horse of Iron', *Tarot Tales*, ed. Pollack & Thomas, 1989
'Gifco' (in a shorter form), *Metahorror*, ed. Etchison, 1992
'Anima', *Interzone*, ed. Pringle, 1992
'Empty', *Sisters of the Night*, ed. Hambly, 1995
'Seven Guesses of the Heart', *Sorceries*, ed. Kerr, 1996
'I Did It', *A Book of Two Halves*, ed. Royle, 1997
'The East', *Interzone*, ed. Royle, 1999
'Suicide Coast', *Fantasy & Science Fiction*, ed. van Gelder, 1999
'The Neon Heart Murders', *Fantasy & Science Fiction*, ed. van Gelder, 2000
'Black Houses', *The Ex Files*, ed. Royle, 1998
'Science & the Arts', *Times Literary Supplement*, 1999

Contents

Old Women

Elizabeth's first marriage had connected her to some remote part of my family. She had once looked after us for a year or two when I was a boy, one of those colourless, very kind women, always ironing, giving up her character to mine because of some tragedy in her life the family never talked about: a miscarriage, a cot death, an infidelity. In late middle age she suddenly became thinner, more active and independent. Her second husband left her a pension of some sort.

Like her friends she had short, roughly cut hair. They were all vegetarians and this gave them the energy of girls. They wore quilted Chinese silk jackets with a yellow woollen tam o' shanter and a long squarish skirt they had made themselves from some odd black dressy material. (Under this their knees appeared at surprising angles when they sat down.) They went regularly to church, but, to the suppressed fury of the vicar, would not repeat the parts of the creed that offended them. They believed in the power of mussel shell extract, and the imminent arrival of a 'Master' who would come from Venus; they believed that the military aircraft which roared all day a hundred feet above the moor were knocking holes in the atmosphere.

They had an immense faith in people.

'I don't believe those jets can really be said to be knocking holes in anything,' I once challenged Elizabeth.

'Oh but you *do*!' she cried. 'You do believe it. Only you don't realise it yet.'

This suggestion made me look quickly at her face for the signs of an irony I had never noticed as a boy. But it was as open as ever. She simply trusted everyone to come round in the end.

3

'There,' she said. 'What do you think of that?'

She was trying to paint, in acrylic paints on a piece of hardboard, some marguerites which the overnight rain had reduced to damp lumps with a fringe of bedraggled petals. She had taken them out of someone's garden without permission at six o'clock that morning, on her way back from one of her restless walks down by the reservoir, and put them in an enamel vase with four or five elder twigs and a few other drying sticks I couldn't identify. After that she had been heavily influenced by one English post-Impressionist or another.

'Nothing looks uglier, does it, than the remains of something so bright and simple?' she said. 'I despair of being able to love them enough to get them down at all.'

'It's not one of your best,' I agreed weakly.

'When I first came here they grew wild all over the dry bank by the post office, right in among the willow herb and bracken. They were in most of the gardens, too.' She stared at her painting, surprised by an afterthought. 'Nobody seems to bother with them now.'

I was embarrassed by her passion for things, in the way you often are by the enthusiasms of people you have looked up to as a child. She had no objectivity. She filled the house with runny-eyed tomcats she had coaxed in from the dustbins. She re-papered the walls bright yellow, with window blinds the colour of Carnation milk. She wouldn't throw away the weediest geranium cutting. It was contained, like the black kitten juggling madly with a bit of lamb bone in the hall, in the intense sympathy she had for everything in the world.

To temper this she overcharged me so savagely for the two furnished rooms I had at the top of her house that I had to do two days a week at a bookshop in the town to eke out my income. I was supposed to do my work up there under the roof, but it was draughty, and you could hear the starlings buzzing and clicking mechanically to one another in the gutters, so more often than not I would go down to Elizabeth's sitting room on the floor beneath, where she would be waiting for me to light the fire.

4

She could never get it to burn. It had a tiny Victorian grate, the fire basket was broken, the chimney always needed sweeping. When the wind blew from the east, which was when you needed a fire most, it wouldn't draw at all; and it went reluctantly even on a good day, puffing out clouds of tarry smoke while a few flames nosed over the surface of Elizabeth's cheap coal, and smuts drifted about the small room in the weak beams of sunlight. Despite this, we often spent all afternoon there, talking desultorily; and had breakfast there in summer, with the windows open to catch the early warmth. There was a coloured rug, a little carved table, a neat pot of Persian violets. Elizabeth kept most of her books along one wall, though the air always smelled a little of damp and Costa Rica coffee. One morning we had been sitting there for a few minutes when she said,

'I see your friend Ashman has gone to Korea, then?'

I decided to keep my face completely still.

'Oh yes?' I said.

She gave herself some more coffee and folded back the arts page of the *Guardian*. 'It says here he's going out to study their traditional drama.'

I carefully put marmalade on a piece of bread. One of the cats, which had been expecting this move, waddled over and fell heavily on my feet, gazing at me with feigned affection and sending up a haunted smell.

'That doesn't sound like him,' I said.

'Oh, there's a photograph and everything. The National Theatre are sending him, apparently. You can have a look in a minute.'

'I don't think I've got time,' I said. I ate the bread and went to my bedroom.

'Fuck,' I said to myself, staring out of the window. 'Fucking blasted hell.' It was early September. A faint haze lay over the other side of the valley, incandescent where the sun poured down through it. Circling against it were some large birds, crows or gulls. I closed my eyes. 'Ashman's never been inside a theatre in his life,' I thought. A dog was barking in the distance, and I could hear the putter of

5

machinery in the bottom of the valley. I didn't know whether to laugh or cry. 'Good luck to him.'

I had a sudden memory of him years ago, after we had just left university. He was already living in derelict buildings, day-centres and institutions as one of the homeless single men who would eventually provide him with the material for *The Incurables*. He huddled in the doorway of Lewis's in central Manchester to light a cigarette, holding it in one hand at waist level out of the wind, his whole upper body bent protectively over it while he turned it in the flame of the match he held in his other hand. There was an indescribable pallor beneath the dirt on his fingers. He caught me looking at him and laughed. 'Lend me two pounds,' he said. 'I'll pay you back. I want it for a book.' He was reading to some dossers, he said, on the canal bank at night. They built a fire when it got dark and he read to them while they sat round it half asleep. He went into Lewis's and came out with a paperback about Japanese atrocities in World War Two. 'The old bastards love it,' he said. 'They'd beat shit out of me if I gave them anything else. They love this stuff better than anything.'

'You'll be late for the shop!' Elizabeth called up the stairs.

I opened my eyes again.

As I went out she said, 'Have you seen the petals falling off the flowering privet? It looks exactly as if it's trying to snow out there – a few bits of snow coming down on a cold day.'

Then she said, 'Cheer up.'

I hadn't seen Ashman for years. In the shop he looked out at me from the dustwrappers of his early books, the eyes screwed up against a strong light. Thick stubble made the lower half of the face seem grimy. It might have belonged to one of his own subjects: in those days he had cultivated – perhaps as a means of survival, perhaps simply by the accident of being so close to them for so long – their furtive, dispossessed air, and turned it into a badge. Yet when you read *In a Prison Hospital* with its famous closing line, 'All we can do now is watch,' you knew that he was more complicated than that. It was full of fragmentary gestures, abortive movements,

6

half-spoken sentences. You could never say 'the point is this' or 'the point is that'. In those days he made you feel that some revelation was imminent, something that had little to do with our social conscience, or even our society, something about being human that it was intolerable for us, in this century, not to know.

Once or twice a week I met Elizabeth for lunch. She liked the restaurant on the third floor of Marsden's, in Huddersfield. This place, which was entered through the underwear department, would be packed at lunchtime with fifty or sixty old women, crouching among the pot plants on uncomfortable chrome chairs. They wore huge silver crucifixes and imitation silk scarves, neck-braces, velvet turban hats, coats like blankets with voluminous sleeves, and they made a sound like a distant lunatic asylum. Only thick carpets and the vestiges of their own caution muted the shrieks of greed and envy, dismay and growing formless horror.

'Anyway,' they would say to one another, getting up clumsily and staring across the table with groans of covert violence, 'it's really been very nice.'

Pictures by local artists hung in brushed aluminium frames on the bamboo-patterned walls: a famous bridge, under which flowed some curiously gelid water; water again, banking like a race track round the curves of the woodland; and the abandoned railway station in Holmfirth, with its platforms vanishing into a greenish infinity. Curious failures of perspective led your eye into impossible positions behind or to the left of each scene, suggesting that the real world lies oblique to our own.

I was looking up at these one day while I waited for Elizabeth, when I heard a voice say desperately from somewhere near me, 'Lymeswolde. It *is* creamy, but not too creamy.' And then: 'Are all the seats at this table taken?'

'No,' I said, before I could stop myself. 'I'm only saving this one.'

They pushed past and sat down facing me, a middle-aged woman in a smart green tailored suit, and a much older one whose whitish silky hair, parted on one side and brushed back over her red ears, gave her a mannish look, like a retired librarian who writes verse in his spare time and is never quite sure whether to put 'poet' or 'civil servant' on his passport. Throughout their meal they sat very close together, bolt upright, and stared blankly ahead, chewing slowly. The older one made an inadvertent snarl every time the fork touched her lips, though while she was actually chewing her mouth remained pursed tight, as if she was unaccustomed to the workings of her own jaw.

('Food, that is,' I heard someone say at another table, with the air of finishing a sentence begun somewhere else.)

They were eating salad. The woman in the green suit finished first and sat back. She took out of her handbag a thin gold chain, which she ran backwards and forwards through her fingers while a sharp, contented expression crossed her well-made-up face. She smiled at me once or twice, so imperceptibly that it might have been to herself. I couldn't settle with them sitting there. I swilled the remains of my coffee round the cup, wishing Elizabeth would come and rescue me. The woman in the green suit put on a pair of half-round spectacles and, wetting her thumb to separate the pages, began to consult a railway timetable.

'Why on earth have you had your hair cut like that?' she said to me.

'I'm sorry?'

'Is it supposed to make you look rough?'

By the time Elizabeth had arrived, the older one had finished eating and struggled back into her loose grey raincoat. She was sitting with a handbag like a music case on her knees, still staring vaguely into the air ahead of her.

'I'm sorry,' Elizabeth said. 'I got held up at the bus station. Aren't they horrible places? It's something to do with people in queues. All the cheerful clothes suddenly look cheap and shoddy, and the girls who wear them seem so shifty and unhappy.' She smiled at the two women. 'I think I'll have a salad too.'

'Where are all these flies coming from?' said the older woman to her friend.

That afternoon I stared at the blond wood shelves with the strip lights above them, at the biographies of Edith Sitwell and Kingsley Martin and Hugh MacDiarmid; I read the titles of the pamphlets on the Yorkshire Arts Association display stand. 'Ashman is in Korea,' I told myself. 'When he gets back he'll write some fatuous thing about the food and drink there for the *Sunday Times* colour supplement, and his publishers will fall over themselves to buy the book.' Nobody was coming into the shop.

October was perfect, with early frosts, still, transparent air, and a bright blue sky almost incandescent towards the south. Chimney smoke hung in the hollow by the milking shed. Tortoiseshell butterflies repopulated the garden briefly; the cats stalked them in a fury of concentration. Inside, Elizabeth had pot-marigold a thick ochre colour, geraniums pink and red, ageratum with strange purplish flowers like sea-anemones. She painted the window frames in her bedroom. She sent me down the hill to look at some cottages where, she told me, she had seen the ivy 'heaving' with insects: when I got back we read, '. . . the yellow blooms of the ivy itself are full of nectar – the last feeding place of wasps before they die.'

'How depressing,' she said.

She was never lonely. She would put on her German boots and walk for miles across the moors in the direction of Greenfield, where Autumn was well advanced in the sheltered cloughs, bringing back a handful of green acorns. 'Look how *finished* they are,' she urged. 'Like proper little manufactured products! When I was a girl it disappointed me to find there was nothing you could do with them. Children always confuse gloss with usefulness, don't they?' She loved the valley, with its three-storey weavers' houses and its air of decline from some high water mark of prosperity and energy in the '20s, like a slowly emptying bath. She loved it when the farmer's wife drove sheep down the road outside with, 'Kew! Kew! Kew! Kew! Kew! Come on then! Kew! Kew!'; although she was not beyond complaining, especially after some ideological difference with her CND group, 'I've no patience with the local people, none.'

9

Her relatives came from Bacup or Mytholmroyd once or twice a month to tea.

I knew them only slightly, and never felt entirely comfortable with them. Because I was closer to their age then hers I found myself wondering what they thought of my being there.

They never mentioned it. For the most part they were nieces and nephews from her second marriage. They had children of their own now, to whom they had given the brisk practical names you give sheepdogs – Bob and Jan and Sam. One Saturday afternoon just before the weather broke for good, they all arrived at once. The children excitedly rubbed butter into the television screen and knocked over Elizabeth's easel. They were as yet unsteady on their feet: chasing the cats upstairs, they fell from about halfway, screaming with real fear and rage as they bumped back down from step to step. A babble of talk and laughter came from their parents, who had flung all the windows open and were drinking instant coffee at the kitchen table. The air was full of the smell of spilled orange juice. One couple had brought some Sainsbury's pâté and a bottle of home-made wine, but left them for the moment unopened. Above the clatter of crockery I heard someone say,

'Well it would make a bit of a change from camping in the south of France!'

I was anxious to see who had spoken. It turned out to be a blonde girl, a little younger than the rest and wearing faded corduroy dungarees, who had driven over without her husband, in a Morris Minor with NUCLEAR POWER? NO THANKS! stickers. He was at home servicing the brakes of their Fiat, so she had brought the twins herself. 'I thought I might as well.' She looked tired. The twins were about one and a half years old, and when they crawled about on the floor she called, 'Dan! Meg! Oh Dan, what have you done now?' (Her pale exasperated face gave the impression that she found life unsatisfactory and difficult, coming as it had done so soon after teacher-training college. Though, as Elizabeth suggested afterwards, she might just have had the beginnings of a cold.)

'It's not going to be cheap though, is it, Puffa?' said another woman challengingly. This raised a general laugh, and some murmurs of agreement. 'A lot of people will be lucky to get three weeks in Cornwall this year!'

'We thought – well, Peter thought – we'd take a rucksack each, and just wander round. That way we'd only have to find the fare there. We're all for just packing up and going, taking a chance on it. When the package tour people really move in they'll spoil it for everybody. It just won't be the same.'

'But what would you do with the twins, Puffa?' said the other woman. 'The poor little tykes!'

There was a silence.

All at once a foul smell filled every corner of the room. The girl in the corduroy dungarees, who had been looking rather defiantly round the table, raised her head and sniffed, 'Meg? Dan? Oh, you *bloody* little thing!' she shouted. The child stared up at her from its squatting position in the middle of the carpet, smiling weakly and patting the bottom of its plum-coloured velour pants. At this the conversation started up again in a relieved way, with a man's voice saying, 'Oh, we'll manage Cornwall all right. Ally's just exaggerating, as usual.' (There was broad agreement among the men that they would be able to afford some sort of holiday that year: although they would prefer to put in a week's work on the pointing at the back of the house before they went.) 'When's this bottle going to get opened then? Eh?'

I went over and said, 'You're quite right. A friend of mine is out there at the moment—'

'Look,' said the girl in the corduroy dungarees, 'could you just *hold* him a minute while I fetch a nappy, please?' Later, as she got into her car, I heard her tell someone, 'Well, they're going to be blowing the world up soon enough. I don't understand why we can't see a bit more of it before they bloody well blow it up, do you?'

When they had gone Elizabeth stared round at the disorder with an expression I couldn't interpret and said, 'Watching Ben open the biscuit tin this afternoon, I saw his father in him so clearly.' We vacuumed her sitting room. Cool autumn air poured in through the windows, to mix with the smell of lemon geraniums and cigarette smoke. One by one, sniffing the floors and flattening themselves warily at any sudden noise, the cats were coming back from the garden, where they had been having some success with the late insects. 'He has the same extraordinary smile when he thinks he's going to get what he wants.' When I didn't answer she said, 'They were talking about Korea, were they?'

'Yes.'

'Oh dear.'

I thought she was going to add something to this, but she only looked thoughtfully at the shelves of books.

'I'm going down to London when Ashman gets back,' I said. 'Perhaps for good. I feel out of it up here. I just feel as if I'm missing out on it all.'

That evening the temperature fell suddenly, and it rained. A thundery yellow twilight set in. But once or twice before it got properly dark the sun broke through the clouds to silver the water-filled ruts round the farm, and during one of these lulls a flock of starlings was blown like smoke into the field behind Elizabeth's house. For a moment you could hear nothing but their energetic mechanical twittering. You couldn't see what they were eating: each bird pecked around in the mud with a determined but apparently fruitless violence for thirty or forty seconds, then flew to the next field. No sooner had the stragglers arrived than the vanguard were taking off into the wind and rain.

Elizabeth went to bed early but got up again almost straight away. I was sitting in one of my rooms under the roof. I heard her go into the kitchen, where she boiled the automatic kettle, then into her studio. (She often moved about like this at night. In the morning she would say, 'Do you know, I spent all night in a chair – and it was really very comfortable!' Neither of us slept well. Meeting on the stairs in the early hours we would politely ignore one another like two species of animals in the same field.) The rain stopped at about half past one, giving way to a moonlight I could have written by. It cast the shadows of walls and bushes on the grass and lit up the

12

puddles in the farm gateways a dull colour like iron. I thought I might go out for a walk in it, but in the end I went to bed. Just before I drifted off I thought I heard something fall over downstairs.

I woke up with Elizabeth bending over me. She had put on a faded peach nightdress which had a V-shaped panel of lace at the front. Her face swam above me in the peculiar light, strange, self-involved. I had the impression that she had been whispering while I was asleep. I thought at first she was tucking in my covers, I had had a nightmare and she had heard, but she was pulling them back, and before I could say anything she had got into bed with me. Her feet were cold. She touched my face with her fingers. I woke up properly and remembered her ironing clothes in the evening in September. I was nine years old: craneflies tapped at the kitchen window: my father was away.

'For God's sake Elizabeth what are you doing now?' I said. I got out of the other side of the bed and stood with my back to her. 'I'm staying here until you've gone.'

After a moment or two I heard her get up and walk over to the window. She was looking out across the fields. 'I often wonder why I shut myself away here when Arthur died,' she said. Then: 'I was so bored with Harrogate.' The nightdress fell straight down from her wide, bony shoulders. 'This geranium looks like an artificial flower,' she said. 'That's what people would say if you painted it in moonlight like this.' She went out.

'I'm sorry,' I called.

I went to see Ashman in London a day or two later. Since he would have to come in on a suburban line train, I arranged to meet him in the 'Bistro Europa' at King's Cross Station. Out of nervousness I got there an hour early. I didn't want him to arrive without my seeing him.

The 'Bistro Europa' is really just a sort of fake-exotic station buffet where they will give you white wine with a rubbery pizza: its walls are a mauvish brown with cream Edwardian-looking panels let into them and wall-lights on curved brass stems. It was full of steam from the coffee-maker behind the counter. One or two sleepy tourists on their way back from Majorca were sprawled on the nylon plush banquettes waiting for a train to Glasgow. Across from me lolled a fat man wearing a two-piece beige suit with the jacket flung open; he was reading a paperback which he had bent back on itself so the title couldn't be seen. I found it hard to settle down. I went out and studied the arrivals board: came back in: bought a cup of coffee: sat down again. Behind me a boy from some local office said in a loud voice, 'Did the *Times* crossword this morning in ten minutes flat. What do you make of that?'

'Clever chap!' squealed his girlfriend.

At this the man in the beige suit sat up suddenly. He took a notebook out of his jacket pocket and began to write hurriedly in it with a gold fountain pen. There were two or three other fountain pens, I saw, in the top pocket of his open-necked cheesecloth shirt. One of them had leaked. Every so often he paused as if he was listening, and a sharp contented expression crossed his pink face. I realised it was Ashman. He looked fifty years old. His belly hung over the waistband of his trousers.

'I'm sorry,' I said, holding out my hand and laughing. 'I didn't recognise you. We nearly missed one another.'

'For Christ's sake,' he hissed. 'Fifty quid's worth of subject matter boasting about crossword puzzles behind you and you aren't getting it down? You might be able to afford to pass it up, but I can't! Just listen to the little fucker.' He chuckled. 'Now he's talking about a *tied cottage*!'

I went out on to the platform and left the station as quickly as I could. I spent the afternoon wandering about King's Cross in the rain and didn't go back until five o'clock when I could be certain he would have given up waiting.

The return train had trouble with its gas turbines, and crawled through the Midlands stopping and starting nervously. In Doncaster the streets were black with damp; HILTON SCHOOL OF DANCING, announced a blue neon sign in an upper window, wincing and blinking behind the rain on the glass. A woman came out of the house, tugged the lid off a dustbin and stared uncomprehendingly into it for a few seconds before going back in. All the way to Wakefield water vapour clung to everything, and when I got there I had missed my connection.

There is nothing emptier or more meaningless than a small station at night. The staff move slowly to conserve energy. No one will tell you anything. Towards either end of the platform the lights seem to grow dimmer, as if a certain distance away from you the world has started to fade. Everything looks new but filthy. All that could be seen out of the waiting-room window was a wet road junction, a set of traffic lights always on red, and the 'Shalamar' take-away, Asian and Continental dishes. The walls were thick with graffiti. An old woman I thought I recognised sat bolt upright on one of the benches, her short white hair parted like a man's, her mouth tightly pursed, a handbag as big as a music case on her knee.

'Excuse me,' I said. 'Do you know when the train to Huddersfield is due?'

She stared at me.

'I've seen you before,' she said. 'That's a very rough haircut.'

'I—'

'They never gave it out when the train was going,' she said, and turned her head away. 'They never gave it out.'

I got a bar of chocolate from a machine and sat down to read the *TLS*. The old woman rummaged suddenly in her handbag. Once or twice she cleared her throat as if she was about to speak; but when I looked up she was still staring blankly ahead of her into the middle distance. This became a strain, so I said:

'They don't seem to be able to tell us anything.'

'They ought to be shot,' she said. 'Is that a paper you're reading? I don't know the name of it. Could I have a look?'

She took it away from me quickly and awkwardly before I could open my mouth to say yes, crumpling the edges in her big clean hands. Her handbag fell on the floor with a loud bang; two or three sheets of the *TLS*, coming loose under the force of her attack, drifted down on top of it. While I was picking them up she licked

15

her lips and turned to a piece which seemed to be about the development of Cretan civilisation six or seven hundred years BC. I looked at her thin ankles in their curious fawn stockings.

'Now that's interesting,' she said. 'I wonder if you'll be interested in this? I'm not talking to a Jew, am I?'

'No . . .' I said cautiously.

'Ah, well, you'll be interested in this, then.' She jabbed at the article with her finger. 'Do you know anything about it?'

I hadn't read that particular piece, I said. History wasn't so much my subject as literature. 'I'm a—'

'Ah, well, you'll be interested then. It's about how the Jews got themselves into Europe in the first place.' In a breathless, rapid murmur, like a child reciting something that has been impressed upon her by a kind teacher, she said: 'It was the Romans' fault, you see, allowing them to get away with everything like that. I mean they got away with everything. You see, they were excused *military service* and everything, just because of that one little talent they had with money—'. When she saw that I had no idea of what she was talking about or what I was required to say, she burst out quietly, as if overcome by the immediacy of an injustice we could now both share, 'Well it's not *fair*, is it?'

'I only buy this to read the book reviews,' I said at last. 'I'm – I work in a bookshop. Is that the train?'

'Ooh,' she said. She snatched up her handbag, crumpled the TLS into a ball and, using it to thrust me away from the waiting-room door, made off down the platform. 'They never gave it out,' I heard her say. She looked back at me with undisguised ferocity. 'Never.'

Diesel smoke poured out of the exhaust stacks of the train; under the battered carriages the engines jerked and roared; oily light glistened on the sleepers. I sat as far away from her as I could, and she soon began to talk to a girl in a football scarf. 'Tights with a double gusset,' the girl said.

When I got home it was about half past nine and Elizabeth was out. She had made some attempt to light the fire in her sitting room before she went, but the wind was blowing from the southeast and all she had managed to do was fill the room with smuts. We usually cover the books and records with an old tablecloth when it is like this. The coals were still clicking and creaking musically as they contracted, so I guessed that she hadn't been out for long. I lit them again, coughing as the smoke and fumes were forced back down into the room. It was quite cold: my hands were shrivelled up, and hundreds of tiny white creases had appeared in the skin. The cats ran in and out of the room behind me, making sudden little noises of encouragement to one another. Fights started, raced up and down the stairs like a burning fuse, then fizzled out. They were hungry. After I had got the fire going I went to the kitchen and fed them.

When the place was warmed up again I sat by the fire reading Olivia Manning and listening to Corelli on the stereo. The warm orange light flickered on the shiny dustjackets of the books. The young cat tried vainly to get one of the older ones to play by wriggling about in front of it on the floor, then gave up and washed.

'Its purr is like the coo of a pigeon,' Elizabeth had told me a few days before. (One of those late October days with transparent air and a light blue sky; sharp enough to need a fire but bright enough to believe you can keep the windows open. Elizabeth dropped a paintbrush into the garden, where it left an indelible mark on the concrete path.) 'Just like a pigeon. Aren't you surprised how many gardens still have flowers in them? I've seen snapdragons, nasturtiums, even pansies!'

At about eleven I left her a note saying that I was going to bed. 'You forgot to cover the books up, but I dusted them. Cats fed.'

In my rooms under the roof the windows were wide open. She had thrown some of the chair covers and cushions out. The others were still draped over the sills, soaked. The wind had scattered my typing paper and manuscripts everywhere. There were coffee-grounds all over the carpet, and long smears on the wall. She had bent and strained methodically at my desk lamp until it stood out at an odd angle by the typewriter, like a heron with a broken neck. In the typewriter was a piece of paper on which she had endlessly typed, fuck off fuck off fuck off fuck. I stared at it tiredly. She had dragged the covers off the bed and, I found, urinated on some of them. I put the clean ones back on and curled up under them; but I hadn't closed the windows and I had to get up again. One of the cats came and sat by me. I thought I might be able to peel some of the damp manuscript sheets apart; but I would leave it.

When the wind is like this I am stupid and depressed. I once woke up in the middle of the night in a panic because I had forgotten how old I was. Worse, I thought I had repressed the truth, and even though I knew it would make me miserable I had to get at it: I was thirty-nine, not thirty-eight, next birthday. I lay there for what could have been an hour or only half a minute, saddened by that awful logic. The curious thing is that I *am* only thirty-eight next birthday, and in the morning I knew that perfectly well.

Small Heirlooms

In his thorough but ironic way, Kit discovered, her brother had named her his executor. This meant she would have to go through the mass of papers he had left. In a way she was pleased, although his books, with their mixture of autobiography and fiction, had always seemed to her hurtful and embarrassing. 'You never know,' she had often said to people, with a lightness she didn't feel, 'when you might open the latest one and see yourself! And really: some of the things he invented are easily taken for fact.' He had kept up writing until the day of his death.

It was a long journey from where she lived. All one December day she connected station to station like someone connecting up dots to make a picture. The different trains seemed to pass again and again through the same landscape; and although she would later say to someone, 'I saw the most marvellous faces on Peterborough station – full of character!' she could hardly distinguish between the different travellers either.

She always tried to get a window seat, which she occupied in a slumped, awkward way, as if over the last decade she had become unused to herself. Her face, though still attractive, had also a kind of slumped heaviness; she had made it up carefully before she left home. The boy who sat across the table from her between Grantham and London found himself thinking: 'She's older than you realise at first.' Front face she had a perceptible thickening of the neck; her lips drooped at the corners. At the moment the breadth of her back was muscular, but in four or five years it would soften and thicken further. Rather than being fat she had a kind of mass, accentuated by her clumsy, often irritable gestures. 'She's a powerful old thing,' he thought. But the power of her body was beginning to be put solely into moving it around. He took out his cheque book and began to go through the stubs.

Kit ate a sweet, looking out at the unending procession of suburban golf courses and sodden recreation grounds; the lines of disused rolling stock in sidings; bits of woodland where ivy fattened the tree-trunks mysteriously in the dark winter air. She was bored and hot. A mile outside King's Cross people began putting their coats on. You could see them all along the carriage, all reaching up to the luggage rack at the same time, with a movement they were unused to making, their sudden clumsiness compounded by the swaying of the train. She pushed her handbag away from her across the table.

'I'm sorry,' she said absently to the boy.

Waiting for the train to stop, she heaved a sigh.

As she got to her feet her fur coat was thrown against his leg. Under the thick make-up, he saw, her skin was as coarsely textured as his mother's. 'She *is* fat,' he told himself, 'after all. Her heaviness is only that, and two vodkas from the buffet in less than an hour.' Even so he still saw it as a kind of repose, a kind of strength in repose; and surprised himself by thinking obscurely that it would get her through.

Dragging a battered canvas bag on a trolley behind her, she trudged slowly along the platform and vanished into the brightness of the Euston Road.

The last part of the journey turned out to be the quickest: nevertheless it was dark by the time she arrived in Reading. 'Don't get on the train standing at Number Five, love,' a guard warned her. 'Unless you want to go straight to Portsmuff.'

'Oh no,' she explained, looking puzzledly at him. 'I'm coming here. I'm definitely coming to Reading.'

At John's small house in Darlington Gardens she found some washing-up in the sink and water in the electric kettle. The little bathroom next door to the kitchen had, in addition to its plastic containers of Flash and Fine Fare disinfectant, a fresh towel arranged neatly on the side of the bath, as if he had expected Kit, which in a way, she supposed, he had. The house was orderly, clean, but as dusty as it had been when he was alive. She made a cup of tea and took it into the lounge where she could drink it in front of the gas fire. Shelves of paperbacks, mostly detective stories arranged carefully by author, lined the two long sides of the room. The carpet and curtain fabrics were rough-textured, a comfortable mealy colour popular in contract furnishing. In the centre of the room on a low bamboo table was a pile of French and Spanish film magazines. Actresses had fascinated him.

Kit was tired. In the spare room the actresses stared at her levelly from the walls. He had favoured girls with a Slavic or Balkan look. She remembered him once saying to her sadly, 'I suppose I shall soon have lived a whole life without ever having worn an earring.' She couldn't find any blankets, and she was too fastidious to sleep on the mattress without a sheet, so she went downstairs again and spent the night on the sofa, under her coat.

In the morning she felt stronger and went straight into the room he had used as an office and began to empty out the two grey metal filing cabinets she found there.

Most of the material was in envelope wallets stuffed with undated sheets. There was an intermittent diary in spiral-bound and loose-leaf notebooks: 1948 to 1960, with huge gaps where years had been removed or never written in. The oldest stuff, which went back to before the war, he had kept in four or five deteriorating 'East Light' box files, their fastenings all broken, their marbled boards warped with damp and sunshine.

He had kept the curious, muddled, sporadic commentary on the world any novelist keeps. 'This morning I saw from the top deck of a bus a woman sitting by a window using a magnifying glass to help her thread a needle.' There were fragments he had never used, as in, ' "It's not my alcoholism he hates, it's my personality—" ', dialogue evidently intended for Anais Tate in *Saint Govan's Head*, though she never spoke it; or which found their way into a book in modified form. Kit came across a title or two, like 'The Empty Sign' (this had been written several times, over two or three journal entries, sometimes in capitals, sometimes in quote marks, sometimes in what appeared to be someone else's handwriting, as if John had been playing with a new pen; he had never, to Kit's knowledge, called any piece 'The Empty Sign'); and some criticism – '*Once Upon a Time in America*, another film devoted to the proposition that human beings are cannibals with faces the colour of putty.'

Every so often she would find something so disconcerting it hardly seemed to qualify as any of these things:

'The Expressionists chained to their mirrors – Rilke and Munch, Schiele and Kafka – never able to turn away for a moment. A column of doomed and disintegrating soldiers in the long war against the father and the society he has created to imprison them. The mirror is not a simple weapon. It is their only means of defence, their plan of attack. In it they are allowed to reassure themselves: their nightmare is always of an identity so subsumed under the father's that it becomes invisible to normal light, causing them to vanish as they watch.'

Kit thought this unfair to their own father. She put it aside. Later it would have to be burned, in the waste bin or the grate according to how much more she had collected. She decided she could familiarise herself with the diaries, in a superficial way, in a morning. She found nothing that referred to her at all.

At half past ten she had to go out for shopping. It was one of those clear December mornings with pale but distinct shadows. After the small northern towns Kit was used to, the Reading streets seemed wide and endless, the red brick houses tall and elegant. Christmas trees were in all the shops, and bunches of holly which reminded her of something else John had written, in a letter to her while he was still up at Cambridge before the war: ' "The holly bears a berry as bright as any wound." Every time you hear that carol you take the full weight of the Medieval experience, which was just like a childhood. To them the words seemed mysterious and valuable in their own right, the berries so bright against the dark foliage of the tree. Rowan and yew berries are just as bright. So are hawthorn berries, especially when they are new. Hips and haws are as bright. All are instrumental and have their magical and symbolic associations, but none as dark and childlike as this myth of conscious sacrifice, organised, performed, *expressed*, as the matrix of a culture.'

'John, you put yourself in such a bad light with things like this,' she had written back to him, unable to explain that it wasn't so much his atheism that dismayed her as his sudden articulacy, which had emptied Christmas for her as memory. She felt that she had lost all the holly they had collected as children together. Hadn't he even enjoyed singing the carols?

'You always used to love Christmas.'

She bought sheets, bread, milk. She was away from Darlington Gardens for less than an hour. The moment she opened the front door again she knew someone was in the house. Along the narrow hall and on the stairs hung the smell of some unfashionably heavy perfume – thick, Byzantine, yet not at all unpleasant. The impression it gave of occupancy was so strong that Kit stood there on the doormat for a few seconds calling cheerfully, 'Hello. Hello?' Had a neighbour come in while she was at the shops? 'Hello?' But there was no answer. She went puzzledly in and out of the dusty rooms; looked from a window up and down the street. Later, in the bathroom, she discovered that one of the little round cakes of air-freshener had come unwrapped from its cellophane. At first she wasn't convinced that this powerful reek of violets, with its hard chemical edge, was what she had smelt. Then she was.

That afternoon, already bored with her brother's notebooks, she turned to the expensive black Twinlock binder which held the journal of his last three years, and almost immediately came upon this: 'Concrete only yields more concrete. Since the war the cities of the Danube all look like Birmingham.'

She bent her head over it.

When I was a boy (he went on), you could still see how they had once been the dark core of Europe. If you travelled south and east, the new Austria went behind you like a Bauhaus cakestand full of the same old stale Viennese Whirls, and you were lost in the steep cobbled streets which smelt of charcoal smoke and paprika, fresh leather from the saddler's. The children were throwing buttons against the walls as you passed, staring intently at them where they lay, as if trying to read the future from a stone. You could hear Magyar and Slovak spoken not just as languages but as incitements. There in the toe of Austria, at that three-way confluence of borders, you could see a dancing bear: and though the dance was rarely more than a kind of sore lumbering, with the feet turned in, to a few slaps on a tambourine, it was still impressive to see one of these big bemused animals appear among the gypsy girls on the pavement. They would take turns to dance in front of it; stare comically into its small eyes to make it notice them; then pirouette away. As performers themselves, they regarded it with grave affection and delight.

I loved sights like this and sought them out. I had some money. Being English gave me a sense of having escaped.

By day the girls often told fortunes with cards, favouring a discredited but popular Etteilla. (I don't know how old it was. Among its major arcana it included a symbol I have never seen in any traditional pack, but its *langue* was that of post-Napoleonic France: 'Within a year your case will come up and you will acquire money'; 'You will suffer an illness which will cost considerable money without efficacy. Finally a faith-healer will restore your health with a cheap remedy'; 'Upside down, this card signifies payment of a debt you thought completely lost'; and so on. It was like having bits of Balzac, or Balzac's letters, read out to you.) They would stand curiously immobile in the street with its seventy-odd unwieldy cards displayed in a beautiful fan, while the crowds whirled round them head down into the cold wind of early spring. By night many of them were prostitutes. This other duty encouraged them to exchange their earrings and astonishing tiered skirts for an overcoat and a poor satin slip, but they were in no way diminished by it.

To me, anyway, the two services seemed complementary, and I saw in the needs they fulfilled a symmetry the excitement of which, though it escapes me now, I could hardly contain. Huts and caravans amid the rubbish at the edge of a town or under the arches of some huge bleak railway viaduct, fires which made the night ambiguous, musical instruments which hardly belonged in Europe at all: increasingly I was drawn to the gypsy encampments.

Was I more than eighteen years old? It seems unlikely. Nevertheless I could tell, by the way the dim light pooled in the hollow of her collar bones, that the girl was less. She raised one arm in a quick ungainly motion to slide the curtain shut across the doorway; the satin lifted across her ribby sides. I thought her eyes vague, shortsighted. When she discovered I was English she showed me a newspaper clipping, a photograph of Thomas Masaryk, pinned to the wall above the bed. 'Good,' she said sadly; she shook her head then nodded it immediately, as if she wasn't sure which gesture was appropriate. We laughed. It was February: you could hear the dogs barking in the night forty miles up and down the river, where the floodwater was frozen in mile-wide lakes. She lay down and opened her legs and they made the same shape as a fan of cards when it first begins to spread in the hand. I shivered and looked away.

'Tell our fortunes first.'

Masaryk had died not long before; the war was rehearsing itself with increasing confidence. Like many of the European gypsies, I suppose, she ended up in some camp or oven.

The afternoon was nearly over.

Kit sat on in her brother's cold front room, with its photo-magazines and dust, unable somehow to reach over and switch on the lights or the gas fire, while the bright inks he had used, a fresh colour for every entry, fluoresced like a beacon in the last of the winter daylight.

'Years later,' she read, 'I could only think that Birkenau had been in the room with us even then. A burial kommando drunk on petrol and formalin was already waiting rowdily outside like the relatives at the door of the bridal suite, as she closed the curtain, spread the cards, then knelt over me thoughtfully to bring me off in the glum light with a quick, limping flick of the pelvis. However often I traced the line of her breastbone with my fingers, however much she smiled, the death camp was in there with us.'

And then, almost wonderingly:

'Any child we might have had would have lived out its time not in the Theresienstadt, the family camp, but in Mengele's block.'

She read and re-read this and then sat slumped in the chair, legs stuck out in front of her like an old woman until there was only time to get up, put on the light and the fire, make something to eat, and go to bed. She felt slow and exhausted, as if she had finally used up some great resource. Before she could go to sleep she had to hear a human voice. 'Book at Bedtime' was *Le Grand Meaulnes*. She listened to a weather report. 'Visibility nil.'

In bed she decided over and over again, 'He poisoned his own memories too.'

Eventually she dropped off and after some time dreamed – if that was the right word for it – she was listening to a woman's footsteps tap-tapping on a polished wood-block floor. This took place in the lounge of some comfortable 'country' hotel, with its low ceiling, panelled walls and red velvet sofa. It was full of great exotic indoor plants which had been planted in brass jugs, casseroles, bits of terracotta balanced on tall awkward wooden stands, even a coal scuttle made of some orange-blonde wood, anything but proper pots. Kit heard herself say reasonably to the other woman:

'Why don't you sit down?'

Cars were parked in the driveway outside. Through the open French windows – it was a warm night – she could see a Devon Rex cat moving thoughtfully from car to car, marking each bumper with a copious greenish spray. Suddenly it became bored and jumped in through the window. It was old, blind-looking. Brindled and slow, it weaved about in the open spaces of the wood-block as if it were pushing its way through a thicket of long entangled grass.

'Do you think he's in pain?' the other woman asked.

She had difficulty ordering her dinner.

'Mm . . . I think . . . yes, soup I think . . .'

Her voice became almost inaudible. She would like her steak spoiled, she admitted, 'overdone. Sorry.' She laughed apologetically.

Kit wanted to tell her: 'The waiter doesn't care how you have your steak. You can see he is young and shy, but a little impatient too – he's used to people who know quite well what they want.'

When the waiter had gone the heels began again, tap tap indecisively round the room. She rustled the newspapers and magazines in the wicker basket; went from picture to picture on the wall – a head in pencil, turned at an odd angle away from the artist; a still life with two lutes more real than the room; a bridge. In the end she flicked the ash off her cigarette and sat down with a copy of *Vogue* and a dry sherry. In a flash the old cat had jumped lightly on to her lap!

'He's not in pain,' Kit said, 'he only wants attention,' and woke up as soon as she heard it, convinced again that there was someone in the house; that someone had been in the room with her.

She had no idea what the time was. When she switched the lamp on, white light sprayed off the door of the spare room; it was closed. She opened it and went out on to the landing and stood there helplessly, staring at the film posters, the cardboard boxes stuffed with old magazines, the lights in their dusty plastic globes. People say of someone, 'She filled the house with her personality,' without a clue of what they might mean. The perfume Kit had smelled that morning was like a sea around her – she thought that if she couldn't learn to swim in it she would drown – she was gripped by the panic of irreversible events. There was no likelihood, she saw, that it was the smell of an unwrapped air-freshener. It was Persian attar. She was in the heart of a rose. Wherever she looked the sense of occupancy was appalling. Whoever was in the house with her was leaving each room just before Kit went in; or were they coming into it as soon as she had gone? John's desk with its broken IBM; his files and papers where Kit had strewn them over the floor, his bed under its threadbare candlewick cover, were folded into the heart of the rose. She opened the back door and looked out: the concrete path, netted over with suckers from some untended plant, the plumes of pampas grass at the end of the garden, even the rain falling steadily – all enfolded in the heart of a rose.

'Hello?' whispered Kit. No one answered. The house was full.

An hour later it was empty again. She got herself back upstairs, but she knew she wouldn't sleep, and inevitably her brother's papers were waiting there for her, the voice of his despair as his life began to seem more pointless, composed as a mystery—

'You can't cure people of their character,' she read.

After this he had crossed something out then gone on, 'You can't even change yourself. Experiments in that direction soon deteriorate into bitter, infuriated struggles. You haul yourself over the wall and glimpse new country. Good! You can never again be what you were! But even as you are congratulating yourself you discover tied to one leg the string of Christmas cards, gas bills, air letters and family snaps which will never allow you to be anyone else. A forty-year-old woman holds up a doll she has kept in a cardboard box under a bed since she was a child. She touches its clothes, which are falling to pieces; works tenderly its loose arm. The expression that trembles on the edge of realising itself in the slackening muscles of her lips and jaw is indescribably sad. How are you to explain to her that she has lost nothing by living the intervening years of her life? How is *she* to explain this to *you*?'

Kit thought about this until it got light. Who had he been trying to comfort, or separate himself from? Who had held up the doll? Some time after eight she remembered the dream that had woken her to the scent of attar, and saw clearly that both women were herself.

She wept.

'Perspective is unfair,' she had written to him during the war. 'We shouldn't have to live our lives unless we can live in them, thoughtlessly, like the animals.'

By ten o'clock she was standing on the platform at Reading station, waiting for a train to Waterloo. Towards London everything was a blue and grey haze. The rails made a curved perspective into it. The spaces suggested were immense. Kit knew without being told that if she were to go back to Darlington Gardens now, all the doors and windows of her brother's house would be wide open and every piece of paper in it gone, though in the end she had burned nothing. The smell of attar would be so strong it filled the street outside, as if the pavements had suddenly put forth great suffocating masses of flowers. Though she would not be able to see them she would hear the laughter of the children as they threw buttons against the wall; she would hear the tambourine keep time for the dancing bear.

'In the heart of the rose,' she whispered to herself.

Sitting in the 12.15 p.m. King's Cross to Leeds the next day, she caught herself repeating this, like a line from a song. Unable to face the whole journey at once she had broken it with an old friend who lived in North London. Now she settled herself and got her luggage on to the rack. The train was crowded. While she was waiting for it to pull out she watched two girls on the platform kissing one another. One of them was wearing a man's thick grey overcoat much too large for her. 'Those two imagine they've discovered something new.'

So as to have eaten something before her vodka-and-tonic at half past eleven she brought back with it from the buffet two slices of toast. They lay thick and white under the BR paper napkin, in every way as much of a mistake as the book Judith had lent her to read on the way back: *Voyage in the Dark*. Every page or two she looked at her wrist watch. She gave up before the train had reached Stevenage, and instead tried to carry on with the letter she had already begun, 'Dear Judith, I saw a boy with the face of your new painting. He was taking the money in the station café at King's Cross. His head was turned at the exact same angle; the exact same half-smile was on his face.'

To this, before she could change her mind, she added quickly,

'Does Pentonville Road go to Pentonville? Who knows? (I expect you do, Judith!) If it does, Pentonville is some misty attractive distance where you can see a junction, trees, a white cupola. Everything goes away to there from the doors of King's Cross, through a foreground with choked buses in shadow, narrow-looking pavements.' It was always difficult to write to people who had lived and worked all their lives in London. You tried to bring it alive for them, but how could you? Judith lived in Highgate, had said as they talked late into the night, 'Don't think of getting up early in the morning.' Kit looked out of the window. 'For a moment,' she wrote, 'I was tempted not to go inside and catch the Leeds train, but to walk a little and see what happened to me.'

After three quarters of an hour the train was halted (as the guard said) by a 'lineside fire'. The fire brigade was out, he reassured everyone, trying to find some means by which the train could pass. It was cold, and there was some weak sunshine. Out of the window Kit could see ploughed fields, trees, a stream; then in the distance lorries and cars on a motorway. When the train began to move again there were neither fire nor engine to be seen, only some factories and houses which looked like the outskirts of a town but weren't, and in the end the fire turned out to be a lot further ahead than anyone had expected. The landscape became very flat, although its sense of emptiness was relieved by birchwoods and spinneys. The sun went in again; a power station loomed up suddenly out of a thin local mist. 'Ladies and gentlemen,' the guard said without warning, 'we are now approaching the scene of the fire. This will be visible on your right hand side in the direction of travel.' A second or two later he came back on the loudspeaker and said, 'It will be on your *left* hand side in the direction of travel.' There was some laughter. Passengers began leaving their seats so they could poke their heads out of the windows in the doorways between the carriages. From half a mile you could see dark grey smoke rising a hundred and fifty or two hundred feet in the air above the edge of some small town or village. The train slowed, jerked forward suddenly, slowed again. Old women walked up and down the gangway with vague, loose, expectant smiles on their faces, like backward children at a pantomime. As the train rolled closer, at perhaps ten or fifteen miles an hour, you could see that the smoke cast a shadow across the empty fields: by now it looked much blacker and denser. The fire engines, two of them, were parked at the bottom of the railway embankment, on a bridge over a culverted stream. This made them look like toys with little flickering blue lights, arranged in a model of a landscape; all the values of the real landscape shifted suddenly to fit. The fire itself was disappointing – a small dump of discarded agricultural tyres in an old siding forty or fifty yards long, only a section of which had caught. It was a toy fire: but even though the deep red flames were twenty yards off, blown back on themselves by the wind, over the dump and away from the train, you could still feel the heat on the side of your face through the double glazed window. The firemen moved easily through the smoke, stepping in and out of the flames as they dragged the smouldering tyres apart, occasionally staring in at the passengers. Though the smoke had looked so black and thick, Kit had been protected from it to some extent by the air conditioning. Now, with the fire falling behind and the old ladies trooping back smiling to sit down, a movement of the air in the carriage seemed to bring it to her suddenly. She had expected the heavy, acrid odour of burning rubber: but the smoke smelled first of attar of roses, and then after that of something utterly disgusting, and Kit thought, ' "At Birkenau the human fat is wasted; they do not manufacture soap",' and had to get up and push her way down the carriage and into the lavatory, where she leaned over the washbasin in the corner and was copiously sick into it.

'The war ended,' John had written. 'The cold war began. Not long after the Communist seizure of power in Czechoslovakia, Thomas Masaryk's son Jan, then Foreign Minister, was found dead in the courtyard beneath an open window in the ministry. This came home to me among all the other events, I think, not because I had any interest in Czech affairs but simply because I remembered the faith the girl had put in his father. We don't so much impose our concerns on others as bequeath them, like small heirlooms. They lose one significance then, discovered in a drawer years after, suddenly gain another.'

Shivering defiantly, Kit wiped her mouth and looked round the lavatory.

'I know you're there,' she said.

The Gift

1: *The Rainbow Shuts Its Gate Against You*

If you probe in the ashes, they say, you will never learn anything about the fire; its meaning has passed on.

There are as many as seventeen good hotels in the city. On the 'entresol' floor of one of them, the Central, a woman lounges in the tropical heat of her single room, drinking rum. The TV is on, the sound turned down. It's eleven o'clock at night. Downstairs, the railway station from which the Central takes its name is almost deserted. When a train arrives the air is filled for a few minutes with shouts, laughter, people calling to one another in the crush, and the concourse sounds like a zoo or an asylum. As if to soothe the inmates the concourse muzak will suddenly play a schmalzy, faraway version of 'Rhapsody in Blue'. To this the woman in room 236 listens only briefly, tilting her head at an intent angle as though she is trying to catch some tune underneath the music, before she shrugs and turns away from the window.

'"Black Heart Rum",' she reads aloud from the bottle in her hand. '"the Heart of Darkness".' She laughs and adds, '"All the sweet lacunae of the Caribbean Sea—"'

Now it is the television that captures her attention, and she turns up the sound just in time to hear '—unease in the minds of ladies. Considerable unease in the minds of ladies.' But this sentence, read out in a bright yet concerned voice, is the end of the item, and the scene changes abruptly to some grainy night footage of lorries being manoeuvred in and out of a shed. 'Real unease in the minds of some ladies,' she thinks, sitting on the bed with her shoes off and allowing her arm to rest briefly along the padded headboard. In this position she is revealed as a tall woman whose clothes – a black two-piece suit with lightly padded shoulders, a striped grey and black blouse of some glazed material – scarcely hide a kind of untidy sexuality, a gawky and almost absent-minded sleepiness of the limbs.

Her eyes are blue, a little watery and indirect. Her age is hard to tell.

Wherever you are at night in the city you can always see, beyond the roof of the next building, the faint glow of the floodlights of some monument. This is less a light than a sort of luminescence of the air itself, soft and tremulous, as if it is full of mist or water. Out of it rises a Victorian minaret, which you cannot quite see; the crenellations of a castle, which you can; or a flagpole. The parks are full of statuary.

The woman in room 236 remembers how, at the end of a holiday in Europe, she flew back into the city on board a jet: first passing over the great cool neon signs hanging in the air at its outskirts – TEXACO, MOWLEM, ALFA-LAVAL, the Internationals signalling steady as beacons into the night – then entering that soft meniscus of light, that city of floodlit monuments as far as the eye can see. Her loneliness, she felt at the time, was complete.

Now, with the room darkened and the television turned off, she lies back on the bed and allows this faint illumination to fall on her from the open window. Turning restlessly one way and then the other, as if she were trying to sleep in her clothes, on the undisturbed counterpane in the trembling light, she stares up at the ceiling. At first her hands are quite still at her sides. Soon though they draw themselves up along her thighs, flat, palm down, pulling the hem of the skirt up with them. They are tender but nearly impersonal. With the skirt bundled awkwardly around her waist, and her silk knickers rolled down round her ankles, she seems to be offering her sex not so much to her own hands as to the room, the city, anything as long as it is beyond herself. 'Oh,' she says quietly after a minute or two, 'it's so beautiful!' But then a train clatters into Central Station, and the Muzak plays 'Rhapsody in Blue', and she gets up from the bed in despair or rage and switches on the fluorescent lamp above the make-up mirror.

Her name is Sophia. She was disfigured at birth by a mark like a splash – as if, her parents said, someone threw red ink in her face the very day she was born – down the right side of the nose, all round the eye on that side, and across the right cheek. Splatters and dots radiate from the raw-looking central stain like the headlands and islands of some heavily fjorded coast.

2: Narcissus Fires

At this time of night Peter Ebert can usually be found at the Doric Restaurant, which is not far away across the city at the corner of Acol Street.

The Doric is often crowded with young men like himself. Hands thrust into the pockets of their baggy black trousers, they wait for a table, gazing at the bottles above the bar with the musing expression you give to art, while the pictures – gigantic loving pencil sketches of a link of dockyard chain, which looks pumped-up and organic and about to explode, like a black pudding or a huge turd – go unnoticed on the walls. Bottles are a feature of the décor: spirit bottles in optics over the bar, green ends of wine bottles goggling into the room from racks, empty bottles stuck with cheap white candles to light the long oilcloth-covered tables. At the height of the evening, waitresses are running in and out distractedly, the room becomes suffocatingly hot, the air stuffed to bursting with the smell of choux pastry with ham and cheese in a gooseberry sauce, the walls yellow with cigarette smoke.

'After all,' someone shouts across the racket, 'it's no good cutting the Speak Your Weight machine out of your will because you don't like everything it says about you!'

'I know.'

At Peter Ebert's table a girl passes her finger through the candle flame, an expression on her face of distant enquiry, as if objectivity were not so much an act as a very faint emotion: one so removed from humanity – or at least everyday humanity – as to be hardly detectable in oneself without special training; yet an emotion nonetheless. Ebert stares at her.

This morning someone gave him a book.

It was such a curious transaction – hermetic, contingent, having its own rules, like a bubble of meaning in the ordinary events of life – that even now he feels tempted to tell someone, 'I bet this has never happened to you. At the station this morning' – Ebert means not Central but the city's less important station, Eastern, popularly known as Regent's – 'a man I had never seen before came up and offered me a book.'

Between the end of Regent's platform 4 and the mouth of the tunnel which takes the line out of the city centre, there is a deep walled cutting. On a wet day rain blows about in this space; as it circulates there, the light striking into it from the street above the station makes it seem distinct and photographic, as romantic as rain falling in a new Russian film. Watching from the dim, sheltered platform, you have the impression of an illuminated curtain, out of which noses every so often the yellow front of a train, streaked with oil, shiny with water, and bringing with it a cold stream of air. People waiting near the edge of the platform step back momentarily to let the carriage doors swing open; passengers alight and rush away.

Making room like this with all the others, Peter Ebert found himself staring at someone's face. It was quite close to his: one of those old or ill-looking faces at whose salient points small tight lumps of muscle seem to have gathered, as if the flesh had retreated there to leave the bones prominent and bare – or as if blobs of putty had been arranged on the jaw and cheekbones of a skull, then covered with white pancake make-up. Later he was to say 'a man', but in fact he was never sure whether it belonged to a man or a woman. Of the body beneath it he caught only confused impressions – a pale brown raincoat, thin shoulders, a leather case or bag. A hand, its knuckles reddened and enlarged by years of work or illness, offered him the book. He took it without thinking: imagined he heard someone say in a contemptuous, dismissive voice, 'Narcissus' or 'Narcissus Fire': lost sight of the figure in the crowd pressing towards the ticket barrier.

He stared at the book in his hand. He was suddenly convinced that there must be some other way to live. What he meant by this he couldn't think; except that it wasn't what you would normally mean. He had to catch the train, or he would have dropped the book into the nearest waste bin. When he got out at the other end it was in his pocket.

'All at once,' he now thinks of saying to the girl at his table, 'you can't make head or tail of anything, can you?'

As he opens his mouth to speak she smiles at him and pinches out the candle flame. He sees how the naked small of her back would curve up out of the waistband of her skirt, how astonishingly real and human its warmth would make her seem to him. But the book is in his pocket – though its cover has fallen off long since, he thinks it was a paperback, quite an old one from the '30s or '40s – and he knows he will be going home to read it. It is Ebert's belief that understanding ought to come by epiphany rather than by increments: it has never occurred to him how completely this might limit his intellectual reach. Behind him the waitress says,

'Whose was the plain chocolate mousse?'

3: *Sophia's Gift*

Every story is a cup so empty it can be drunk from again and again.

Once or twice a week she brings a man home to room 236 at the Central Hotel. If men see too much of her face they sometimes become puzzled and unkind, so out of consideration she keeps it turned away when she can, and on the way home tries as often as possible to be looking at something on the other side of the road: an old bicycle propped against a wall, the brightly lit shop window where a display of popular wedding stationery seems to merge indistinguishably with the cigarette ends and chip wrappers on the pavement outside. She always leaves the door of the room open a crack, so there will be no need for a light.

Tonight she is with a man called Dave.

When they got inside the room he wouldn't lie down. He had been drinking whisky and Coke, so she had to struggle with his clothes as well as her own. 'I love you, Dave,' she said, kissing his face. 'At least do something to help,' she said. 'Dave, I love you.' He kept trying to find the light switch. Eventually he managed to put one of the bedside lamps on. Please don't change your mind now, she thought, and looked away so quickly that the tendons stood out in her neck. But he only said, 'Women!' and switched the light out himself. Then he fell on to the bed, where – after trying to lever her legs apart, unaware that they had become fastened together at the knees by the muddle of tights and underwear she had not had time to push down any further – he made a few disconnected movements, came with a groan between her closed thighs, and fell asleep. 'No, wait,' she was still whispering, 'you're not—'. She held his head tenderly.

Dave's semen is drying in the warm hotel air, tautening a patch of her skin. A hotel is so comfortable, she thinks: if you had really wanted to do that I could have helped you, and now we could be having a bath together or anything. Sophia stares at the diffuse line of light round the open door. The last train has come in, and now the station concourse is so quiet you can hear someone's shoes squeaking across the polished floor. This faint dry sound reminds her of her holiday in Norway: the sound of feet on the shiny museum floors of Oslo, which smell of care and polish and respect.

She loves pictures. At the Munchmuseet she was careful to see *Consolation, Madonna,* and *The Mountain Path*; at the Nasjonal Galleriet, *Den Sarede Engell.* A friend took her to the Vikingskip-museet so she should have a chance to see the Oseberg Ship before she left. He showed her a runic inscription scratched on a piece of black wood one thousand years old. 'It means,' he told her, ' "Mankind knows so little".' He was a quiet man, a little younger than herself and determined to entertain her, who sold books in Scandinavia for a firm of English academic publishers, and lectured at the Universitet on the early film documentarists with their theories of 'camera eye' and 'redemption of reality'. He had made short films for a living, and still wrote scripts. 'I read everything about this once,' he said. 'I think that's what it means.' The old ships, their planks laid together in bunches of hurtling curves like diagrams of a slipstream, sailed round her through the dim light of the museum, ignoring her.

'It's hard to imagine them buried,' she said. 'How they must have flown across the sea!'

'A boat like this was built only for funerals I'm afraid.'

Later she had to wait for him in the darkened cafeteria of one of the university buildings. There, a boy with long red hair played desultorily on an out-of-tune piano; after a moment he got up with an exclamation of impatience and went out into the corridor. Outside, the rain was falling into a courtyard the high brick walls of which, though quite new, looked authentically old and tranquil. To foster this impression weeds had been allowed to grow between the unworn cobbles. The rain turned to hail, then after a moment of violence passed over; the fountain bubbled up. Yellow roses and dark earth. The red-haired boy came in again and said with Norwegian irony, 'I suppose we are all waiting for something!'

That was the last day of the holiday. When they drove back to her friend's home along the coast it was late. On one side of the Drammensveien the moon hung diffused and dark orange, bloated like a bag; on the other, the morning light, clean and green. The moon, though, would not set; and the dawn, endlessly promised, was endlessly incomplete. She was so tired and happy. They had stayed on in the cafés of Tingvallakaia, which at half past two every morning begin to empty themselves of couples so drunk they could only look straight ahead.

The next day, through the scratched and smeary window of a British Airways 757, she caught sight of the great granite rock of Kōlsas. Because she had stared at it so often from the balcony of his flat, she was eager for it to be the last thing she saw in Norway. Touching her face gently at the airport, he had promised her: 'This is not a birthmark. It's a map.'

4: *The Precious Discoveries of the Senses*

At three in the morning Peter Ebert makes himself a cup of tea.

The hotel is quiet. At this time of night you might hear a door open then close, a muffled laugh from another room: but though the lights burn in the carpeted corridors, no one is walking along them. The central heating touches your skin gently and evenly. Ebert loves the sense of freedom this gives him; he loves nothing better than to be awake at night and let the hotel press round him its padded silence.

At six, grey light comes through the curtain, and he opens his window. Cold air spills over his feet; pigeons clatter away between the buildings, a sound unannounced and without issue; somewhere out of sight a pink and gold dawn is colouring the edges of the statues in the city's hilly little parks. Ebert rubs his hands over his eyes.

At nine o'clock he telephones his office.

'Another puzzle,' he thinks as he waits for his secretary to answer, 'is the *title*.'

What sort of book has he been given? Peter Ebert is unable to say. It lies open on the table in front of him amid a litter of crumpled hotel notepaper, empty cups, and torn sachets of non-dairy creamer: a hundred and thirty pages which end in the middle of a sentence – 'the precious discoveries of the senses—'. Even the surviving text is incomplete. Some pages are missing, others have been torn in half longitudinally, to leave only curious groups of words: 'years of swill', 'the subsoil account' and 'comically little value'.

Everyone who has owned it has stained and defaced it with his humanity, thinks Ebert. They have annotated it in pencil too faint

44

to read, spattered it with food, slashed it in straight careful lines with a razor blade on a wet Monday in a bus station. They've sweated into it and worse whilst reading listlessly, sick in bed in Mottingham or Manchester. They've rubbed tomato sauce into it in thumbprints, and left impacted in its central creases cigarette ash like the grey flock which bursts from padded bags. Its outer pages are a pissy yellow colour, glazed with grease yet furry from being handled, their corners rounded-off and thick as felt. Its spine is rotten. All that remains of its title pages is a blank leaf on which is printed centrally in bold letters EON HEART; and even there they have spilled bleach or semen on it, Ebert thinks, so that 'eon' is only part of a word which might as easily have read 'Simeon' as 'Pantheon'.

'I'm not coming in today,' he says suddenly into the telephone. Then: 'Tell him no.'

His eye has been caught by the words,

'. . . the little Fennec with its beautiful ears!'

Last night, though he had no idea what they meant, he gave a shiver of delight every time he read these words.

'To make the little white Fennec, butterflies mated themselves to foxes, fluttering into their uplifted faces in the desert air at evening. The faces of the foxes were like flowers to them, they circled closer.'

Ebert's hotel room looks out on a deep four-sided yard built in Victorian Gothic, with pointed windows, peaked gables and brick finials. The lower part of the yard – where, less than thirty years ago, traffic still went in and out – has become choked with small buildings. Wires sag aimlessly from wall to wall above them, rotten ladders run over their roofs. Where hotel guests once stepped down from cars and taxis, moss thickens the rusting gutters. Where laughter once flew up like birds, everything is indescribably filthy. Every flat surface – even the collars which hold the drainpipes against the walls – is covered with a soft roll of pigeon shit, which hangs beneath each window ledge like a cream-coloured beard.

When he first got the book home, his excitement was so intense that he could feel the whole of his upper body rocking slightly and rhythmically to the beat of his heart. All the way home he had looked forward to the moment when he could open it. At every junction the familiar streets had seemed to lurch into new arrangements, as if he was seeing them after a long absence or from an unexpected angle.

5: 'As if by Moonlight'

'If my face was a map,' Sophia wonders, 'what kind of country would it reveal?'

An island, with other islands outlying, in a warm sea.

From its central highlands fissures and ridges radiate, mapped with jungle: green velour sleeves which fall right down to the tide. Coral snakes curl up like strings of lacquered beads, water lizards bask in the sun, macaws thicken the noon sky in flocks. Up there in the highlands the light slants between the trees in distinct beams. At night you dream you are down in the island's fever-haunted valleys, where the aboriginals – painted ash-white with blackened eye-sockets – pursue you without mercy to the shore. 'While the currents are generally labyrinthine,' the guidebooks promise, 'the water unforgiving and wine-dark, you can sometimes find a shallow bay filled with water of an intense blue.'

She stares into the make-up mirror.

'I'm like a whitewashed wall,' she decides. 'Should I go to the zoo?'

On the way she thinks of Dave, who never got in touch.

The streets smell of burning rubber, and cold has made the air transparent. You can see every building in the city centre – every duct and aluminium window frame, the gilded iron on every old bridge – from miles away, and sense the river flowing grey and gelid to the sea. At the zoo a few Japanese and Italian tourists shiver from cage to cage, photographing one another while waste paper and empty peanut shells blow about their ankles. Wherever you go in

the zoo you can hear the strange, carrying, bird-like cry of the lar
gibbons.

These coffee-coloured animals huddle like lookouts among the
metal struts in the ceiling of their tall cage. They hold their delicate
hands curved in front of them as if the joints are painful. Their eyes
look bruised. They face steadily into the cold wind and cry out as
though there is some message in it they cannot understand, only
celebrate. Sophia can't bear this. To escape them she takes the
underpass to the Nocturnal Mammal House, thinking:

'If my face is a map, it must never show a wilderness—'

All down the west coast of the island at night glitter the lights of a
modern city five miles long, its towers like black and gold cigarette
packets standing on end. In its shopping malls fluorescent light
catches the surfaces of hard and soft designer goods: matte plastics,
foams of lace and oyster satin, the precise curves of cars and shoes
and shoulder pads. This city is well known for the scent of Anaïs-
Anaïs in the streets; stacked video screens in the cocktail lounges;
and, down by the sea-front, where men push past you smelling of
sweat and Chinese food, neon of green, red or frosty blue. Music
pulses from its amusement arcades and night clubs. In the jazz bars
they serve only Black Heart rum, and you can hear the intricate bass
and saxophone lines twenty miles out to sea.

'It's none of these things,' she admits to herself. She laughs.

'My face is the map to an island off the coast of Norway. A few
quiet people from Oslo live there at weekends, in coloured wooden
houses. To get there you first catch a train to Sandvika, where a
bank of wild flowers comes right down to the station platform.'

The further you go into the mammal house, with its walls of
undressed brick, the darker it gets. The Moonlight World itself is
illuminated only by the dim yellow lamps in each specimen
compartment. Its air is full of the recorded blips and warbles of
nocturnal insects or birds. Groups of people come and go
preoccupiedly in front of the animals; pause silhouetted on the
edge of vision; vanish murmuring round an unexpected corner. It
is quite crowded: attracted immediately by the most beautiful

miniature fox with creamy beige fur, soft thick tail and enormous ears, Sophia finds herself standing next to a young man.

'Isn't it lovely?' she exclaims, for something to say.

But he seems less interested in the fox than its compartment, in which has been reconstructed – with a bit of stone, brushwood, and the skull of a camel embedded in fine sand – a dreary little corner of some desert. The fox trots so intelligently about this lost or reduced territory! You can feel its warmth and liveliness even when it curls up and goes to sleep. At first Sophia is delighted like this by every animal she sees – lemurs, echidnae like soft toys, civet cats and desert mice. But soon the air feels too warm. It smells increasingly like sawdust and urine. The animals, she notices suddenly, often move in agitated, repetitive patterns behind the smeary, finger-printed glass. A child, laughing shrilly, makes claws of its hands and runs up and down in front of a puzzled cat.

On her way out, Sophia has to pass the young man.

'Still looking?' she calls, but he doesn't seem to hear. In the feeble light from the compartment she can see how tight he grips the plastic rail; how drawn his face is, how wide and tired his eyes. He takes out a notebook and begins to write intently in it. He is copying down the details of the animal, which are recorded on a small plaque.

6: In Omber Grove

Whatever else it may be, EON HEART is the record of a journey, made some time during the last fifty or sixty years, into one of the less-travelled countries of the world. And often a plain record, too:

'For four miles round the bay at Enchidoche,' the author tells his readers, 'where the deeper water runs inshore, will be found meat-packing plants and sheds which, until recently, were used for drying fish.' He includes specific sailing instructions – 'Half a mile from Tharasalla Point, sandbars and wrecks show themselves at half tide. We went in boldly and got ten feet of clearance at low water. Keep

Mutton Rock in line with the derelict flensing factory on Auxilliadora Island and it will take you clear of the sand' – though they are not for major ports; and clear sketches in pen and ink of items of special interest:

'A diadem of yellow and blue macaw feathers, with the Clan Sign.'

Yet this country is never referred to by name. And if, in its original condition, Peter Ebert's copy contained a map, it has been lost with the title pages. The surviving text, a description of the interior, speaks only of villages, minor towns and rivers too small for any atlas to record. The kinds of clues it might offer are obscured by the author's style:

> Exploration, anthropology, natural history. Metaphysics, poetry and fear. A travel book should be about all these. But then it must whirl itself away beyond them; and, at once runaway boat and racing current, plunge between the dark walls of its own silence until it becomes only a spume of visions and metaphors – so that its reader, gripped by the vertigo of new experiences, is compelled to close it suddenly and walk away in an attempt to control his own excitement. In short, it must address our *desire*.

– or lost among the partly torn pages, stains and defacings, of which Ebert has now compiled a list so exhaustive it defeats any use he might make of it. 'p43: two words of text heavily deleted in red ball point pen, and another word – perhaps "fugazi" – inserted above.' 'p53/9 missing.' 'p60 detached, folded in half, and reinserted between pp75/6. Scrawled across it in black marker pen the words, "Mary I cant believe this. See you at ten." This unsigned, and the ink has deeply penetrated the paper.'

Peter no longer eats out in the evenings. He has exchanged his room at the Midland Hotel for a cheaper one in a boarding house a short way out of the city centre. From his window he can now see: a short stretch of cracked, littered pavement (Omber Grove), curving away to a junction (with Quex Road); a unisex hairdresser's called *Nueva Swing*; and a newsagent owned by an old man with the acronym FUGA tattooed on the inside of his left wrist. Though Peter still wears the expensive, generously cut suits and striped shirts you would expect to see at the Doric Restaurant, he no longer shaves every day and even forgets to wash. Obsessed by a puzzle his intelligence is unequal to, he has resigned from his job, and goes agitatedly from one lending library to another, from reference library to museum, looking for a complete copy of the book.

He has often wondered why it was given to him, speculating, 'It's not uncommon for a commuter to pass on, say, a newspaper he's finished with.' But when he reviews the circumstances of the gift – the crowd, the train, that white face with its shiny lumps of flesh – he understands that this is too simple an answer. His notebook describes a visit to the zoo, concluding disappointedly:

'After all, the Fennec is only a kind of fox.'

Every morning the pale light throws on to the wall of his room the shadow of a tree outside in Omber Grove. At first this image is so clear and sharp that Ebert can make out the patches of condensation on the window pane and construct the whole depth of the tree – its nearer branches sharp and black, the further ones less and less distinct. Later it fades until you have to work just to see it. Before it vanishes altogether it seems more like a product of the wall than of optics: as if, lighted by a very faint inner radiance, the wall has offered some memory of its own as a curio, as an almost random pattern. Someone pushes a pram down the street outside.

7: The Truth Which Most Contradicts Itself

Sophia often gets up late and walks about the city in her fur coat, watching the afternoon light die out of the residential streets. From the recreation grounds come the shouts and whistles, the tragic howls of some football game. At this time of year, with the sun setting at half past three behind a frieze of bare sycamores, the big red-brick houses round the parks have a comfortable November style: yew, holly and privet make their gardens mysterious, their lighted front rooms warm and inviting, as if Christmas had already come.

On the pavement one woman says to another:

'He's had no proper dinner then?'

'No, he's like a whitewashed wall. Eating chocolate all the time, well it's no good, is it? Just no good at all. All he thinks about is that CD.'

This reminds Sophia of Oslo. The phrase 'en koppe caffe og en koppe sjokolade' comes back to her very clearly. 'The morning we went to Toyen,' she thinks, 'to the Munchmuseet, we sat in an upstairs café. He looked into his cup and said in a lugubrious, Norwegian voice, "Nothing lasts forever!" and we laughed.'

Whenever she recalls something like this a shiver of excitement runs through her, itself an echo of the excitement she felt every moment in those days. '"Nothing lasts, especially a cup of chocolate!" He was so clever at mimicking himself.' Her own cup, she remembers, was decorated with three thin horizontal lines: pink, maroon, pastel blue. 'They seemed so precise and yet so fragile against the bluish-white depths of the china. I was afraid to move the saucer in case they rippled and broke.' She felt the tendency of all things to quiver without warning and fall away from perfection. But as long as she left her coffee untouched, and the sun continued to pour in so brightly across the marble table-top, the world would remain fixed. It would maintain its exact edges.

At Oslo airport, waiting for the flight back, she bought a box of matches. On its label an attractive little landscape – a tree, some low hills, a lake – was silhouetted in black against an ochre ground. 'Bruks-Eske,' ran the legend. She had no idea what it meant. 'Hjelpestikker.' For a long time she kept it on the make-up table in 236. It was an impulse of love not so much for him, she recognised, as for Oslo itself: she never used the matches, but the box could make her think so suddenly of the view from Holmenkollen, or the seagulls in Pipervika harbour, that everything seemed to rush out of her and empty itself away like water.

'En koppe caffe og en koppe sjokolade: that's what we had.'

Though which of them gave the order to the waitress she is no longer sure. Weakened and tranquillised by these memories, Sophia stands in the middle of the pavement, staring helplessly over some railings at a strip of grass strewn with fallen leaves where two dogs are running in opposite circles in the gathering dark. Then, wondering what people must think of her, she walks off quickly towards the city centre and goes into the first bar she finds.

'Black Heart rum, please.'

Leaving it two or three hours later, she wishes she could fly up into the trembling meniscus of light over the city. Some rain has fallen and the air is warmer. High up there are a few clouds like ribs. From above, she imagines, they must look like something drawn on a transparency between the aeroplane and the earth.

'I did think it would last forever,' she admits. 'I did think it would.'

8: Peter Ebert's Gift

Meanwhile Ebert lurches about the city, the EON HEART clutched to his chest, now in one hand, now in the other. The streets are glassed with rain, the long cotton coat he often wore to the Doric is sodden and filthy, his route has become as habitual as any dosser's. By seven or eight a.m. he's on the pavement outside the Midland Hotel where he used to live. He spends much of the morning at Regent's, shuffling his feet in the cold draughts under the great Victorian vault. At lunchtime he takes himself off to one or another of the city's little parks. He has stopped pretending that by this means he can 'understand' the book. Neither is he driven any longer by the urge to revisit, venue by venue, the stages of his own descent – the platform where he was given it, the libraries in which he searched for it, the rooms in which he copied it out.

Instead he reads the book to himself for itself. Mid-afternoon finds him in the Natural History Museum, moving his lips over the words 'fly down mass' (p62) or returning to the most resistant passage of all:

> After all why *should* our goal be the reinstatement of an illusory 'exact' relationship between events and words? If you probe in the ashes you will never learn anything about the fire: by the time the ashes can be handled the meaning has passed on. Every adventure is a cup so empty it can be drunk from again and again and again. Every adventure is so perfect it verges on silence. (p112)

His hair has gone grey.

Perhaps from all this reading, his eyes are inflamed, caked at the corners, deeper-set than he remembers. If he is ever frightened it is not when he smells his own breath in the morning. Or when in the mirror he sees a man twenty years older than the one who, in an unguarded moment a month or two ago, accepted a book just because it was offered him. These shocks soon pass. He slides them over his real fear, that he will begin to read the book aloud to passers-by. There are days when every park bench is a pulpit. He feels himself begin to speak. If he did, how could he bear their contempt?

Regent's Station, 4.30: commuters prowl uneasily beneath its scrolled iron girders in the bitter cold. The arrivals board makes a fluttering, disappointed noise and a train is wiped off as they watch. In his turn, Ebert watches them, looking for the one he could talk to; makes off, limping, just in time. He has the intolerable sense of being at a locus, where something is struggling to be revealed.

'I—'

Every adventure verges on silence.

Trapped by the rhetoric of the EON HEART he sees how impossible it will be to say anything ever again, and by nightfall finds himself standing on an obscure corner in the pool of light outside the *New Venus* dry cleaner's. Across the road a few market stalls are closing down for the night. There is a smell of rain, leather, soapsuds, food; in a gust of wind the plastic over the stalls shifts uneasily; a tortoiseshell cat is staring intently down a drain. Inside the *New Venus* a woman in a fur coat is arguing with the proprietor.

'What colour were the trousers?'

'There weren't any trousers,' she repeats tiredly.

Ebert sees a tall untidy woman with brown hair and wide shoulders, whose age is hard to guess because her face is turned away from him. Beneath the bulky fur, which is itself in need of a clean, her body has heavy, relaxed qualities, as if she has always been comfortable with it. Her shoes are scuffed, black suede peeling off to reveal the plastic heel; and wet pavements have left little pale splashes of mud on her stockings. In one hand she holds a pair of gloves, in the other a carrier bag printed with the name of a well known off-licence.

'Ah,' says the proprietor, an elderly Asian. '*No* trousers.'

He takes her ticket and stares at it for some moments.

'One white shirt. Two pullovers. A blue dress,' she reminds him. 'You said I could have them before six.' But the proprietor can find none of these garments on the rack behind the counter. Instead he keeps offering her quite different ones.

'This?'

'No.'

'This?'

Making a gesture of disgust she walks quickly to the door. Ebert, who has been following their exchange as if it represented some warm real world from which he is now endlessly separated by the existence of the book, turns guiltily away from the window. He hears the door of the *New Venus* swing open. In a gust of heated, solvent-laden air she crosses the road. Heels click, bottles clink. Before he can stop himself Ebert has pushed his way between the market stalls and is hurrying after her. Bare electric bulbs illuminate his face, her retreating back. Spoiled vegetables slither under their feet. He hears himself call out.

'Wait! I was given a book!' And then, managing at last to touch her arm shyly, 'Please let me read you this—'

Horrified by his fatal loss of self control, and hallucinating in his anxiety to escape before he can add anything more, a strong smell of rum, Ebert dodges away from her and runs blindly into a brick wall.

9: The Hearts of Things

'All at once you can't make head or tail of anything, can you?'

Tonight Sophia is with a man whose name she doesn't know. This has happened before, if not often. When they got back to the Central Hotel the bar was still open.

'Would you like a drink?'

'It's kind of you,' he said. 'No.'

He was so preoccupied she found it easy to keep her face turned away from him. While she collected her room key he sat on the edge of a chair in the foyer, staring down between his shoes at the design in the carpet as though he were trying to see past it. Every time the door opened, a cold draught came into the foyer and he looked up suddenly. He was thinner than she'd thought, and his coat was ruined.

'I hope you didn't hurt yourself too much,' she apologised. 'I thought you were the man from the dry cleaner's. I was so angry with him!'

'It's a relief to talk to someone,' he said obscurely.

'Didn't I once see you at the zoo?'

He passed his hand puzzledly across his face.

Now they are up in 236, with the door a little open so that the room is filled with a brown light. She has helped him off with his coat. He doesn't say much, but sits there on the bed, leaning forward with his hands between his knees. She likes his face, which though young is so tired it seems all bone, stubble, grey eyes; which is incapable of taking shelter; which admits desire but never alleviation. She wants to touch it gently round the eyes and cheeks, and at the same time say, 'You can just sleep if that's what you'd like. I mean, we don't have to do anything at first.' She can imagine herself saying just those words: 'I mean.' Then a couple go past in the corridor outside, talking and laughing quietly. At this a shiver runs through him and he pulls away from her.

'All at once you can't make head or tail of anything—'

Out of the pocket of his coat comes an old book; and before she has time to realise what he is going to do, he has reached out and switched on the bedside light—

—To Peter Ebert the lamp seems brighter than it can possibly be, a kind of lightning flash that splits the air diagonally between them to reveal the appalling rose-coloured *map* which obscures her face.

He recalls the words, 'Instants of self-awareness too confused to be of any use.'

The book has become agitated in his hands, leafing through its own pages with increasing hysteria until they flicker and blur like destinations on the 'departures' board at Regent's Station. In slow motion Sophia averts her face from the light, turning her head to the left and dropping it forward and down so that her chin will be tucked protectively into the hollow of the clavicle on that side. Before she can complete this characteristic passive gesture, it seems to Ebert that the EON HEART has left his hands and embedded itself in her face. As it is sucked away, a white arc hangs fluorescing in its wake, overlapping images of an open book fossilised in the very air of the room.

Sophia opens to it like a flower—

—Every story is so perfect it verges on silence: in this moment none of us can ever be sure whether the map receives the book or is received by it. The light flares up, room 236 is filled with the strange, carrying, bird-like cry of the lar gibbons, while a voice repeats endlessly:

'It's lovely. It's so lovely—'

—It isn't a dream. The book lies on the bed, its accumulated defacements glowing like stigmata. With the light dying out of the air between them, Peter and Sophia are flung apart. They will find

one another again confidently enough. She will be surprised by the
heat of his skin and whisper, 'I only felt the slightest touch.' The way
the hollow of her back curves up out of the waistband of her slip
will make her seem astonishingly real and human to him. Just
before dawn there will steal over the 'entresol' floor of the Central
Hotel that silence which enfolds lovers and lovers' cries and is only
deepened by them.

Aware of it pressing upon them its padded warmth, they will
go to the window of 236 and smile out at the city – five miles of
coloured neon where the jungle comes down to the sea, buildings
like elegant black and gold cigarette packets standing on end, music
from the amusement arcades trailing out like lights across the water:
the smell of Black Heart rum and the scent of Anaïs-Anaïs in the
streets.

Sophia will sit before the mirror in the morning, while Peter
reads (already planning how to pass the book on, in some jazz bar
or pizzeria) and then scribbles on the fly-leaf, just under the title in
that intense, endlessly expectant white space—

Take me aside. Tell me a sign.
Send me a neon heart. Seek me inside.

The Horse of Iron and
How We Can Know It
and Be Changed By It Forever

Recently I switched on in the middle of a television arts programme. Two men were moulding in brass something which looked at first sight like the stripped carcass of a turkey, that exact, sharp-edged cage of bone which reveals itself so thoroughly through all the strips and flaps of flesh after Christmas dinner. It turned out, though, to be something less interesting, a classical figurine, a Poseidon or Prometheus which systematically lost its magic as the layers of casting material were knocked off carefully with the back of an axe. This was so essentially disappointing – a striptease by which, by removing veils of strangeness and alien signification, the sculptor revealed a value ordinary and easily understood – that to replace it I turned off the TV and imagined this:

Another foundry, somewhere in the night, somewhere in history, in which something like a horse's skull (not a horse's *head*: a skull, which looks nothing like a horse at all, but like an enormous curved shears, or a bone beak whose two halves meet only at the tip, a wicked, intelligent-looking purposeless thing which cannot speak) came out of the mould, and all the founders were immediately executed to keep the secret. They had known all along this would happen to them. These men were the great craftsmen and engineers of their day. They could have looked for more from life. Yet they crammed down their fear, and got on with the work, and afterwards made no attempt to escape.

This was how I learned the secret of the horse, which I now give here, after first folding it across itself like a slip of paper, in a further intricating gesture:

1: THE FOOL

A young man, in whose dark hair a single strand of grey has recently appeared, decides to set out on a series of excursions suggested by the fall of the cards.

Complex rules will determine the direction of each journey. For instance, the suit being WANDS, he will only go North if the journey is to take place in the second half of the year; or if the next card turned up is a *Knight.*

Equally intricate rules, whose algebraic clauses and counter-clauses he intuits with each new cast of the cards, cover the choice of South, West and East; of destination; even of the clothes he will wear: but he will always travel by train. This decision is based on the relationship he has identified between the flutter of cards falling in a quiet cold room and the flutter of changing destinations on the mechanical indicator boards at railway stations. This similarity rests, he is willing to admit, on a metaphor: for while the fall of the cards is – or seems – random, the sequence of destinations is – or seems – controlled.

To represent himself in this affair, the young man – or 'Ephebe' – has chosen THE FOOL. This card, therefore, will never turn up. He has subtracted it from the deck and keeps it beside him; each afternoon, as the light goes out of the room, it seems to fluoresce up at him from the table or the arm of his chair, more an event than a picture. We move forward through time by the deeply undercutting action of Desire. As THE FOOL steps continually off his cliff and into space, so the Ephebe is always a presence attempting to fill the absence that has brought him forth. He is a wave tumbling constantly forward into each new moment, and his journeys are thus in every sense a trip. By following the journeys as they fall out, he believes, he will open for himself a fifth direction; and to help identify it he will bring back from each journey an object. These objects or *donnés* will eventually comprise both a 'compass' and a set of instructions for its use.

All the Ephebe's journeys begin from London.

2: THE MAGUS *representing Heterodox Skills*

Some are no more than commuter trips, on trains with automatic sliding doors and the interior design of buses. They arrive at the platform loaded with well-groomed, purposive people who seem prosperous but new to it: clerks and estate agents already a bit pouchy in the face, doing all they can with a shirt and a tie and a padded shoulder to pass themselves off as dangerous, successful accountants from the City – men and women in their early twenties who pride themselves on looking like self-satisfied bullies.

Trains like this run hourly between Harrow and Euston, through a station called Kilburn High Road, the high walls of which are covered with the most beautiful graffiti. They are not scrawls whose content – 'LUFC wankers die tomorrow' 'No brains rule' – and context are their only significance, but explosions of red and purple and green done with great deliberation and exuberance, shapes like fireworks going off, shapes that bulge like damp tropical fruit, with an effect of glistening surfaces. They are names – 'Eddie' 'Daggo' 'Mince' – but names which have been transformed from sign or label into illustration: *pictures* of names. After them everything else looks dull, the high brick walls of the next station – Hampstead South – resembling the walls of some great windowless linear prison. The children who do this call it 'bombing'; they bomb their personalities on to the walls.

When the train stops at Kilburn High Road the doors slide open as if it is waiting for someone and after a long time an old man gets on and goes to an empty seat. His overcoat is belted but he has no shirt on, so you can see clearly the mass of springy yellowish-white hairs between his withered old pectoral muscles. A rank smell comes up from him. As soon as the doors close, he rolls a cigarette and smokes it with relish, smiling and nodding around at the other passengers. The men stare at their polished shoes. The women draw away and look angrily at one another as he pulls back his cuff to consult his watch. This grand gesture reveals the word FUGA tattooed inside his grimy wrist. 'No one dare remind him,' the

Ephebe muses, 'that this is a No Smoking carriage.' And then: 'We should live our lives the way those children sign themselves, bombing our names on to the prison walls inside our heads.'

From this, his first excursion, he brings back a flattened cigarette stub, porous and stained brown at the end where the old man has held it gently between his lips.

3: THE HANGED MAN, *representing the descent of light into darkness in order to redeem it; in its female aspect, the Sophia of Valentinus*

New trains run on the line between Wakefield and Huddersfield. Inside them, next to every door, is a sign which reads PRESS WHEN ILLUMINATED TO OPEN. Illuminati everywhere should know about this sign. Between Wakefield and Huddersfield illumination is likely to come as a corollary of the abandoned factories visible from the train; the rubbish that clogs the shallow river; the dour failed lives in the houses beyond. What is the Ephebe to do on receiving it? Press the button and jump out of the train?

In the overheated carriages of the 22.01 his journey pulls out like chewing gum; then snaps.

At Dewsbury a tired-looking woman gets up to leave the train. Round her neck she is wearing five or six gold chains, each bearing either her initial or her Christian name. They cling and spill between the tendons of her neck like a delicate gold net. She stands in front of the doors, which will not open for her. The sign is illuminated but she has not noticed it. Soon the train will pull away again and she will still be on it. She looks around with growing agitation.

'I can't just work these doors out. Can you?'

The Ephebe would like to be able to reply:

'What you call yourself, who you claim yourself to be by putting on all your necklaces, is not as important as the act itself.' That gesture, of netting or fixing, he believes, is what actually identifies her. He would like to be able to explain, 'People love you for the identity in the act, an identity so frail they must constantly help affirm it.' But all he actually says is,

'I think you have to press the button.'

At this the train gives a lurch, as if it has lost its patience.

From this journey the Ephebe brings back an item of personalised jewellery in the form of the name SOPHIA. The Aeon called Sophia, Valentinus reminds us, astonished to find herself separate from the Good, mistook for its light the tawdry, bluish flicker of the created world, and flung herself towards it. By desiring God so strongly she fell away from Him and into the city of Alexandria, where she still redeems herself daily as a prostitute. (In some versions of her agony, Sophia *becomes* the city, and as library, language, labyrinth, is thus the instrument of Mankind's redemption. In others, rather than falling away from the Father, she denies herself to Him in reprisal for some never-defined unkindness to His children.

4: THE LOVERS, *representing Alchemical Marriage and the Concordance of Opposites*

Now the Ephebe lives along the line.

His journeys divide themselves between those on routes he has never travelled in his life – such as the one that worms its way, stopping at every station from Shotton on round the coast, from Crewe to Bangor – and those he already knows by heart, so that he can recognise every power pylon, substation or battery hen house between, say, London St Pancras and Sheffield Central.

He delights in the surprises of an unknown line.

Suddenly the sea is racing along by his shoulder, light spattering off it like frying fat. Later the train crawls past container depots, and a tank farm lit up mysteriously in the night. The guard announces, 'Once again lays n gem I do apologise your late arrival and inconvenient cause,' and the Ephebe wakes next morning in the Rose & Crown: where like some travelling salesman he feels obliged to guzzle bacon, eggs, sausage and hot tea while he looks speculatively out at the wet provincial street.

As a result of one of these journeys he drifts into a tranced, sensual affair with a young woman a little older than himself who runs her mother's boarding house. In the mornings she serves breakfast to the guests, while he lies in bed imagining the men as they watch her moving about the room with her tray. Though she has already brought him his own breakfast in bed, kissed him, watched him eat it with a kind of unfashionable pride in his appetite, the Ephebe sometimes finds himself envying them what he thinks of as an intensely *formal* experience of her. They see her only once or twice a year, at the beginning and end of a day. Some of them try to look down her blouse as she puts the crockery on the table; others are content to talk to her about the weather; yet others are hypnotised by the quick deftness of her hands as she lays out knife, fork and serviette, or calmed by the smell of her body beneath the smell of her perfume.

When he tries to explain this to her she laughs and tells him, 'You're so greedy!'

This goes some way towards understanding, though perhaps not far enough. Increasingly, after she has taken away his breakfast tray, the Ephebe catches himself staring up through the attic skylight at the heavy white clouds, wondering if he can disguise himself and, like some boy out of a Medieval poem, appear one morning among the commercial travellers at the breakfast table to observe her unobserved: and from this journey he brings back only the sound of her voice as she urges him, 'Fuck me. Fuck me,' in the night.

5: THE CHARIOT, *representing Self-Expression*

All journeys are enchanted.

It isn't so much that the landscape distracts you, as that something about the motion of the train – something about the very idea of constant, rushing, forward movement – makes you restless and slow to settle to anything. You read a few pages of a book and look out at some swans on a canal. A newspaper opened suddenly just down the carriage sounds like rain spattering on the window. Another chapter and you make your way down to the buffet or the lavatory. Between each event a reverie pours itself, as seamless as Golden Syrup, as smooth as the motion of the train. You wonder what the weather will be like in Leeds or Newcastle, turn to the *Independent* to find out, read: 'The world economy is likely to remain subdued.'

Looking up from these words to a landscape of hedges and ponds, copses and little embankments, the Ephebe sees with amazement a strange vehicle bounding along beside the railway line.

In a long, complex frame of metal tubing, suspended on four tractor wheels, are cradled: an engine wrapped round with copper pipes and sheaves of old electrical wiring; clusters of what seem to be household butane gas bottles; and, well to the rear, the padded seat of some old-fashioned military jet, into which is strapped a man. Gouts of earth and water spray up from its enormous wheels. From time to time this whole machine seems to be consumed by a kind of radiant discharge, through which its driver or pilot can be seen helplessly or furiously waving his arms.

Is he a prisoner of his vehicle? Or does he prefer to drive on the edge of disaster like this? He is a wasted old man. When it can be seen, his face runs the gamut of expression, wild with fear one moment, laughing with excitement the next. His long grey hair blows back in the slipstream. His lips contort. He has fastened himself into a tight brown leather suit along the arms and legs of which run clusters of neoprene tubing. Out of these at intervals erupt thick coloured fluids, which splatter over his chest or into his eyes. Though he blinks furiously, he suffers the indignity without harm: but wherever the machine is touched it blackens and smokes briefly, and lightning writhes along its chassis members.

One huge wheel flies off suddenly into the air. The old man claps his hands to his face. At that moment the train enters a tunnel, and the Ephebe can see only himself, reflected in the window.

If the appearance of the machine has filled him with astonishment, its disappearance leaves him with a curious mixture of elation and anger he can neither understand nor resolve. By the time he is able to unclench his hands and wipe his forehead, the train has left the tunnel for open ploughland across which spills a tranquil evening light. Wrestling desperately with one another, the old man and his machine have passed back into the dimension from which they came, where they leap and bucket and belly their way forever through rural England, scattering clods of earth, steam, small bushes and dead animals. But in the palm of the Ephebe's hand remains a small, intricately machined metal item, melted at one end to slag.

This he brings home with him. For months it remains warm to the touch, as if it had only lately been thrown out of the hearth of the heart.

6: THE TWO OF DISCS, *representing Change*

Some journeys encourage a different kind of fantasy.

In his journal the Ephebe records:

'For some time I was enchanted by a tiny station called Long Eaton on the main line between Derby and Loughborough. Here, two slatted wooden platforms surrounded by larch, pine and variegated holly gave the air of a rural halt at once bijou and mysterious: the last place you would expect an Inter-City turbine to stop. Sitting in the train, you had no idea what sort of landscape lay behind the woods. The wind rushed through them, so that you thought of yourself as being on some sandy eminence away from which spread an intimately folded arrangement of orchards and lanes, of broad heathland stretching off to other hills. Afternoon light enamelled the leaves of the holly. Owls and wood pigeons moved amid the branches. Everything was possible in the country – or garden – beyond.

'Then the light passed, the wind dropped and the train began to move again: you saw that the trees were dusty and birdlimed, and that they had hidden only housing estates, allotments, and a light engineering plant. A fat woman with a hyperactive child came into the carriage, sneezed in your face. "Just sit down," she warned the child. Instead it stared defiantly into her eyes for a moment then wandered off to make noises with the automatic door.

'Despite this I always looked forward to Long Eaton, as if I hoped each time that the enchantment would be maintained. Then one day I glimpsed, fleetingly, through the windows of a train speeding in the opposite direction, a station called Haywards Heath (it was on the line between London and Brighton), and realised immediately that both it and Long Eaton were references to a lost type, that intimate little station of middle-class children's fiction forty years ago. Conifers and sandy soil; foxes and owls and stolen ponies; gorse and gypsy caravans in a rough field: then some mystery about a pile of railway sleepers near the tracks, shiny with rain in the green light at the edge of the woods.'

The Ephebe has recognised his mistake. But is he cured of it? Or does he still hope that one day he will abandon his life as it now is, some freak fall of the cards throwing him into another one in which he gets down from a train at just such a fictional station without even a suitcase and walks towards some granite tor steeped in evening light? Whatever the answer to this question, he brings back from a subsequent journey a children's novel called *Island of Adventure* – though to give him credit he does not actually read it.

7: THE QUEEN OF SWORDS, *'We are the words; we are the music; we are the thing itself.'*

Long journeys encourage the Ephebe to read and write: but they also outline the great gap between the lived and the written. Under a railway bridge at night, in Glasgow perhaps, he finds himself staring into the window of *Appollo Video Supplies*. There on a large screen, the following video clip repeats itself endlessly and silently to the drunks who stagger past:

In front of an Asian boy who watches captivated, a sword is beaten into existence out of the sparks of the anvil. The boy's father lies dead. The boy will grow up to be a Ninja fighter, and avenge him. His eyes are huge now as he discerns his uncertain yet triumphant future in the steel. The sparks stream past.

Exactly what you would expect, thinks the Ephebe, and indeed this boy is only a cliché: but look up from the screen and you can see the orange sparks fly out of it and down the road, where amid the dancing hailstones they light up in other dreary shopfronts something more than 'Winter Woollens – Reduced'.

Language is a scandal because it can make connections like these. Stories pass the experienced world back and forth between them as a metaphor, until it is worn out. Only then do we realise that meaning is an *act*. We must repossess it, instant to instant in our lives.

8: DEATH. *Everything opens to contain its opposite.*

Whenever the Ephebe looks up there is something new in the landscape – gorse spilling down the side of a steep little hill with a farm on top; factory chimneys dissolving in a blaze of sun he can't bear to look at; a clear night somewhere up north, with contrails drawn across Orion and the Dog – but eventually journeys like this must become tiring. The clean yellow front of an Inter-City train, rushing towards the platform in the sunlight, no longer fills him with excitement. He's slept in too many overheated rooms, under thick continental quilts; eaten in too many station cafés; awaited too many connections. He is losing faith in the insights he had, the relationships he formed.

All he remembers about the city he's in is a display of popular wedding stationery – 20% off – which, as he walked past it, seemed for a moment to merge indistinguishably with the cigarette ends, burger cartons and supermarket receipts on the pavement: so that for a moment everything became illegible to him, because the floor of the display window and the street, the inside and the outside, were only extensions of each other. He yawns and stares in the mirror. Behind him his bag is packed.

Later, the 5.18 Sheffield/St Pancras is delayed by repair works along the line, then again by a fault in one of its power cars. It's Sunday. The Ephebe dozes and then wakes up abruptly. The train isn't moving and he has no idea where he is. He looks for lights or signs in the night: only dark fields. He has no watch – it was broken in Edinburgh – and the only one he can see belongs to a woman sitting across the aisle. Made of plastic, this has a dial transparent to its own works, greenish flickering cogs in the complexity of which your eye loses the position of the hands. The Ephebe falls asleep again for a moment, dreams briefly of the old man and his strange energetic machine, racing alongside the train but this time looking in, then wakes suddenly in the horrified knowledge that he has cried out in his sleep and the whole carriage has heard him. He has become someone who makes noises in his sleep on the London express: a worn-out middle-aged man with bad teeth and a cloth briefcase, his head resting uncomfortably in the corner between the seat-back and the window.

From this journey, though, he brings back a memory of his childhood in Warwickshire.

One July morning, sitting hypnotised by the sound and weight of the river in Stoneleigh Park, he watched the hot sunlight spilling and foaming off the weir until he could no longer separate the look of the water from its strange, powerful, almost yeasty smell. Most of the objects of his childhood, he remembers, were transfigured in this way for him; and he notes in his journal that night:

'Little earthy lanes and banks become secret entryways into the warm fields and bemused emotional states of childhood, when in a kind of excited fatigue you watch your own hand come closer and closer to the dry grey wood of an old gate, and find yourself unable for a second to context the one by the other or find a single context – unless it is something as huge and general as "the world" – which will accept both. In the end you are able to understand only the intense *existence*, the photographic actuality of such objects. In that kind of childhood everything is fused into the light like flowers fused into a glass paperweight. At first I thought this light was in itself a fusing-together of other states or qualities which I could only vaguely label – "self awareness" "growing sexual curiosity" "the unconditional trances of narcissism". Now I see that the child is contrived wholly of the things he has already experienced: a spider web in the grass, a jet flying overhead; a cocoon of cuckoo-spit, the flare of light off the windscreen of a designer car. These elements are reassembled as a way of looking at other things. It was this continual fusing and re-fusing – this infolding – of experience which I perceived as a light bathing the landscape.

'What we call "meaning" is not what the light discovers, because what it discovers is itself. Now cast by the adult on new objects, it is valuable only for its very act of illumination. *Perception* is meaning. Meaning is an act.'

9: THE MOON, *representing the state of impure horror; human faculties reach their limit and collapse before the Inward Light*

As soon as the journeys are over, the cards can be laid to rest.

The Ephebe waits in the taxi rank outside Charing Cross Station after his last trip. A short, badly dressed woman of about twenty-five or thirty is walking up and down the station forecourt shouting 'You bloody piece of paper, you bloody piece of paper' at a letter she holds in her right hand. Her face is red with effort, her hair straggles down around it. A maroon wool coat like a carpet compresses her fat breasts. 'You *bloody* piece of paper!' Eventually she varies the emphasis on this accusation until it has illuminated briefly every word; as if trying for the feel of some final, indisputable delivery. Her sense of drama, the transparency of her emotion (whether it is unaffected misery or something more complex and theatrical declaring itself) leaves him unnerved.

No one else seems bothered. Out on the Strand the taxis continue to drive homicidally at one another. The people waiting for them laugh and talk about the price of things. But as his cab arrives, and he sees the light dancing in the raindrops on its bonnet, the Ephebe cannot repress a shudder. Later, when he tries to recall the incident, he will be able to fasten only on the minor details – the minicab touts, for instance, mooching up and down the queue pleading in soft voices, 'Any long jobs?' while the woman stares down at her bit of paper like Ellen Terry as Joan of Arc and rubs her free hand in the food stains down the front of her coat.

'You bloody piece of *paper*!'

That afternoon he sits by the downstairs front window of his small house, looking out into the street. Rain drips steadily on the window sill. 'This drip, which is sometimes doubled, sometimes trebled, syncopated,' he once wrote to a friend, 'is all that is most monotonous about London residential streets.'

In fact it is a street he rather likes: in summer all rain and sunshine and every minute the most surprising and confusing changes of light.

Over the road from the Ephebe's window two beautifully trimmed bushes stand out against a brick wall. He has no idea what they are. The word 'buddleia' comes to mind when he looks at them; but they are evidently conifers. Under certain lights, especially in the morning – 'When the world looks promising again despite what we know about it' – the brick takes on an old warm red colour. The wall itself seems to recede a little, as if the street had widened, and at the same time it becomes taller and longer. At that, the bushes no longer seem like bushes at all. Rather than being in front of the wall, they define two arch-like spaces *in* it. It is an illusion: but suddenly the Ephebe seems to be looking through two arches at a hedge some way behind the wall. The effect of this is of a glimpse in the well-matured garden of some great house near Warwick or Leamington, and it always delights him.

Tired out now by his journeys, unable to convince himself of the need to unpack his case, unsure of the success of his experiment, he makes himself a cup of coffee, then another. The room behind him is dim and quiet, full of secondhand furniture.

On a little veneered table he has arranged the incomplete Tarot, THE FOOL which represents himself, and the objects of his search – a flattened cigarette end stained with nicotine and spittle; an item of personalised jewellery in the form of the name SOPHIA; the vulnerable but determined whisper of a woman approaching her climax in the middle of the night; a small, intricately machined metal object, melted at one end; the children's novel *Island of Adventure*; particles of sleet billowing down an empty pavement; a page from his journal – though he cannot yet bring himself to do anything with them. Instead, he finds himself watching the school children running up and down the street. At half past four there is an increase in traffic. The rush hour has begun.

About fifteen minutes later the woman he watched this morning outside Charing Cross Station waddles into view from the junction with Harrow Road, crosses on to the opposite pavement and, going through one of the 'arches' in the wall, disappears from view. Sunlight splashes the pavement. Rain falls through it like a shower of sparks. Without thinking, the Ephebe leaves his house and rushes after her. The 'arch' is closing again even as he passes it. He has the sense of penetrating some material halfway between wood and stone, then something which is neither, something membraneous which clings for a moment round his face.

Now he is in the garden. Paths race out everywhere in front of him, across great lawns, between high topiary hedges, over patios paved black and white like chessboards surrounded by grey stone urns and leaden statuary. In this confused, ideal moment, the Ephebe believes he may go anywhere. With a shout of elation he attempts to fall forward instantly and endlessly in all possible directions; only to find to his dismay that in the very exercise of this privilege he has selected one of them.

The house, in all respects the same as his own, is empty.

Though the carpets have been removed, odd items of furniture remain – a small inlaid table, an old-fashioned brass fender with grotesque mouldings, an ironing board folded up in a corner – as if some tenant is still in transit.

He sees the woman he has been pursuing, standing quite still in her maroon coat staring out of a bay window in an upstairs room; he sees her through the open door, lumpen and heavy, from the landing at the top of the stairs. Light pours round her thickened, monolithic silhouette, transfiguring the bare floor of the room, illuminating where it spills out on to the landing rolls of dust beneath cream painted skirting boards. He knows that if he was able to enter the room and look over her shoulder now, he would not see North London or his own house. The light fixes him, photographic, frozen; it is the same hot, silvery light which falls on the dense trees on the other side of the valley, giving them the look of giant mosses, thick clumps and curtains of moss of the sort that drips down the ornamental waterfalls in old gardens.

'All the things it might be,' a voice says clearly. 'The one thing it is.'

At this a white bird flies past the three panes of the bay window, its shadow flickering between elongated bars of light over the walls of the room: entering the first pane from the left and leaving from the right, it crosses the third in the same direction, only then flying across the central pane from right to left, after which it vanishes.

'The one thing it is.'

The Ephebe knows that he must cross the doorway of this room. He must pass through the moment he finds himself in. Before he can do this, though, the woman must turn towards him, so that he sees balanced on her shoulders the skull of a horse. It is not a horse's *head*, but a skull, which looks nothing like a horse at all; and out of this enormous curved shears, this wicked bone beak whose two halves meet only at the tip, will come words. 'You bloody piece of paper,' she must admonish him. Only then will he be able to pass.

'You bloody written thing.'

10: THE HIEROPHANT, *representing occult force, voluntarily evoked*

The journeys are over.

The Ephebe, having returned to the front room of his own house and made himself another cup of coffee, has arranged on the veneered table – alongside the incomplete Tarot, THE FOOL which represented himself, and the objects of his search already noted – a further nine cards. For each card of the original spread, we discover, he drew an alternative which has remained unconsulted until now.

These blind or uncommunicating cards provoke completely different interpretations of his journeys, and of their 'meaning' for him and for us. For instance, as an alternative card to THE CHARIOT he drew THE AEON ('God has deconstructed the Old Universe and has learned too much to be able to build another'). Had he looked out of the opposite window of the railway carriage that day, he would have seen only a toddler with a string of snot at its nose, pedalling its plastic tricycle through the weeds, the heaps of dried mud and discarded plasterboard in the back garden of a newly completed council house in the Midlands. To simulate speed, the child kicks out violently with its little legs, while from its open mouth comes a constant high-pitched imitation of the roar of a jet fighter overhead – 'Nnnnneeaaaa!'

Here are the alternative cards he drew, in order:

The Nine of Discs; the Six of Wands; the Four of Swords; THE AEON; the Ten of Discs; the Ace of Swords; THE DEVIL; the Princess of Wands; FORTUNE. He is left only with the card he chose to represent himself. This was the Knight of Swords. As he turns it up, THE FOOL, which it replaces, charred and curled as if by some great heat or light, vanishes in incense smoke! He hears the horse repeat gently,

'All the things it might have been.'

Initiated now, the Ephebe smiles thoughtfully. Next to THE LOVERS he places the Four of Swords. He remembers the young woman whispering, 'Fuck me, fuck me,' in the night. What would he have seen if he had turned his head away from her then and looked into the quiet darkness of their upstairs room? The journeys are over. They have just begun.

Gifco

A few months after the death of our teenage daughter, we left her –
as we thought – safely buried in St Anne's churchyard, Barnes, and
bought a house in Peckham.

'My God,' my wife said, the day we moved in.

She wasn't keen. But Peckham suited me. Its main street was full
of cheap hardware shops. Fast-food wrappers blew about in the
sunshine. Driving past the Leisure Centre that first afternoon, we
noticed that part of its signboard had fallen off. The next day it had
lost the whole of the first E in 'leisure'. Peckham leaned up against
the rich suburb of East Dulwich (where at that time the Prime
Minister still lived) like some old bag lady against a West End shop
window. Every morning its rich complement of lunatics and
failures would begin to make their hesitant way down Rye Lane
into Peckham itself to do their shopping. There were halfway
housers, psychotics released suddenly into the community with a
carrier bag and a strange list to the left, failed old criminals with
eyes huddled and blank, fat women in jogging pants and carpet
slippers. They shambled and loped, or walked sideways like
Martinique land crabs. Shouts were drawn from them inadvertently
as their dreams and anxieties ebbed or flowed. They talked to
themselves without let.

Down the length of the lane massive horse chestnuts were in
blossom, their leaves so densely packed it was evening outside the
Jet paper factory at 9 a.m. The chestnut flowers looked like strange
little flickering pagodas of light. They always reminded me of
William Blake's 'tree full of angels'. Further down Rye Lane stood
the remains of an old hedge made up of holly, hawthorn and elder.
It was dusty, broken, full of gaps, full of rubbish from the house

behind it. Builders had been working on the house for months, perhaps years. The collapse of the property market towards the end of the '80s had made them desultory, half-hearted.

When I first went past, its windows were boarded over with panels of cheap blond wood. Across one of them had been scrawled in grey cellulose primer: GIFCO WE ARE HERE. This message began high up on the left of the panel but rapidly lost confidence and toppled away towards the right-hand bottom corner, the letters becoming smaller and harder to make out. It had a desperate air and I wondered who had written it. They weren't there any more. The house was silent. Gifco had never arrived. Or perhaps he had. Perhaps, waiting it seemed interminably in the dark behind the boards, they had made some essential mistake about his nature, about his plan and their part in it. Walking past among all the other lunatics I caught the corrupt, sweet scent of hawthorn blossom, and paused fractionally as if I had heard someone call my name.

Later that day a young policeman rang my doorbell. Anxious to do things properly, he showed me his warrant card twice: once on the doorstep and then again inside on the stairs. He was quietly spoken; dressed in jeans, a thick pullover and oxblood Dr Marten's shoes, not a colour you see much recently. He explained that he wanted to use my second-floor balcony to get a view of some houses further down the Rye. That was all right, I said. But would he be comfortable?

Showing me a cheap airline bag, he said:

'I could survive for days with what I've got in here.'

He didn't seem to have much more than a pale blue nylon rally-jacket and a two-way radio. 'Hello?' he said into the radio. 'I think I've got an OP.' He had a boyish look, an undiminished sense of the excitement of what he was doing. 'This'll be great,' he said. 'Great.'

I took him a dining chair to sit on, and a cup of tea. I found that he had camouflaged himself by hanging up two large squares of black plastic material and rearranging some flower pots along the low wall of the balcony. The radio was in front of him. He was grateful for the tea. 'It's a real sun-trap out here,' he said.

'I love the sun,' I told him immediately. 'I'm out here a lot.'

'If anything exciting happens I'll give you a shout,' he promised. He grinned.

'Better than watching it on the telly.'

After that, things were quiet. From the front room I heard him speak once or twice into the radio.

About half an hour later he went away again for ten minutes, then came back. 'Sorry about this,' he said, as I let him in. 'Something has happened. Not very spectacular, but something.' He had another cup of tea, and this time he spent much longer out there. He spoke into his radio.

'Control, control from Colin.

'I've just seen an IC3 climb up some ladders at the back of the house. Control, did you get that? Yes, yes, I can confirm that.

'No, he's gone up a ladder and through a door at the rear. Wearing a blue jacket: a ski jacket: an IC3.'

His voice became lively.

'Second floor, window on the right. Yes!' he shouted. Then:

'To your left, to your left!'

I was excited too. We huddled behind the camouflage plastic, craning our necks to see what was going on. I heard some faint shouts from down in the street. I thought I could see a lightly built figure running about in a back garden: a child or a teenager: an IC3.

Suddenly I realised the direction I was looking in. I said:

'Isn't that the house with the boarded-up windows?'

He stared at me.

'I wouldn't say anything about that.'

Later he added, as he put his things one by one back in the airline bag:

'After all, you've got to live round here.'

The radio fizzed and spluttered to itself from inside the bag. Every so often a woman's voice assembled itself out of this noise, like a child speaking into an empty tin to make itself important. It sounded like 'Paul? Paul?'

He zipped the bag shut.

'Can I use your loo, please?' he asked. He laughed. 'I think I'm going to be busy for the rest of the day and this is going to be my last chance.'

'He was nice,' I told my wife when she got home. She wasn't so sure.

'It never occurs to you to hold anything back,' she said.

That night I had a nightmare, in which, believing I had contracted angina, I visited several doctors. None of them could find anything to explain my symptoms. I became increasingly agitated. Finally I stopped in at a small chemist's shop somewhere in Bethnal Green. There, the pharmacist asked me to kneel in a bath of warm water while he made his examination. At first he could find nothing. 'She's been fairly thorough,' he said, of the last consultant I had seen. Then he inserted his fingers into my anus and began to pull. Why he would search there for the source of a pain in the heart, I have no idea. In the dream it seemed clear that this was the medicine of the East. Anyway, without much discomfort, out came a rolled-up copy of *The Spectator*, a journal to which I have contributed the occasional review.

'I swallowed *The Spectator*?' I said.

I burst out laughing. The pharmacist laughed too. There we were as the dream came to an end, in a shop smelling of coal tar soap and medicated shampoo, roaring with laughter like two naughty boys. But I woke up sweating. It was five o'clock in the morning; my wife was shaking me. Somehow, in the zone of slippage between dreaming and waking, 'spectator' had become 'watcher'. I was full of terror.

Next morning my wife asked:

'How do you feel?'

When I was a younger man I was very shy. I was frightened of being sick, having diarrhoea or fainting, especially in front of people. None of those things ever happened. Supposing there was something so deep inside you that you never heard from it, something so intricately woven into your personality that it was hidden, something which had nothing but contempt for you. Suppose one day it spoke quite clearly to you, with perhaps a shade of an echo, as if it came from a well, and told you in a clever voice that the things you did were shit. Would you want to hear it speak again?

'I feel fine,' I told her.

'I hope you do,' she said.

'You know what the funny thing is?' I said.

'No.'

'The funny thing is that the doctor had Allo Johnnie's voice.'

'Who's Allo Johnnie?'

'Don't you remember?'

After that I set up my own OP on the balcony at nights. It was hard to see clearly. But I thought I could make out a constant quiet coming and going at the Gifco house. There were visits and deliveries. Black plastic rubbish bags were manhandled into the garden and perhaps buried. By day, though, it lay hot and deserted behind its hawthorn hedge in the sun. Late one morning curiosity made me push my way through the hedge, prise the hardboard off one of the ground-floor windows, and climb inside. The air lay hot and heavy in the corners of the room. After a moment I could feel it in my chest, in my heart, all the lobes of my body. A single thin bar of light fell molten yellow across the concrete floor, revealing shreds of green linoleum, a dusty old three-seat sofa, its threadbare velvet covers faded from maroon to orange. I stood there for some time, lapped in the most perfect silence though the lunchtime traffic was already backing up on Rye Lane, heat shimmering off the bonnets of the little modern cars.

Peckham is always full of temporary bookstalls which appear and disappear in a day – one table pushed up against the window of a hairdresser or furniture shop, with perhaps thirty or forty dog-eared paperbacks on it. They are the result of house clearances: the books of the deceased, the evicted, the permanently hospitalised. That morning I had bought an old novel from one of them. I took it out, and, squatting down in that perfect ray of sun, began to read the first page – 'When I was a tiny boy I often sat motionless in the garden, bathed in sunshine, hands flat on the rough brick of the garden path, waiting with a prolonged, almost painful expectation for whatever would happen, whatever event was contained by that moment, whatever revelation lay dormant in it.'

As I read the word 'revelation' I heard someone come in through the front door. Feet scraped in the hall. I closed the book and stood up.

'I wondered if I'd find you here.'

It was the policeman, Colin.

'When did you begin to work for Gifco?'

We talked for so long that first morning I was late for lunch. When I got home I found a Ford van parked outside the house next to mine. 'Houses Cleared', was painted on its side in fake Edwardian script: 'Furniture Bought'. An oldish man, very active, with a pink face, grey hair and spectacles, wearing Marks & Spencer's joggers, a cardigan and a neck scarf, was making a pile of the stuff on the pavement while a younger one threw it into the van. The older man laughed and joked a lot.

'Lucky?' I heard him say. 'I'm not lucky!'

Cushions off a chair, a wooden ironing board, two black tin boxes about eighteen inches on a side and rusty at the corners; a grey double-breasted jacket and a pink shirt; old aluminium saucepans, plastic supermarket bags stuffed with clothes: everything went in, even the tangle of wire coat-hangers left behind in the wardrobe. A pair of stepladders was hurled in like a javelin.

Upstairs I found my wife.

'Someone's died next door,' she said.

She was standing at the window looking down into the street. I could hardly hear her over the sound of the television.

'Perhaps they're just moving,' I said.

84

'If he's just moving, why are they throwing his mattress into the back of the van like that? Look at that sock! If you're moving you don't just drop a sock in the road and leave it there.'

She rubbed the window with her hand.

'Those are someone's things.'

Through our wall you could hear the older man run energetically up and down the stairs inside the house, then shout:

'Here, catch this!'

'Christ!' my wife said disgustedly.

The pile in the back of the van grew unstable. For a moment it looked as if everything would totter and fall. With an intelligent, attentive expression on his face, shifting his balance like a goal-keeper intent on saving a penalty, the younger man watched it for a moment. But everything settled down again suddenly. He shrugged and walked away.

'They're just taking aim and throwing it in,' my wife whispered to herself. 'Those are someone's things,' she repeated, then:

'Can't you switch that fucking TV off?'

'It was you who put it on,' I said. 'You put it on yourself.'

'We'll be next. Don't worry about that. They'll be throwing us in the back of a van next.'

In a second, more formal dream of angina, I kept an appointment at King's College Hospital.

In the dream it was night-time. The hospital's bleak annexes straggled down Denmark Hill towards Camberwell in the curious bluish moonlight, buildings like shoeboxes, as shabby, bashed and precarious as the people they were supposed to rescue. From Mental Health to Cardiac, their corridors were all the same: stale cream glazed with dirt: cobwebs high up. At Cardiac Reception I counted the plastic chairs. There were sixteen, arranged in four rows on the faded blue lino. SOMETIMES, advised the poster above them, AN ACCIDENT AT WORK IS NO ACCIDENT. The rest of the furniture consisted of some white cupboards with curious sloping tops; a filing cabinet labelled 'Liver Clinic'. Long ago, the room had been part of a children's department. Blue and green tiles told the story of Jack and Jill. Beneath them, the receptionist whispered:

'Yes?'

'The Nine Stations of the ECG.'

'Pardon?'

'One dab of gel at each wrist, one at each ankle; five beneath the heart,' I explained. 'It's the heart that counts.' Too late now I saw that the Jack and Jill story had been compressed into just two lobes, 'Jack and Jill went up the hill' being followed instantly by 'Jack and Jill fell down the hill.' Act and consequence. The heart of events.

'It's hardly a matter of that,' the receptionist tried to explain. She could not find my file. Suddenly she raised her head and called:

'Mr Petorni?'

The waiting patients shifted uncomfortably in their seats. No Mr Petorni here.

'Doris Mullins? Doris Mullins?'

'No Doris Mullins here,' said a very old man, neatly dressed in tweed jacket and polished brown shoes, looking up briefly from *Aspects of Antiquity* in the Penguin edition. The rest of the patients – three women, twelve men – sat staring ahead with their arms folded or their hands in their laps. They looked used up, at the end of things. Yet among them sat one younger man, whose remaining hair was combed from left to right across his bald head. Whose blue *sta-prest* trousers covered his foreshortened thighs, on which rested hands abbreviated by fat, with signet rings. Whose soft leather jacket was zipped reverently over his fat little belly. Whose feet were clasped by oxblood shoes with a brogue detail. Like the shoes, his face was heavier at the bottom, thickening out and concentrating in the area of the neck. Deep lines slanted from the nose to the ends of the downturned mouth, so that lips, lines, eyebags, fat cheeks and all seemed to drape over the chin in a sequence of inverted V-shapes suspended from somewhere near his prominent ears. It was an extraordinary engineering solution, which gave him an expression of permanent dissatisfaction and anger. At the same time fear and genuine puzzlement made him look boyish and sad, and you saw that his lips had once been rather full and well-shaped.

'Colin!' I cried. 'Good to see you.'

Instantly, he opened his mouth and said:

'These people might be your mum and dad before they died. They haven't had much to do with hospitals. They haven't been out much except to the shops. They haven't had much in their lives at all. Now they find themselves on the edge of a transformation so great they have to sit down to face it. It is as full of vertigo as sin or birth or marriage; or their first job as a railway electrician. They fluff up like sparrows on these plastic chairs here at the cardiac clinic, looking around passively and yet with suspicion. They suppose they'll have to wait. Their heads go up at every name called, every new arrival at reception. Weak sympathies cross their faces. Then they go back to working out their place in the queue.'

'Colin!' I called. 'Don't you remember me?'

'You have slaughtered your child.'

He became a baby, asleep across its mother's knees, hands held in lax fists each side of its lolling unsupported head. Nauseated, I looked down at my own feet. They were bare and gnarled, the feet of a very old man, yellowed, dirty and covered with veins as thick as the cables that run in the tunnels alongside the Underground trains. Between them, on the dusty, dented wooden floor, lay two Polaroid photographs. I reached down to pick these up, my hand becoming huge in my own sight, pink, magnificently lined, and with the clarity of a thing seen through optical plastic.

'Mr Hamilton?'

'Thomas Daley, please!'

'Mr Marchant?'

The patients conferred.

'Did she say Markham?'

'Merchant. I think it was Merchant.'

'Or was it Martin?'

'Mr Marchant?'

'Mr Marchant?'

'Mr Marchant?'

This dream took place, as far as I can establish, at about 2.15 in the morning. As soon as I woke up from it I phoned Colin. Forty-five minutes later he turned up at the Gifco house, where he undid his coat nervously, gawping like a tourist at the rows of books I had arranged around the skirting boards.

'Where we going?' he said.

Gifco had told him nothing. I showed him the two Polaroids I had been provided with.

'You were in my dream,' I said, while he was examining them. 'You didn't look well. We're going to St Anne's churchyard.'

'Where's that?'

'Barnes,' I told him. I said: 'Gifco wants us to check something.'

'Fetch something?'

'Check something,' I corrected him. But immediately I began to wonder.

'I'm ready if you are,' said Colin.

On Rye Lane we got a minicab. The night was like oil, moving slowly down pipes. Camberwell, visually simplified by its own streetlights, gave way to the brutal sloping ramps of the Elephant. Each time I looked into the back of another car, a single passenger was looking out at me, warm and comfortable yet white-faced and uneasy.

'Where you want to go?' the driver asked eventually, with a kind of neutral exasperation.

'I'll tell you when we get there,' I said.

'Look at that,' said Colin suddenly. 'BMW 850i. Nice car.' Then: 'Wow! Houses of Parliament!'

Half an hour later he was running about in St Anne's graveyard in the dark. He ran with a strange, gliding gait, his head thrown back and his toes pointed. His breath steamed out in the cold air. He was pleased with himself. He had told the cab driver:

'We're not fucking paying that, mate.'

The moon cast the pale but definite shadows of trees across the bulk of the church. There were dead leaves scattered on the grass. Flowers in cellophane decorated a new grave. Many of the grave-stones – whose unreadable inscriptions all seemed to face away from me – were engraved with pictures: a tall arched window, with a ray of light striking through it on to an altar; stairs, rising to a rising sun, and the words 'Adele Junck'; an angel, with its head bowed and one hand offered to the spectator, palm outwards, as if to bar the way. I sat down companionably at the grave of Adele Junck, a woman who had died early of some dysmenorrhoeaic condition now easily remedied. If anyone could understand me it would be Adele.

I said:

'My name is Jack, and I am fifty years old. I was once a political commentator and literary critic. I was once a person. Once I had a daughter, with hair as red as your own (though her complexion was never so pale). We called her Sofia, because when she was a baby her eyes were direct enough to damage you if you looked into them without using a mirror. She grew up and went to school and at thirteen years began to listen to music which left me puzzled, cold and angry all at the same time. I loved her dearly for that, too. Now where the fuck is she? Tell me that.'

I began to cry.

'Here!' called Colin, his voice moving about erratically behind me in the darkness, like a voice from a broken stereo. He was trying to draw my attention to a grave decorated with brand new white chippings.

'Has it snowed, or what?'

He laughed uneasily.

'I thought this was snow!' he said.

Was that the moment I began to dig? Or was I already digging by then, forcing my stiffened fingers hurriedly into the dry fibrous earth like garden forks? I don't know. Was I digging at all? I have to say that I believe I was: I was scraping like a dog. I could hear myself panting and whimpering, off in some faraway night. Eventually Colin moved away, and everything was silent. When I looked up again, the stone ivy on the graves was sculptured perfectly by the moonlight. Moonlight slicked off it like the light on the polished leaves of house plants. Do we build big, ornamental walls round cemeteries just to keep the dead in? Is it that simple, after all?

I did dig. But it was Colin who beat up the cab driver.

After I got home I lay awake the rest of the night. My wife turned restlessly beside me. 'Can't you keep still?' she asked me.

'I'm going to make a cup of tea.'

'Don't use all the bloody milk.'

The next morning I made my way reluctantly to the Gifco house. Whatever I had expected, I found neither Colin nor the girl. The room we used was dark and empty except for its rows of books. Over the weeks, heat and humidity had piled up into it until the air seemed saturated and heavy, hard to breathe, on the verge of being something other than air. It had a distinctive odour. But above that I could smell something else. Perfume. Sweat. Some sharp bodily smell which made me shiver with the ghost of old anticipation. One ray of light lanced across the centre of the floor, where it found among the blackened flakes of linoleum two Polaroid photographs. I picked them up. One was of a girl. It was of a daughter. In it she was shown sprawled, legs apart, in one corner of the room. She was naked but for a pair of white briefs designed for someone twice her age, with lace detail and legs cut very high to accentuate the pubic mound. Her ribcage and immature nipples stood out in the forty-watt light. Shadows pooled in the hollow of her collar bone. A musing, inturned expression was on her face; but you could almost hear her laughing inappropriately at something an adult had said.

The other picture was of a woman who bore a strong resemblance to my wife. She wore a long pink satin slip, and her hair was disordered. Her expression was hard to read. I remembered how my wife had said to me some time after the death of our daughter, 'Why don't we fuck any more?' And then:

'Oh for God's sake, it doesn't matter.'

I waited for Colin, but he didn't come. Halfway through the

afternoon I left the house and walked back up Rye Lane. Women were toiling up the hill in the hot sunshine, laden with plastic supermarket bags.

'I think David's going to let me buy that clock,' I heard one of them say. 'You know, that hippo clock. Because he was having a look at it in the Argos catalogue.'

When I got home, my wife had gone. I went through each room, calling, 'Jill? Jill?' The bedroom was in a mess, the curtains half-drawn, make-up and underclothes pulled out of drawers and strewn over the carpets. There were signs of a struggle, but not necessarily with someone else. The bath was full of hot water, the bathroom full of steam. It smelled strongly of rose bath-oil, which she loved. In the condensation on the bathroom mirror she had written, making careful, reversed capitals, so that it could read from outside: GIFCO LEAVE US ALONE. The door to the balcony was open.

The first time I ever saw my wife, whose name is Jill, was in late 1989, in the breakfast room of a hotel in Los Cristianos, Tenerife. She was trying to order a boiled egg. The waiter, a Portuguese, seemed not to understand some distinction she was trying to make. As she began to explain to him, 'The way I normally do them at home—' the man sitting next to her interrupted tiredly:

'Why not just ask him for a soft-boiled egg?'

'A soft-boiled egg,' the waiter repeated in a relieved voice, and left the breakfast room instantly in case things became complicated again. She stared after him in a vague way, then at her companion. You could hear her thinking, 'I didn't really mean that. That wasn't really what I meant at all.'

Suddenly she said in a low but distinct voice:

'Why don't you fuck off, Jeremy?'

He stared at her.

'Just fuck off.'

'Well, look, I'm sorry.'

She didn't answer.

'Look, I honestly thought that's what you meant. A soft-boiled egg.'

After a moment she snatched the paper out of his hands and began to read it. When the egg came it remained in front of her, cooling and unopened.

It was my first morning in the Hotel Mirador. I had arrived the previous evening by air from England, and then, ambushed by the situation in Europe, spent all night watching satellite news footage of East Berliners pouring into West Berlin. At five in the morning I had finished an article I was writing with the words: 'When you see East Germans staring entranced into the jewellers' shops and restaurants of the West, the illusion is complete. Late 1989: the poor children of Europe have come to the windows and are yearning for the toys. Eventually, I suppose, they will look through windows in Huddersfield or the valleys of South Wales, and discover only other poor children staring out.'

After breakfast I went out to buy some sun tan oil. The air was still cool, but you could feel the heat building up. The sea crackled with light. The sky was already violet and harsh, just like the sky in the bad paintings outside the sea-front cafés. I stopped to rub the oil into my face, arms and legs, then walked along the beach in the opposite direction to Playa las Americas, until I found a cove with some low volcanic rocks, a promontory from which I could look back up at the town. There were lizards everywhere on the rocks and among the prickly pear, basking in the sun. Some of them were four or five inches long. I felt relaxed and excited at the same time, as if anything could happen. After half an hour, when nothing had, I made my way across some waste land, up through the self-catering apartments at Tenerife Sur and thence to the swimming pool of the Hotel Mirador, where the sun was falling vertically on the pink terracotta surround, silvering the tiles with heat.

The shouts, squeals and laughter of the children echoed back off the stacked balconies above, while the adults lay as stunned as lizards under the orange and green beach umbrellas in a light so hard you had to squint even through your sunglasses: ancient

Germans massaging their lost or sagging flesh; young French-women with muscles like wires on parched-looking emaciated legs; salesmen from Droitwich or Gravesend, reddened bellies hanging over their extraordinary 'surf' shorts. Among them, not far from the pool itself, I spotted the couple from the breakfast room.

She had not forgiven him, but lay turned away on her side, with her hair hanging over the edge of the sunbed. Her hand rested on the tiles, next to an open paperback book, a novel by Isabel Allende. He was pretending to read the *Daily Mail*, wincing at the bedlam of the children. As I watched, he reached over her and brushed her skin very lightly with the back of his fingers, just where it tightened between her prominent pelvic bones. She rolled away from him immediately, got to her feet and went towards the swimming pool. 'I'm not having a month of this,' I thought I heard him say. For a moment she stared straight at me. Then her eyes went blank, and she walked past and jumped into the pool.

Two Spanish boys began to ride a hired motor-scooter up and down the hotel steps.

At eight o'clock that evening the pedestrianised streets around Baranquillo and the Valle Menendez were suddenly suffused with people in new clothes. Attracted by the dreamy sound of guitar music and the smell of seafood on the soft warm evening air, the holidaymakers were leaving their hotels and drifting slowly down-hill past shop windows full of silk underwear, ethnic leather and electrical goods, towards the Los Cristianos beachfront. There in the dusk they found a wind from Africa blowing sand across the café tables. Children, their energy undiminished – though their cries had become soft and chirruping, made thoughtful by the night and their sense of the Atlantic stretching away west to nowhere – jumped up and down on the beach trampolines in the twilight. It was the month before Christmas, and the plaza muzak, barely a whisper, followed 'Silent Night' with a reggae version of 'Jingle Bells'. Say what you like, all this had a kind of rough magic, orchestrated by waiters, street musicians and trinket salesmen who made their way from table to table.

'Allo Johnnie, what you like?'

'You like this?'

'No problem, nice price.'

And then, sung out as if to a dawdling child:

'Come on, Johnnie!'

The voice belonged to a tall West African in a steel blue shirt. All afternoon I had watched him with amusement as he loped unassuagedly up and down the sea-front with his goods wrapped like a glamorous encrustation round one fist. His energy was extraordinary, his insincerity grotesque. He offered bracelets plated with nine carat gold, Spanish chokers made of jet beads, phony Cartier watches and little flasks of a perfume which had never breathed the breath of Chanel: his goods made a kind of gauntlet, a gilded prosthetic, of his forearm. He had disappeared during the empty hour between afternoon and evening, when the wind drove the dogs about the plaza in silent packs and the waiters dragged the café tables about in a kind of suppressed, meaningless rage. Now he was plying the outdoor tables of the beach cafés, his teeth white in the twilight and a curious sense of urgency in every movement of his body.

'2000? OK? Nice price, no problem.'

'OK, come on Johnnie.'

A German couple, eating goat and heavily salted Canary potatoes two or three tables in front of me at the Café Amarillas, tried for a while to bargain him down to 1000 pesetas. Then, after he had said something in a low voice to the woman, paid their bill abruptly and walked away.

He said quietly, 'Fuck off then,' spun on his heel and began again with someone else:

'Allo Johnnie! Allo Johnnie!'

This emerged in such a sweet childish voice its hypocrisy sent a shiver of fear through you.

'Look, old son,' I heard his new mark say, in a voice I recognised, 'we're just not interested.' It was fat Jeremy, from the Hotel Mirador.

'How you know, Johnnie? How you know until you know?'

Suddenly, Jeremy pushed his chair back and got to his feet.

'Because I'm bloody psychic, Johnnie,' he said. And then more quietly: 'Because this stuff is crap, that's all.' He looked away from Allo Johnnie and down at the woman. For a moment it was as if he had never seen her before. He looked lost. Then a flicker of bemused recognition seemed to go over his face: I had the feeling he was remembering a whole life, element by painful element. 'I'd rather eat at a bloody Harvester in Gravesend,' he told her, 'than in this shit heap.' And he walked off.

She waited until he had got ten yards away and called after him quietly:

'I know you would.'

He came back to their table.

'Are you coming?'

'No.'

'You can fuck off then,' he shouted. He bent over the table, leaned his weight on it so that the unused cutlery slid towards him, and put his face close to hers. I often ask myself if that man was me; if my behaviour to that date had really been any different to that man's. Do you know what I mean? He leaned harder on the table, so that everything spilled off it, and shouted: 'It's your turn to fuck off now.'

Quite suddenly she began to cry.

Later, she came over to my table and leaned on it the way he had leant on theirs, body bent forward from the waist, arms spread wide. The effect of this was aggressively sexual. At the same time, it made her seem vulnerable: her long breasts, a little reddened by the sun, fell towards me against the thin Indian cotton of her blouse; her shoulders and inner elbows shook faintly with the physical effort of supporting her. I had a sensation of thin cotton touching my skin, a foretaste of that envelope of warmth so hard to separate from someone's odour, as if I had already brought my face close to her breasts. I smelled sweat, wine, après sun. She laughed, looking over my head at something behind me; a waiter, perhaps.

'I've seen you watching me.'

'I—'

'Don't think,' she said, pulling a chair out unsteadily and dropping into it, 'I give a fuck—'

'Would you like to sit down?'

'— because I don't.'

'Have some wine.'

'I don't give a fuck about anything, especially that fucker,' she said.

'I'm sure you don't,' I said.

'Just tell me one thing, yes or no,' she said. 'Do you come from Colchester? If not, let's go back to the hotel.'

Once this had been understood there was no need to hurry. The waiters fussed around us. The children quietened. The warm air licked the backs of our hands, moved off into the palm fronds. Eventually, we moved off too. In some alley on the way back to the Mirador we heard a cicada. Drawn by the volume of its extraordinary mechanical call, we stood in the soft rosy daylight of a single halogen lamp.

'It's there!' she said excitedly. 'There, on the floor!'

By then she had to hang on to my upper arm to stay on her feet. Later, crouching over me in the hot darkness, she rallied – pushing me into her, moving strongly up and down, groaning and panting until she came. But one come was only the beginning for her. Instead of falling forward on to me and going to sleep – so that my cock detumesced and slowly fell out of her and the juices ran out to cool and dry between my pubic hair and hers – she set her face and kept moving up and down, grinding her pubic bone into mine, staring ahead with her eyes blank and preoccupied, until the spasm began again. It was as if I wasn't there. When I came too, and lost my erection, she pulled herself off me with an urgent groan and whispered, 'Lick me. Lick me. No. Put your fingers in. Quick! Something! Something!'

She seemed trapped inside herself. Orgasm was easy, but it was all empty space in which nothing ever happened to relieve her. The loneliness of her desire made me feel guilty.

'What about Jeremy?' I asked her.

'Who's Jeremy?' she said; and: 'Let him bugger off.' So for the rest of the week we lived in my little suite on the fifth floor, directly under the great sign which says "Hotel Mirador". We were so happy. We drove up to Tiede and trudged about on the edges of the permanent snow. We visited the basilica at Candelaria and the Dragon Tree gardens at Icod de los Vinos; we caught the ferry over to La Gomera and walked about for an afternoon in the stunning heat of the laurel forests. We took a camel ride, up through the banana trees, with their greasy trunks like large badly wrapped cigars, and out on to the blasted, cindery landscape south of Los Cristianos. The camels wore a kind of wire-netting muzzle. It was easy to get used to their rocking gait, the squeak of the saddle, the warm sandy smell of the animal itself.

'Look. Out there. Another island!'

We went everywhere. Everywhere we went, Allo Johnnie got there first. His lean, energetic figure rippled towards us in the coastal mirage. The trade winds flapped the short, carefully pressed sleeves of his steel blue shirt. He welcomed us down off the ferry, the bus, the camel's back. He offered up his arm, prosthetised with goods, and from it we selected an 'antique' jet necklace, two fake sapphires, a fake Rolex with an expanding metal band. Back at the Hotel Mirador, Jill wrapped her own arm with fake things and offered it to me. We laughed. At the end of the day she lay prone on the soft hushed coastal rocks, upper body raised from the waist in the purple light. 'What you like?' she whispered, looking back at me over her shoulder: 'Eh?'

In those days she was always so easy to enter. I could slip into her from the most awkward angles.

*

97

We took the bus to Adeje, Jill and I. Was that the mistake? We took the tourist bus to Adeje and then toiled up the steep, shady little mainstreet, past the Iglesia de Santa Ursula. Up the hill we went, and out, blinking, into the sudden glare, the gaping mouth, of the Barranco del Infierno. There we stopped to gather our breath. Above us stretched the great rock walls, pitted, flakey, resonant with heat. At the mouth they seemed to be miles apart. A great gap of air lay between them like a block of transparent plastic, encasing parched creep-terraces crusted with valo and prickly pear. You could imagine it flowing, glassy, slow and invincible, down the cindery slopes towards the sea. In the opposite direction, the walls leaned in on one another, the high stony path plunged into shadow, the Barranco choked down to a dark cool slit.

'Look!'

There, on a little promontory, steel-coloured shirtsleeves fluttering in the hot wind, stood a single figure.

'It's Allo Johnnie!'

We ran towards him, hand in hand.

'Johnnie! Johnnie!'

'Is he waiting for us?'

If he was, he showed no sign. When we got there, his face was turned away, his expression perfectly blank and hard. He was so still he might have been carved from the same rock as the Barranco. He stared out across the mouth of the gorge, at the town below, or the sea beyond that, or the white ship on the sea. He was staring out into the plastic air, out into nothing at all, and his eyes were wide and empty. Hanging by his side, his prosthetised arm looked as if he had loosely wrapped it in lizards. (They were alive but asleep; it looked too heavy to raise.) His face was varnished with sweat, but that did not make him seem any more human. When we saw this we slowed to a walk. We were reluctant to approach him. We didn't know how to behave. We called:

'What you got for us, Johnnie?'

'What you got for us today?'

After a moment, when we realised that he wasn't going to answer,

98

we stopped and stared at one another like children who begin to panic in the face of the parent's silence. We looked around but we were alone with him. I whispered:

'What are we going to do?'

Jill took my arm.

'Come on.'

'We can't just walk past him.'

'We can.'

We squeezed by on the narrow stony path, trying to make a joke of it. But he ignored us, and in the end we went up silently into the Barranco, and by the time we returned he was gone.

That night, the weather broke, and it poured with rain. I heard nothing, I was too busy. I found myself ten years old, forced to collect rents for a gangster in Chicago. In Chicago each street was seven miles long, with ramshackle housing, small businesses and empty bars at one end and upscale suburbs at the other – there was a lens of banks, office buildings and department stores between. I entered one of these streets I didn't know where, to find it suffused with a kind of vile slippery darkness and a smell of diarrhoea. The buildings were unnumbered. To collect the downscale rents, the low number rents, should I turn right or left? How was I to know? I was a little boy again. It was so important to be right that the little boy couldn't make up his mind. He should have finished an hour ago, and he had barely started. Increasingly panicked, unable to move more than a block or two from his original position without changing his mind, he began to see, in bleak flashes of light, the gangster himself, holding court on the cold Chicago pavement outside a tailor's, a barber's, a café, as he waited for the rents. I turned my face away, pretending to consult the sheet of paper on which he had written the orders. Up the hill or down the hill? He watched with contempt. He knew we were in the high numbers. He knew it would take hours to get where I was supposed to be. Impossible to fool, he had recognised the hot, comforting smell of a wet bed. I woke in the certain knowledge that somehow, in the zone of slippage between dreaming and waking, 'rents' had become 'tears'. Tears were flowing down my cheeks.

Half past ten the next morning, lights were still burning behind the tinted glass of the Tenerife Sur apartments. The maid service was in over there, hanging carpets on the balcony rails in the rain, while the guests stared morosely out at the wet tiles and ruffled water of the swimming pools, the slick palm fronds whipping to and fro in the wind. The woman at the window – she wasn't my wife then – said impatiently:

'It looks like Southend.'

The dream still shifted and turned inside my head, as nauseating as a chrysalis turning on its thread.

'I'm sorry?'

'It looks just like bloody Southend,' she said. 'Southend will follow you wherever you go.' Suddenly she shivered. She turned away from the window and said:

'I touched his arm. It was damp, but like stone.'

Was that the mistake? That we climbed the hill at Adeje and saw Allo Johnnie there and Jill touched his arm? If that was our mistake we soon forgot it.

I won't forget the warm, gritty, evening wind of Los Cristianos. Palm trees with short bulbous trunks the shape of pineapples waved their fronds in it like nervous, landlocked sea-anemones. Nothing in the air tonight, they whispered. Nothing on this wind. But when you heard it, fluting in the halyards of the yachts moored across the bay, it made you think. It made me think, anyway. Our last evening in Tenerife, Jill looked out over the beachfront and said, 'I don't want to leave. I wish we could stay here forever.' Sand trickled across the café tables, the children chirruped from the beach trampolines, 'Silent Night' enfolded each dining couple in wings of tacky magic. Allo Johnnie made his rounds in the half-dark, and soon he stood in front of us.

'Allo Johnnie!'

'Hello.'

'You take me back with you, England: eh?'

'How did you know we were going?'

He looked away into the distance, as if he could already see Peckham Rye, and laughed softly. For a moment we were back at the mouth of the Barranco, the three of us. For a moment there was a kind of heartbeat discontinuity. In it, Allo Johnnie made some kind of unstated, inexplicable offer. He made a gesture with his laden, glittering arm, a gesture of recognition, as if he was recognising us at last. He handed us his card, a scrap of white pasteboard glimmering brighter than a fake Cartier watch, on which we read, 'Gift Company of Los Cristianos,' in an old-fashioned script.

'Gifts,' he said. 'Eh, Johnnie?'

We laughed, and tried to hand it back. He refused it with a grave smile.

'What you like Johnnie? You like this? I go home with you!'

Then sand came up like a fog from the beach and when I next looked he was gone.

I studied the card. 'Gift Company,' I read. What had he offered us? I only knew it was unsuitable and wrong. But sometimes, now, when I look through the notebook in which I wrote all this down, and the dust in its creases – just blown from mainland Africa to make a beach in the Atlantic Ocean – I wish we had accepted.

Again, perhaps we did accept. This is how Tenerife makes you feel. As if there was some residue, some basically insoluble mystery behind or beneath or in some way prior to the rubbishy white hotels, beach bars and endless Cambios. As if even Playa los Americas, one of the trashiest places on earth, had some secret nothing to do with cheap stereos, expensive leather goods and English beer. You can sense it where a brand new road runs out suddenly in builders' waste and prickly pear; or at the top of a low hill, in some unfinished concrete building that looks like a multi-storey car park; or in the amused eyes of the stray dogs of the sea-front.

'Gift Company,' we read.

Perhaps we did accept.

After we returned from Tenerife we moved in together. For perhaps a month I kept clementines in a bowl I had brought back with me. Bright orange against its lively red and green glazes, they reminded me of the light in Los Cristianos, how it would fall on to the balcony in the mornings while you ate breakfast in a pair of shorts or a swimsuit. But by February I had got out of the habit, and in subsequent Februaries there was our marriage, and the birth of our daughter, and her death, and neither of us thought of Allo Johnnie even when we took out the photographs of that holiday.

After I had found the message from my wife – GIFCO LEAVE US ALONE – I stood in the bathroom for what seemed a long time, wondering what to do. Beneath the smells of bath-oil and spilled talcum powder, I detected something more personal: a smell of feet, perhaps, or menstruation, personal, but not necessarily unpleasant because of that. My wife had left her Wilkinson Lady Protector, its shiny blades clotted with soap and tiny hairs, on the edge of the bath. She had left the soap wet, as she often does, so that it dripped a slimy liquor into the bottom of the soap-tray. I pulled the plug, and while the dirty water emptied itself, went out on to the balcony, from which I could look over to where the Gifco house lay silent and empty in the Peckham sunshine.

GIFCO WE ARE HERE.

I found her there a few minutes later. She was lying awkwardly, half on and half off the sofa, masturbating. It was hot in the house, and the air was thick: a bar of incandescent light fell across her white legs. She had turned on to her stomach then half slipped off the sofa, so that one knee was resting on the floor. She was pulling herself up and down against the worn orange dralon, panting and hissing and whispering to herself, 'Come. Come! Oh Christ, come!' Her skirt was up round her waist. The room stank of her. As I stood in the doorway watching quietly, she let go of the sofa-arm with one hand and, reaching down behind her, tried to pull her knickers off.

The elastic got stuck over her hips. After a moment she stopped trying, and her hand reached around underneath her instead.

At first I thought Colin, who was sitting on the floor in the corner, with his back against the wall and his legs straight out in front of him, was watching her. Then I saw that his drill trousers were stiff with blood, brown blood. He was sitting still in a pool of it, holding himself in with one hand, and on his face was fixed an amused expression, quizzical and appreciative at the same time, an expression a little too mature for the Colin I knew. Flies buzzed round him. The traffic droned to and fro outside. I stood in the doorway. My wife grunted and masturbated in the bright light. Colin seemed to watch her. A third party in the room seemed to be watching them both.

People are so frail, wherever in the world they come from. Many of the inhabitants of Barnes, for instance, believe that if you carry a hen's egg about in your armpit for the whole of Lent, it hatches on Easter Morning. Out jumps a naked, deformed human being somewhat less than five inches tall – I imagine it looking a little like Popeye the Sailor – which for the rest of its short, deteriorating existence serves without question the first person it saw when the light pierced its shell. The people who believe this wear classic Guernsey sweaters and drive Volvo 850T estate cars. During the day they go to work on the administrative side of media. But in the evening after dinner – which they often call 'supper' – they tell each other how they have seen a man poisoned with curls of dried wood shaved from a stick thrust into a grave at Putney Cemetery.

'The idea is, I think, that the stick must puncture the chest wall of the corpse.'

'I mean, do you pull it straight out?'

'Oh no, I think it has to stay there a month before it's any good.'

'Extraordinary.'

'It is extraordinary, isn't it?'

In Barnes when I lived there, nobody would believe anyone else was dead until they actually saw the corpse. This meant that their grandmother's husk had to be kept for some time until every relative had – there is no reasonable way to put this – born witness to its emptiness. The corpse would be arranged in a crouching position in a hole under the living room floor, which was closed with loose floorboards and covered with a woollen Berber from Heal's. Only when the whole family, some arriving over the next day or two from as far away as Reigate or Littlehampton, had seen the evidence – the clenched arthritic fist held up to the mouth, the teeth curled back, the old skin like leather – could the poor old thing be buried properly. Someone who died a long way away might still be regarded as alive until their entire family had itself died out. In Barnes they simply couldn't accept death as an abstract idea.

The night of my daughter's funeral, the long cemetery by the river was illuminated by thousands of candles. Some were little more than cheap night lights; others tall, expensive, perfumed. They were collected in apparently random basins of attraction, a hundred candles burning on some graves, only two or three on others. Rich or poor, it seemed to make no difference. It was the vigil called in Barnes 'the Day of the Dead'. The families clustered round the graves were waiting on the mysterious dividing line between All Saints and All Souls. The great white candles filled the air with sweet scents of rose and beeswax. The children laughed softly and chased one another down the paths between the graves, while their elders sat on the grass opening bottles of Chablis they had got from the Thresher on Upper Richmond Road. The effect was of Glynde-bourne, but with less tension perhaps, less need to shine. In Barnes, on the Day of the Dead, you are less on show than you would be at Glyndebourne. Your only purpose is to keep the dead company until dawn.

I walked home from the Gifco house and wiped the condensation off the bathroom windows and vacuumed up the spilt talcum powder; while I was doing that, I thought, I might as well vacuum the living room. My wife returned about two hours later. She never said anything about what had happened, then or later: though I noticed after some months that all the photographs of our daughter were missing. We didn't discuss this, or even refer to it, and for our next holiday chose the island of Jersey. It was a bleak April there, where you might expect spring to be early, with rain and high winds blustering and banging at the dusty granite clifftops. Nevertheless, girls and young women – daughters – were allowing themselves to be led through the streets of St Helier, first two fingers of the right hand linked to the first two fingers of the left of boys with downy brown moustaches. These couples had a hypnotised air despite the cold. Their white trainers and pristine blue windbreakers, box fresh and perhaps – who knows – never worn again, brought a quality of freshness to their flesh too, making it seem plump, unblemished, just-unwrapped, nice.

'I wonder how they'll cope,' said Jill. 'I just wonder how they'll cope.'

Tired of shopping, suddenly unable to distinguish between the scream of the herring gull and the squeal of the revolving postcard stand, we rented a small red saloon and from the car park of the Hotel de France went inland, up the little tight wooded valleys and into the rural hinterland where the money is farmed. We looked out from the north coast and then the south: grey sea, breaking waves, a misty rain driven in like vapour. We visited the German Hospital. We went to the zoo. Even at forty miles an hour, you can drive all the way round the island in a morning. Just outside St Helier, on the way to Three Mile Beach, we passed an abandoned petrol station. It had been designed to fit between some flaking white houses, all curves and balconies in a kind of Bauhaus pastiche. The doors were closed. The pumps were deserted. In a fenced section at one side of the forecourt, perhaps a dozen wrecked vehicles were collected, their broken windscreens glittering in the fitful sunlight.

'Stop!' Jill said.

I stared at her.

'I want to look,' she said. 'Stop.'

So I drove in and we sat there with the engine off and the heater running. Every so often the wind would rock the car, the hanging signs in the forecourt would creak, and Jill would say something like, 'Why do these people buy such fast cars when the speed limit is forty miles an hour?' She might have been watching someone's things being thrown into the back of a van in a Peckham sidestreet. She might have been complaining: 'We'll be next. Don't worry about that. They'll be throwing us in the back of a van next.'

'I don't know,' I said.

'You never know anything,' she said.

She was watching a fattish woman in a pink cardigan and pale blue skirt walking slowly round and round one of the wrecks, staring as intently at it as if she thought of buying it. Its windscreen was crossed with intersecting diagonal fractures. It had been struck suddenly and heavily from the rear-offside, so that the boot and the back seat on that side had been pushed up into the driver's position, exposing the rear-offside wheel, over which was bent and tangled the exhaust system and silencer. The event had wrenched and shortened the whole vehicle so that it seemed to occupy less space than it should. At the same time its new shape captured the vigour of the collision, so that you could feel it happening over and over again, like a recording. Loops of rubber windscreen sealant hung down over the contorted metal. It was an old red Alfasud, V-registered. All the wrecks parked there were rear-end collisions. The woman walked round them staring intently, but as if she was thinking of buying not cars but vegetables or curtain material – something engrossing but not all that important. Eventually she walked off with her arms folded, satisfied.

'I don't either,' said Jill. 'I don't know anything either.'

She shivered.

'We never even had a daughter!' she said.

She said: 'What did we do to that poor girl?'

She said: 'How do you achieve freedom from the future, from endless expectation?'

'I'm not sure I know what you mean.'

After I said that she was silent. Did we have a daughter? What did we do with her? What did we do to each other? What was done to us? You write down what can be remembered: but the day is sufficient to its own illusions. You can never recover them. Memory commits you to the nuance. If you act on memory you act on echoes – unpredictable, faint, fading even as they were generated. Eventually I started the car and drove on to the bleak headland at Rouge Nez, bumping along the track past the racecourse until I found somewhere to park. Rain was blowing diagonally across the pocked and rotten turf. Without speaking, Jill opened her door and got out. She wandered about in the empty car park for a bit, then over to the ruined castle at the cliff edge. There she stood, staring out to sea. I wound the window down.

'You'll get cold if you just keep standing there like that.'

'I don't care.'

We had to shout to be heard.

After about an hour, Allo Johnnie came briskly into view along the coastal path, the short sleeves of his metallic grey shirt flapping in a hot wind. He seemed to float above the ground. Jill waved. He leaned towards her, offering his forearm wrapped in lizards that glittered in the unearthly twilight of a volcanic beach, all impossible harsh violets and greens. She stood waiting for him in the sodden arch of the castle. I watched them embrace, then I started the engine of the car.

Anima

A week ago last Tuesday I dreamed all night of trying to find out what had happened to the woman I loved. She was a pianist and a writer. We had met in New York when she played a concert of American and British music. She had reminded me how I had once been able to dance. Now, some time later, she had come to Britain to find me. But she could no longer speak, only weep. How had she travelled here? Where did she live? What was she trying to say? It was a dream heavy with sadness and urgency. All avenues of enquiry were blocked. There were people who might know about her, but always some reason why they could not be asked, or would not tell. I walked up and down the streets, examining the goods on the market stalls, my only clue the re-issue date of a once-banned medicine.

I never dreamed anything like this until I met Choe Ashton—

Ten past ten on a Saturday night in December, the weekend Bush talked to Gorbachev on the *Maxim Gorki* in half a gale in Valletta Harbour. In the east, governments were going over like tired middleweights – saggy, puzzled, almost apologetic. I sat in the upper rooms of a media drinking club in central London. The occasion was the birthday of a corporate executive called Dawes who sometimes commissioned work from me. Shortly they would be giving him a cake shaped like half a football on which had been iced the words: OVER THE MOON BUT NOT OVER THE HILL!

Meanwhile they were eating pasta.

'Now that's two thousand calories. How much more do you want?'

'So far I've had cheese but not much else, which is interesting—'

'Are we going to get that fettuccine we've paid for?'

The women were in TV: the last of the power dressers. The men were in advertising, balding to a pony tail. Men or women, they all had a Range Rover in the car park at Poland Street. They were already thinking of exchanging it for one of the new Mazdas. I moved away from them and went to stare out of the window. The sky over towards Trafalgar Square looked like a thundery summer afternoon. The buildings, side-lit by street lamps, stood out against it, and against one another, like buildings cut from cardboard. I followed an obscure line of neon. A string of fairy lights slanted away along the edge of a roof. Then cars going to and fro down at the junction by St Martins-in-the-Field, appearing very much smaller than they were. I had been there about a minute when someone came up behind me and said:

'Guess what? I was just in the bog. I switched the hand-drier on and it talked to me. No, come on, it's true! I put my hands under it and it said, "Choe, I really like drying your hands".'

I knew his name, and I had seen him around: no more. He was in his forties, short and wiry, full of energy, with the flat-top haircut and earring of a much younger man. His 501s were ripped at the knees. With them he wore a softly tailored French Connection blouson which made his face, reddened as if by some kind of outdoor work, look incongruous and hard.

'Has anything like that ever happened to you? I'm not kidding you, you know. It talked to me!'

I shrugged.

'OK. Give us a fag then, if you don't believe me. Eh?'

He was delighted by my embarrassment.

'I don't smoke,' I said.

'Come on,' he wheedled. 'Every fucker smokes. Dawsie only knows people who smoke. Give us a fag.'

I had spent all day feeling as if my eyes were focusing at different lengths. Every so often, things – especially print – swam in a way which suggested that though for one eye the ideal distance was eighteen inches, the other felt happier at twelve. Choe Ashton turned out to be the perfect object for this augmented kind of vision, slipping naturally in and out of view, one part of his personality clear and sharp, the rest vague and impressionistic. What did he do? Whose friend was he? Any attempt to bring the whole of him into view produced a constant sense of strain, as your brain fought to equalise the different focal lengths.

'I'm sick of this,' he said. 'Let's fuck off to Lisle Street and have a Chinese. Eh?'

He gave me a sly, beautiful smile. An ageing boy in a French Connection jacket.

'Come on, you know you want to.'

I did. I was bored. As we were leaving, they brought the birthday cake in. People always seem very human on occasions like this. Dawes made several efforts to blow the candles out, to diminishing applause; and ended up pouring wine over them. Then an odd thing happened. The candles, which – blackened, but fizzing and bubbling grossly, dripping thick coloured wax down the sides of the football – had seemed to be completely extinguished, began to burn again. Blinking happily around, Dawes had taken the incident as a powerful metaphor for his own vitality, and was already pouring more wine on them.

'Did you see that?' I asked Choe Ashton.

But he was halfway out of the door.

At first we walked rapidly, not talking. Head down, hands rammed into the pockets of his coat, Ashton paused only to glance at the enormous neon currency symbols above the Bureau de Change on Charing Cross Road. 'Ah, money!' But as soon as he recognised Ed's Easy Diner, he seemed content to slow down and take his time. It was a warm night for December. Soho was full of the most carefully dressed people. Ashton pulled me towards a group standing outside the Groucho, so that he could admire their louche haircuts and beautifully crumpled chinos. 'Can't you feel the light coming off them?' he asked me in a voice loud enough for them to hear. 'I just want to bask in it.' For a moment after he had said this, there did seem to be a light round them – like the soft light in a '70s movie, or the kind of watery nimbus you sometimes see when you are peering through a window in the rain. I pulled him away, but he kept yearning back along the pavement towards them, laughing. 'I love you!' he called to them despairingly. 'I love you!' They moved uncomfortably under his approval, like cattle the other side of a fence.

'The middle classes are always on watch,' he complained.

We dodged briefly into a pick-up bar and tried to talk. The only free table was on a kind of mezzanine floor on the way to the ladies' lavatory. Up there you were on a level with the sound system. Drunken girls pushed past, or fell heavily into the table.

'I love them all!' shouted Ashton.

'Pardon?'

'I love them!'

'What, these too?'

'Everything they do is wonderful!'

Actually they just sat under the ads for Jello-shots, Schlitz and Molson's Canadian and drank Löwenbräu: boys in soft three-button shirts and Timberland boots, girls with tailored jackets over white silk trousers. I couldn't see how they had arrived there from Manor House or Finsbury Park, all those dull, broken, littered places on the Piccadilly line; or why. Eventually we got sick of bawling at one another over the music and let it drive us back out into Cambridge Circus.

'I was here this afternoon,' he said. 'I thought I heard my name called out.'

'Someone you knew.'

'I couldn't see anyone.'

We ended up in one of those Lisle Street restaurants which specialise in degree-zero décor, cheap crockery and grudging service. There were seven tables crammed into an area smaller than a newsagent's shop. The lavatory – with its broken door handle and empty paper roll – was downstairs in the kitchens. Outside it on a hard chair sat a waitress, who stared angrily at you as you went past. They had a payphone: but if you wanted to use it, or even collect your coat from the coat rack, you had to lean over someone else's dinner. Choe Ashton, delighted, went straight to the crêpe paper shrine mounted in the alcove to show me a vase of plastic flowers, a red-and-gold tin censer from which the stubs of old incense sticks protruded like burnt-out fireworks, two boxes of safety matches.

'See this? Make a wish!'

With considerable gentleness he put fresh incense in the censer and struck a match.

'I love these places—' he said.

He sat down and rubbed his hands.

'— but I'm bored with Hot and Sour.'

He stared away from the menu and up at the industrial ceiling, which had been lowered with yellow-painted slats. Through them you could still see wires, bitumen, ventilator boxes. A few faded strings ejected from some exhausted Christmas party-popper still hung up there, as if someone had flung noodles about in a claustrophobic fit or paddy.

'Let's have some Bitter and Unfulfilled here!' he called to the waitress. 'No. Wait a minute. I want Imitation Pine Board Soup, with a Loon Fung calendar.

'But it has to have copulating pandas on it.'

After that we began to drink Tsing Tao beer. Its packaging, he said, the pale grey ground and green, red and gold label, reminded him of something. He arranged several empty cans across the table between us and stared at them thoughtfully for some time, but nothing came of it. I don't remember eating, though we ordered a lot of food. Later he transferred his obsession from the Tsing Tao label to the reflections of the street neon in the mirror behind the bar. SOHO. PEEP SHOW. They were red, greenish-yellow, a cold blue. A strobe flickered inside the door of the peep show. Six people had been in there in two minutes. Two of them had come out again almost immediately. 'Fucking hell, sex, eh? Why do we bother?'

Ashton looked at me. 'I fucking hate it,' he said. Suddenly he stood up and addressed the people at the nearer tables. 'Anyone who hates sex, stand up!' he tried to persuade them. 'Fucking sex.' He laughed. 'Fucking fucking,' he said. 'Get it?' The waitresses began to move towards us.

But they had only come to bring the bill and offer him another beer. He smiled at them, moved his hands apart, palms forward, fingers spread.

'No thanks,' he said shyly.

'The bill's in Chinese!' he shouted. He brandished it delightedly at the rest of the diners. 'Hey!'

I agreed to drive him home. For the first few minutes he showed some interest in my car. At that time I had an Escort RS Turbo. But I didn't drive it fast enough for him, and he was silent again until we were passing The Flying Dutchman in Camberwell. There, he asked in an irritable voice: 'Another thing. Why is this pub always in the same place?' He lived on the other side of Peckham, where it nudges up against Dulwich. It took him some time to find the right street. 'I've only just moved in.' I got him upstairs then consulted my watch. 'I think I'd better sleep on your floor,' I said. But he had passed out. It seemed like a nice flat, although he hadn't bought much furniture.

I woke late the next morning. Ten o'clock. Sleet was falling. A minicab driver had parked his Renault under the front window, switched its engine off, and turned up Capital Radio so that I could hear clearly a preview of a new track by the Psychedelic Furs. Every thirty seconds he leaned on his horn. At that, the woman who had called him leant out of a fourth floor window in one of the point blocks on the other side of the road and shrieked:

'Cammin dahn!'

Beep.

'Cammin dahn!'

Beep. Beep. Beep.

'Cammin dahn! Cammin dahn!'

At the back the flat overlooked a row of gardens. They were long and narrow and generally untended; so choked, some of them, with bramble, elder and buddleia stalks, that they reminded you of overgrown lanes between walls of sagging, sugary old brick. In the bleaker ones, you knew, a dog would trot restlessly all day between piles of household or builders' rubbish, under a complex array of washing lines. Choe Ashton's garden had once been kept in better order. There was a patio of black and white flagstones like a chess board, a few roses pruned savagely back to bare earth. The little pond was full of leaves. Suddenly I saw that there was a fox sniffing round the board fence at the bottom of the garden.

At first I thought it was some breed of cat I had never seen before: long-backed, reddish, brindling towards its hindquarters and long tail. It was moving a bit like a cat, sinuously and close to the ground. After a minute or two it found the pond and drank at length, looking up every so often, but too wet and tired, perhaps too ill, to be wary or nervous.

I watched with my heart in my mouth, afraid to move even behind the window in case it saw me and ran off. Choe Ashton came into the room.

'Fucking hell,' he said. 'Are you still here?'

'Sssh. There's a fox in your garden.'

He stood beside me. As he watched, the fox moved into the middle of the overgrown lawn, pawing and sniffing at the earth. It yawned. I couldn't see anything there it might eat. I wondered if it might have smelt another fox. It sat down suddenly and stared vaguely into the sleet.

'I can't see anything.'

I stared at him.

'Choe, you must be blind—'

He gripped my arm very hard, just above the elbow.

'That hurts,' I said.

'I can't fucking *see* any fucking fox,' he said quietly.

We stood like that for thirty or forty seconds. In that time the fox went all round the lawn, not moving very fast, then crossed the low brick wall into the next garden, where it vanished among some elders, leafless laburnum bushes and apple trees.

'OK, Choe.'

People like Choe are like moths in a restaurant on a summer evening just as it gets dark. They bang from lamp to lamp then streak across the room in long, flat, wounded trajectories. We make a lot of their confusion but less of their rage. They dash themselves to pieces out of sheer need to be more than they are. It would have been better to leave him alone to do it, but I was already fascinated.

I phoned everyone who had been at the Dawes party. No one knew the whole story. But they all agreed he was older than he appeared and, career-wise at least, a bit of a wimp. He was from the North of England. He had taken one of the first really good media degrees – from East Sussex – but never followed it up. He did the odd design job for one of the smaller agencies that operate out of top rooms above Wardour Street. In addition, he had some film work, some advertising work. But who didn't? The interesting thing was how he had filled his time until he appeared in Soho. After East Sussex he had moved back north and taken a job as a scaffolder; then joined a Manchester steeplejacking firm. He had worked in the massive stone quarries around Buxton, and out in the North Sea on the rigs. Returning to London obsessed with motorcycles, he had opened one of the first courier operations of the Thatcher boom. He never kept any job for long. Boredom came too easily to him. Anything hard and dangerous attracted him, and the stories I heard about him, true or not, would have filled a book. He told me some of them himself, later:

Stripping old render near the top of a thirty-storey council high-rise in Glasgow, he found himself working from scaffolding fifty feet above a brick-net. These devices – essentially a few square feet of strong plastic netting stretched on a metal frame – are designed to catch dropped tools or bits of falling masonry. With a brick-net, you don't need safety bunting or a spotter on the ground to protect unwary pedestrians. Ashton quickly became obsessed. He thought

ANIMA

about the brick-net in his digs at night. (Everyone else was watching *Prisoner Cell Block H.*) During the day everything that fell seemed to go down into it in slow motion. Things were slow in his life too. One cold windy Monday ten minutes before lunch, he took a sly look sideways at the other jacks working on the scaffolding. Then he screamed and jumped off, turning over twice in the air and landing flat on his back. The breath went out of him – boof! Everything in the net flew up into the air and fell down again on top of him – old mastic tubes, bits of window frame, half bricks.

'I'd forgotten that stuff,' he said with a grin.

'Were you injured?'

'I walked a bit stiff that week.'

'Was it worth it?'

'It was a fucking trip.'

Later, induced by money to take a long-running steelworks job, he decided to commute to Rotherham from London on a Kawasaki 750 racer. Each working week began in the early hours of Monday morning, when, still wobbly from the excesses of the weekend, he pushed this overpowered bright green monster up the motorway at a hundred and fifty miles an hour in the dark. He was never caught, but quite soon he grew bored. So he taught himself to lie along the Kawa with his feet on the back pegs, wedge the throttle open with a broken matchstick so that he could take both hands off the handlebars, and roll a joint in the tiny pocket of still air behind the fairing. At the right speed, he claimed, Kawasaki engineering was good enough to hold the machine on track.

'The idea,' he said, 'is not to slow down.'

I wasn't sure boredom was entirely the issue. Some form of exploration was taking place, as if Choe Ashton wanted to know the real limits of the world, not in the abstract but by experience. I grew used to identifying the common ground of these stories – the point at which they intersected – because there, I believed, I had found Choe's myth of himself, and it was this myth that energised him. I was quite wrong. He was not going to let himself be seen so easily. But that didn't become plain until later. Meanwhile, when I heard him say, 'We're sitting on the roof one dinner time, and suddenly I've poured lighter fuel on my overalls and set myself on fire,' I would nod sagely and think of Aleister Crowley's friend Russell, discharged from the US Navy after he had shot up forty grains of medical-grade cocaine and tried to set fire to a piece of glass by willpower alone.

'I just did it to see what people would do,' Choe said. 'They had to beat me out with their hands.'

In a broad fake Northern accent he added:

'I'm scared of nowt, me.' Then in a more normal voice: 'Do you believe that?'

'I think I do,' I said, watching with some interest the moth on its flat, savage, wounded trajectory.

He gave me a look of contempt.

This didn't prevent him from flirting all winter, slipping away – but never too far – between the sets of a comically complex personality: always waiting for me to catch up, or catch my breath.

Drunk in bars, he would suggest going to the first night of a photographic exhibition, a new production of Ionescu, ballet at the Royal Opera House: arrive on the night in some immaculate designer two-piece with baggy trousers and immense shoulder pads: and then say—

'I've got the Kawa parked round the corner.'

'I'm sure you have, Choe.'

'You don't believe I came on it, do you?' And again, appealing to a foyer full of people who had arrived in BMWs:

'This fucker doesn't believe I came on me bike!'

To see how far he would go, I took him to a dance version of *Beauty and the Beast*. He sat there quietly, entranced by the colour and movement, quite unconcerned by the awful costumes and Persil-white sentimentality, until the interval. Then he said loudly: 'It's like the fucking fish tank at the dentist's in here. Look at them!' He meant the audience, which, gorgeously dressed and vaguely smiling, had begun to come and go in the depopulated front stalls like moonlight gourami or neon tetras nosing among the silver bubbles of the oxygenator. Quiet, aimless, decorative, they had come, just like the dancers, to be seen.

'They're a bit more self-conscious than fish, Choe.'

'Are they?'

He stood up.

'Let's go and get some fucking beer. I'm bored with this.'

Two or three weeks later, having heard I liked Turgenev, he sent me an expensive old edition of *Sketches from a Hunter's Notebook*, on the front endpapers of which he had written in his careful designer hand:

'Turgenev records how women posted flowers – pressed marguerites and immortelles – to the child-murderer Tropmann in the days before his execution. It was as if Tropmann were going to be "sent on before". Each small bouquet or floret was a confused memory of the pre-Christian plea "Intercede for us" which accompanied the sacrifice of the king or his substitute. But more, it was a special plea: "Intercede for me". These notes, with their careful, complex folds, arrived from the suicide provinces – bare, empty coastal towns, agricultural plains, the suburbs of industrial cities. They had been loaded carefully into their envelopes by white hands whose patience was running out between their own fingers like water.'

I phoned him up.

'Choe, what a weird quote. Where did you find it?'

'I'm not stupid, you know,' he said, and put the phone down. He had written it himself. For two weeks he refused to speak to me, and in the end I won him round only by promising him I would go to the Tate and spend a whole afternoon with the Turners. He shivered his way down to the Embankment from Pimlico tube station to meet me. The sleeves of the French Connection jacket were pushed up to his elbows, to show off slim but powerful forearms tattooed with brilliantly coloured peacock feathers which fanned down the muscle to gently clasp his thin wrists.

'Like them? They're new.'

'Like what, Choe?'

He laughed. I was learning. Inside the gallery, the Turners deliquesced into light: *Procession of Boats with Distant Smoke*, circa 1845; *The Sun of Venice Going Down to Sea*, 1843. He stood reverentially in front of them for a moment or two. Then the tattooed arms flashed, and he dragged me over to *Pilate Washing His Hands*.

'This fucker though! It can't have been painted by the same man!' He looked at me almost plaintively.

'Can it?'

Formless, decaying faces. Light somehow dripping itself apart to reveal its own opposite.

'It looks like an Ensor.'

'It looks like a fucking Emil Nolde. Let's go to the zoo.'

'What?'

He consulted his watch. 'There's still plenty of daylight left,' he said. 'Let's go to the zoo.' On the way out he pulled me over to John Singer Sargent's *Carnation, Lily, Lily, Rose*. 'Isn't that fucking brilliant?' And, as I turned my head up to the painting, 'No, not that, you fucking dickhead, the *title*. Isn't that the most brilliant title in the world? I always come here to read it.'

Regent's Park. Winter. Trees like fan coral. Squirrel monkeys with fur a distinct shade of green scatter and run for their houses, squeaking with one high-pitched voice. A strange, far-off, ululating call – lyrical but animalistic – goes out from the zoo as if something is signalling. Choe took me straight to its source: lar gibbons. 'My favourite fucking animal.' These sad, creamy-coloured little things, with their dark eyes and curved arthritic hands, live in a long tall cage shaped like a sailing vessel. Inside, concrete blocks and hutches give the effect of deck and bridge fittings. The tallest of these is at the prow, where you can often see one gibbon on its own, crouched staring into the distance past the rhino house.

'Just look at them!' Choe said.

He showed me how they fold up when not in use, the curve of their hands and arms fitting exactly into the curve of their thigh.

Knees under their chins, they sit hunched in the last bit of winter sun, picking over a pile of lettuce leaves; or swing through the rigging of their vessel with a kind of absent-minded agility. They send out their call, aching and musical. It is raw speech, the speech of desires that can never be fulfilled, only suffered.

'Aren't they perfect?'

We watched them companionably for a few minutes.

'See the way they move?' Choe said suddenly. Then:

'When someone loves you, you feel this whole marvellous confidence in yourself. In your body, I mean.'

I said nothing. I couldn't think how the two ideas were linked. He had turned his back on the cage and was staring angrily away into the park, where in the distance some children were running and shouting happily. He was inviting me to laugh at him. When I didn't, he relaxed.

'You feel good in it,' he said. 'For once it isn't just some bag of shit that carries you around. I—'

'Is that why you're trying to kill yourself, Choe?'

He stared at me.

'For fuck's sake,' he said wearily.

Behind us the lar gibbons steered their long strange ship into the wind with an enormous effort of will. A small plaque mounted on the wire netting of the cage explained: 'The very loud call is used to tell other gibbons the limit of its territory, especially in the mornings.' I thought that was a pity.

In the spring he gave up his job with the agency and went offshore.

'I need some money,' he said. 'The rigs are the place for that. Besides, I like the helicopter ditching course.'

He wanted to take the Kawa round Europe that summer.

'You need dosh to pay the speeding tickets.' He thought for a moment. 'I like Europe.'

And then, as if trying to sum up an entire continent:

'I once jumped over a dog in Switzerland. It was just lying in the middle of the road asleep. I was doing a hundred and ten. Bloke behind me saw it too late and ran it over.'

He was away for two or three months, but he hadn't forgotten anything. Whatever it was he wanted me for remained as important to him as it had been when he singled me out at the Dawes party. He came back at the height of summer and knocked at my door in Camden, wearing Levi 620s, brand new 16-hole DMs, a black sleeveless T-shirt which had faded to a perfect fusty green, and a single gold earring. We walked up between the market stalls to Camden Lock, where he sat in the sunshine blinking at the old curved bridge which lifts the towpath over the canal. His arms had been baked brown in Provence and Chamonix, but the peacock feathers still rioted down them, purple, green and electric blue, a surf of eyes; and on his upper left arm one tiny perfect rose had appeared, flushed and pink.

'How was Europe?' I asked him.

'Fucking brilliant,' he said absently. 'It was great.'

'Get many tickets?'

'Too fucking right.'

'I like the new tattoo.'

'It's good.'

We were silent for a bit. Then he said:

'I want to show you something.'

'What?'

'It would mean driving up north.'

Determined not to make a mistake this time, I said:

'Would two days' time do?'

'Are you sure you want to know this?'

I wasn't sure. But I said yes anyway. In fact it was four or five days before he was free to leave. He wheedled me into letting him drive. A blip in the weather brought strong southwest winds which butted and banged at the RS as he stroked it up the motorway at a steady hundred and twenty. Plumes of spray drifted across the carriageways, so that even the heaviest vehicle, glimpsed briefly through a streaming windscreen, seemed to be moving sideways as well as

forwards, caught in some long, dreamlike, fatal skid. Beyond
Nottingham, though, where the road petered out into roadworks,
blocked exits and confusing temporary signboards, the cloud
thinned suddenly.

'Blue sky!' said Choe, braking heavily to avoid the back of a fleet
Cavalier, then dipping briefly into the middle lane to overtake it.
Hunched forward over the steering wheel until his face was pressed
against the windscreen, he squinted upwards.

'I can see sunshine!'

'Will you watch where you're fucking going?'

He abandoned the motorway and urged the RS into the curving
back roads of the White Peak, redlining the rev counter between gear
changes, braking only when the bend filled the windscreen with black
and white chevrons, pirouetting out along some undrawn line between will and physics. I should have been frightened, but it was full
summer, and the rain had brought the flowers out, and all I could see
were horses up to their knees in moon-daisies. The verges were fat with
clover and cow parsley. The foxgloves were like girls. Thick clusters of
creamy flowers weighed down the elders, and wherever I looked there
were wild roses the most tremulous pink and white. Every field's edge
was banked with red poppies. That would have been enough – fields
of red poppies – but among them, perhaps one to five hundred, one
to a thousand, there were sports or hybrids of a completely different
colour, a dull waxy purple, rather sombre but fine.

'How odd! Did you see that, Choe?'

'Don't talk.'

After about twenty minutes he stopped the car and switched the
engine off.

'This is near enough for now.'

We were in a long bleak lay-by somewhere on the A6. The road
fell away from us in a gentle curve until it reached the flatter
country west and north. Down there I could see a town – houses for
quarry workers, a junction with traffic lights, a tall steel chimney
designed to pump hot gases up through the chronic inversion layers
of Spring and Autumn.

'When I was a kid,' Choe said, 'I lived a few miles outside that place.' He undid his seatbelt and turned to face me. 'What you've got to understand is that it's a fucking dump. It's got that fucking big chimney, and a Sainsbury's and a Woolworth's, and a fucking bus station.' He adjusted the driving mirror so that he could see his own face in it. 'I hated that fucking bus station. You know why? Because it was the only way in and out. I went in and out on one of those fucking buses every day for ten years, to take exams, look for jobs, go round the record shop on a wet Saturday afternoon.' He pushed the mirror back into its proper place. 'Ever spend any time in bus stations?'

'Never.'

'I didn't think you had. Let me tell you they're death on a stick. Only people who are socially dead use a bus station.'

Everything warm, he said, went on at a distance from people like that. Their lives were at an ebb. At a loss. They had to watch the clean, the happy, the successfully employed, stepping out of new cars and into the lobbies of warm hotels. If the dead had ever been able to do that, they would never be able to do it again. They would never be able to dress out of choice or eat what they would like.

'They're old, or they're bankrupt, or they've just come out of a long-stay mental ward. They're fucked.'

All over the North of England they stood around at ten in the evening waiting for the last bus to places called Chinley Cross, or Farfield or Penistone. By day it was worse.

'Because you can see every fucking back-end village you're going through. The bus is fucked, and it never gets up any speed.' He appealed to me: 'It stinks of diesel and old woollen coats. *And the fuckers who get on are carrying sandwich boxes.*'

I laughed.

'There's nothing intrinsically wrong with a sandwich box,' I said.

'Do you want to hear this or not?'

'Sorry, Choe.'

'I hated those fucking buses except for one thing—'

*

126

He was seventeen or eighteen years old. It was his last summer in the town. By September he would be at East Sussex. He would be free. This only seemed to make him more impatient. Women were everywhere, walking ahead of him on every pavement, packed into the vegetarian coffee-shop at lunchtime, laughing all afternoon on the benches in the new shopping plaza. Plump brown arms, the napes of necks: he could feel their limbs moving beneath the white summer dresses. He didn't want them. At night he fell out with his parents and then went upstairs to masturbate savagely over images of red-haired Pre-Raphaelite women he had cut from a book of prints. He hardly understood himself. One afternoon a girl of his own age got on the bus at Stand 18. She was perfectly plain – a bit short and fat, wearing a cardigan of a colour he described as 'a sort of Huddersfield pink' – until she turned round and he saw that she had the most extraordinary green eyes. 'Every different green was in them.' They were the green of grass, of laurel leaves, the pale green of a bird's egg. They were the deep blue-green of every sea-cliché he had ever read. 'And all at the same time. Not in different lights or on different days. All at the same time.' Eyes intelligent, reflective of the light, not human: the eyes of a bird or an animal. They seemed independent of her, as if they saw things on behalf of someone else: as if whatever intelligence inhabited them was quite different to her own. They examined him briefly. In that glance, he believed, 'she'd seen everything about me. There was nothing left to know.' He was transfixed. If you had ridden that bus as an adult, he said, and seen those eyes, you might have thought that angels travel route X39 to Sheffield in disguise.

'But they don't. They fucking don't.'

After that first afternoon she often travelled from Stand 18. He was so astonished by her that when she got off the bus one day at a place called Jumble Wood, he got off too and followed her. A nice middle-class road wound up between bungalows in the sunshine. Above them, on the lip of a short steep gritstone scarp, hung the trees: green and tangled, rather impenetrable. She walked past the houses and he lost sight of her: so he went up to the wood itself.

Inside, it was smaller than he had expected, full of a kind of hot stillness. He sat down for a minute or two, tranquillised by the greenish gold light filtering down into the gloom between the oaks; then walked on, to find himself suddenly on the edge of a dry limestone valley. There was a white cliff, fringed with yew and whitebeam. There were grassy banks scattered with ferns and sycamore saplings. At his feet purple vetches twined their tendrils like nylon monofilament round the stems of the moon-daisies. He was astonished by the wood avens, pure Art Nouveau with their complaisantly bowed yellow-brown flowerheads and strange spiky seed cases. He had never seen them before, or the heath spotted orchids, tiny delicate patterns like intaglio on each pale violet petal.

When he looked up again, sunshine was pouring into the narrow valley from its southwestern end, spilling through the translucent leaves of young ash trees, transfiguring the stones and illuminating the grassy slopes *as if from inside* – as if the whole landscape might suddenly split open and pour its own mysterious devouring light back into the world.

'So what did happen, Choe?'

Instead of answering he stared away from me through the windscreen, started the car up, and let it roll gently down the hill, until, on the right, I saw the turning and the sign:

JUMBLE WOOD

'You decide,' he said. 'We'll walk up.'

I don't know what he wanted me to see, except what he had seen all those years ago. All I found is what he had already described – the wood, smaller than you would expect, full of dust motes suspended in sunshine – and beyond that, on the knife-edge of the geological interface, the curious little limestone valley with its presiding crag like a white church.

'You're going to have to give me a bit more help,' I said.

He knelt down.

'See this? Wood avens. I had to look it up in a book.'

He picked one and offered it to me.

'It's pretty. Choe, what happened here?'

'Would you believe me if I told you the world really did split open?'

He gazed miserably away from me.

'What?' I said.

'Somehow the light peeled itself open and showed me what was inside. It was her. She walked out of it, with those eyes every green in the world.' He laughed. 'Would you believe me if I said she was naked, and she stank of sex, and she let me push her down there and then and fuck her in the sunshine? And then somehow she went back into the world and it sealed itself up behind her and I never saw her again?'

'Choe—'

'I was eighteen years old,' he said. 'It was my first fuck.'

He turned away suddenly.

'It was my only fuck,' he said. 'I've never done it since. Whatever lives here loves us. I know it does. But it only loves us once.'

He drove back to London in silence, parked the Escort in Camden and walked off to the tube. I telephoned him daily for two weeks, and then weekly for two months. All I got was his answering machine. In the end I gave up. Someone told me he had moved to Chiswick; someone else that he had left Britain altogether. Then one day in December I got a call from him. He was living in Gravesend.

'All that Jumble Wood stuff,' he said. 'I made it up. I only told you that to get you going, you know.'

I said I would still like to talk.

'Can you get down here?'

I said I could, and we arranged a meeting. He rang to cancel three or four times. Each time it was back on within an hour or two. First I was to meet him at the bar of a pub called the Harbour Lights. Then, if I was bringing a car, at his flat. Finally he agreed to be in the main car park at one o'clock.

I drove down there along the coast road, past the rows of empty caravans, exhausted amusement parks and chemical factories which occupied the low ground between the road and the sea. Wet sleet had fallen on them all that month without once turning into snow. You could hear the women in the supermarkets congratulating themselves on being born on a warm coast, though in fact it was quite raw in the town that afternoon. I found Choe sitting on the wall of the car park, kicking his feet, his jeans rolled up to show off a pair of paint-splattered workboots. He had shaved his hair off, then let it grow out two or three millimetres so that the bony plates of his skull showed through, aggressive and vulnerable at the same time. He seemed bored and lonely, as if he had been sitting there all morning, his nose running, his face and arms reddening in the wind from the sea.

He jumped off the wall.

'You'll love the Harbour Lights!' he promised, and we began to walk down through the town towards the sea. Quite soon, everything was exciting him again: a girl getting out of a new car; brilliantly coloured skateboard components displayed in the window of the Surf Shack; an advertisement for a film he hadn't seen. 'See that? Wow!' He waved his arm. 'And look at those fucking gannets up there!' Thinking perhaps that he had thrown them something, the circling birds – they were actually herring gulls – dipped and veered abruptly in their flight.

'They could wait forever!'

'They're big strong birds,' I agreed.

He stared at me.

'I'm fucking scared of them,' he said.

'I thought you were scared of nowt.'

He laughed.

We had come out on to the sea-front, and there was the Harbour Lights, facing out across the bay where a handful of wind-surfers bobbed around on a low swell, their bright sails signalling in acid greens and pinks from a lost summer. 'You should see the pies in here,' Choe said delightedly. 'There's a kind of black residue in them. It's the meat.'

We went in and sat down.

'Tell me about what you do,' he said.

I opened my mouth but he interrupted immediately.

'Look at this place!'

It seemed no different to any other pub on a flat coast, but perhaps that was what he meant. The brewery had put in an imitation ship's bell; a jukebox played '60s surfer classics. At one end of the long cavernous bar were a few empty seafood trays under chipped glass, while at the other the barman was saying to a woman in a torn fur coat, 'You've picked a bad day.' He hurried off down to the other end, where he seemed to fall into a dream. She smiled vaguely after him, then took off one shoe to examine the heel. A small tan and white dog, driven to hysteria by this act, rushed barking at her bare foot. The locals laughed and winked at one another.

Choe stared at them with dislike.

'You went along with all this so you'd have something to write,' he accused me.

I got my notebook out and put it on the table between us.

'It's a living, Choe.'

I went to the bar to get the drinks.

'Write something about me then,' he said when I came back. He grinned. 'Go on! Now! I bet you can!'

'I don't do portraits, Choe.'

The lies liberated from this statement skittered off into infinity like images between two mirrors. He must have sensed them go, because instead of answering he stood up and turned his back on me and pretended to look out of the window at the aimless evolutions of the wind-surfers—

They would tack hesitantly towards one another until they had gathered in a slow drift like a lot of ducks on a pond: then one of them, his sail like neon in the sleety afternoon light, would shoot out of the mass and fly for a quarter of a mile across the bay in a fast, delirious curve, spray shuddering up around him as he leapt from wave to wave. During this drive he seemed to have broken free not just from the other surfers but from Gravesend, winter, everything. Every line of his body tautened against the pull of the sail – braced feet, bent legs, yellow flotation jacket – was like an advert for another climate.

Sooner or later, though, the board would swerve, slow down suddenly, subside. Abandoned by the wind the bright sail, after hunting about for a second or two in surprise, sagged and fell into the water like a butterfly into a bath, clinging to a moment of self-awareness too confused to be of any use. This made Choe Ashton shiver and stare round the bar.

'These fuckers have all committed suicide,' he said. His face was so pale I thought he was going to be sick.

'Be fair, Choe,' I said cruelly. 'You like the pies.'

'I won't let you write anything about me.'

'How can you stop that, Choe?'

He shrugged.

'I could beat the fuck out of you,' he said.

Outside, the tide was coming in resolutely; the light was fading. I went out to the lavatory. Among the stickers on the bar door was one saying, 'Prevent Hangovers – Stay Drunk'. When I got back the woman at the bar was doing up her coat. 'I'd put far too much cayenne in,' she told the barman, 'but we had to eat it anyway!' The tan and white dog was begging from table to table, and Choe Ashton had gone. I found him outside. Twenty or thirty herring gulls had gathered shrieking above him in the darkening air, and he was throwing stones at them with singleminded ferocity. It was some time before he noticed me. He was panting.

'These fuckers,' he said. 'They can wait forever.' He rubbed the inside of his elbow. 'I've hurt my arm.'

'They only live a year or two, Choe.'

He picked up another stone. The gulls shrieked.

'I only told you that stuff to get you going,' he said. 'None of it was true. I never even lived there.'

I have no idea what happened to Choe Ashton in Jumble Wood. Whatever he says now though, I believe he returns there year after year, probably on the day he took me, the anniversary of his first and perhaps single sexual experience. It is as much an attempt to reassure himself of his own existence as that of the girl he believes came out of the inside of the world. I imagine he stands there all afternoon watching the golden light angle moment to moment across the valley. Seen in the promise of this light, the shadows of the sycamore saplings are full of significance; the little crag resembles a white church. Behind him, on the gritstone side of the geological divide, the wood is hot and tranquil and full of insects. His hand resting on the rough bark of an oak, he appeals time and again to whatever lives in that place – 'Bring her back. Bring her back to me.' – only to be hurt time and again by its lack of response.

I understand that. I understand why he might want to obscure it. From me. From himself. What I don't understand is my own dream.

I've lost no one. My life is perfectly whole. I never dreamed anything like this until I met Choe Ashton. It's since then that I can no longer accept a universe empty of meaning, even if I must put it there myself.

Empty

Not everyone looks in a mirror one day and sees they've grown old. But we all get some reminder.

You slip off the kerb and break your ankle. Or you suffer something you think is angina, a pain in the heart, on a wet Monday morning. Or someone you depended on leaves you. ('Our marriage always stifled me.') Your whole life lurches, and that's when you get your glimpse of the doorway between the two big rooms of existence. Suddenly your confidence has gone. You were middle-aged: now you're old.

I can always tell when this has happened to someone I know. They get well, remarry, beat the clock: but their eyes take on a wounded, flabby look. They've stopped trusting other people, perhaps. Certainly they've stopped trusting themselves. Most of all they've stopped trusting life. Young people can shrug things off, shave their heads, queue in the rain for hours for tickets, crash a motorcycle, juggle with a gun. But the rest of us are just standing there in rows, with a nice touch of grey in the hair, watching the cars rush past and wondering if we'll ever dare cross the road again.

Some people go longer than others before that pain in the heart knocks them down. I lasted a long time; and in the end none of those ordinary things happened to me. The shock I got was in some ways easier to understand.

In some ways it was harder.

My name is Jacob Wishart. I find other people for a living. Kids especially. They go off-course, they bolt and get lost. Perhaps that was never their real intention, perhaps it was just language, a confused emotional invitation, 'Follow me.' So I follow them into the bash cities in Birmingham, Leeds and London; tell them my favourite band is Pearl Jam, which is not entirely a lie; then entice them back to their middle-class parents. Cruel, I know: but by the time I get to them they're sick of living in a cardboard box anyway. And yet sometimes you think these kids have eyes like old glass beads. If they're looking at anything, it isn't you. They hear music in their heads all the time: you forgot it long ago. Worse than that, you can't get over the feeling that they would eat you if they refocused, if they woke up long enough. No: that they have already eaten you. But this is to jump the gun. And to be honest I never found a runaway that didn't really want to go back.

Most of my clients are private, although I get the occasional case from the social services. My office is in King's Cross, but I don't keep paper there. To tell the truth I throw away anything that bores me. I once began a CV, 'My name is Jacob Wishart and I don't own much. Live alone, travel light, never sign your own name.' They didn't give me the job. I dress twenty, pass for thirty, but the day Ann McGrath phoned me from Manchester, I was forty-seven years old.

'Annie!' I said. 'Hiya!'

We talked for a moment about the weather, the job. Then she said:

'I've got work for you if you want it. I need someone to charm a runaway. She won't open up for us.'

'You've already got her back?' I said.

There was a silence.

'Yes,' she admitted.

'I find the kids,' I pointed out. 'Someone else can counsel them. Life's too short.'

'It's not like that.'

'So what is it like, Annie?'

When she didn't answer I said: 'How long was she away?'

Another pause.

'Two days.'

'Two *days?* Don't waste my time.'

'She can't tell us what happened to her.'

'They keep it to themselves, Annie. They want to forget it.'

'I won't be happy until I know.'

'Annie, you already know. You know what the luckier ones do. They take the paytrain into Manchester. They dance. They get lost looking for crack. The real street kids steal their money the first night. They try begging and it makes them feel sick. They spend the rest of the weekend in the bus station and the rest of their lives trying to guess if they caught Aids from someone's dreadlocks—'

'Jake, will you listen for once?'

'I always listen.'

She put the phone down. I heard it go down, click.

'Annie?'

I rang her back.

'I'm sorry,' I said. 'What happened to her?'

'She got lost on the moors between Manchester and Sheffield, Jake.'

'So?'

'So it's the back end of nothing up there. Just a lot of empty hills. She spent two nights wandering about without even a coat. When we ask her what happened she says, "A lady looked after me." Do you understand, Jake? No crack, no dreadlocks. Just, "A lady looked after me." It's not that she won't tell. It's that she can't. She doesn't seem to *know* what happened to her.'

I thought about it.

'Who would be paying me for this?' I said.

'Oh, so now you're interested.'

'Who would be paying?'

'The department.'

'Try again, Annie. Remember me? I'm Jake.'

'All right,' she said tiredly. 'I'm paying for it.'

'You really do want to know, don't you?'

I drove up two days later with my real office, a fifty megabyte Dell laptop, beside me on the front seat of the car. I took the M1, then swung west from Sheffield along Woodhead Road to get some feel for the scene. It was late March, the weather by turns squally and bright; very cold. The moors unfolded suddenly in front of me – long black slopes dotted with sheep, a chain of reservoirs like molten tin, the big quarries glittering with icy rock against dirty blue clouds. I thought about the girl stumbling around on her own, able to make out the city lights one minute, the next staring into darkness. Snow had fallen while she was missing. You could see the remains of it salted across the upper curves of the moor. Further down it had already cleared.

I shivered and turned the heater up. The roads were empty. By midday I had checked into the Britannia Hotel. From there I phoned Ann McGrath.

'You were right,' I admitted. 'It's the last place God made.'

'Never doubt me,' she said.

She gave me an address in Hyde, a burnt-out industrial suburb which had somehow spawned middle-class suburbs of its own.

'Talk to the girl,' she said. 'But don't upset the parents.'

'Are we sure she was really up there?'

'Yes. Don't upset the parents, Jake.'

In the event I didn't see them. Not then.

Their house was about five years old. The stonework looked raw and new, but the 'Georgian' window frames were already peeling in the Pennine weather. Like many of the other houses on the estate, it was for sale. There was a strip of bare lawn at the front; and at the back double-glazed patio doors from which you had a view north and east to Harrop Edge. As I knocked on the door a bitterly cold wind was blowing down off the moor. The girl herself let me in and showed me to the dining room. There, the afternoon light lay obliquely across a reproduction refectory table, where it discovered kitchen scissors, a white vase half full of water, and two or three bunches of orange lilies recently unwrapped from florists' paper. As we talked, the girl busied herself with the flowers. She stared dreamily out of the windows. The first thing she said to me after she let me in was:

'These moors used to be a sea.'

She waved her arm towards Harrop Edge, as if she could still make out the brackish Carboniferous shallows lapping there.

'Did you know that? Of course you'll say you did.'

'Adults know everything,' I said. 'I thought you understood that.' We laughed.

'The lilies are nice,' I said.

'They are, aren't they?'

She was perhaps sixteen years old, eager to talk one moment, a bit detached the next. Of her parents she said apologetically, 'They take too much care of me.' She found her first night on the moor easy to explain, her subsequent disorientation more difficult. This had so shocked her mother and father she was reduced to denying it, insisting instead, 'I got a bit muddy, that's all. They shouldn't have been so upset. I got a bit tired, wandering about all night.' She assured me several times, 'I wasn't drunk. You couldn't have been drunk on what I had.' I didn't think she was lying.

There had been an end-of-term party at Ashton Technical College on the Friday; an anarchic affair which lasted all afternoon. Suddenly some of her friends, growing bored, had decided to drive down Longdendale to the big quarry above Crowden. 'They had this idea of watching the sunset from the top,' she told me, with a kind of musing pride, as if she was bringing them out to show me. 'They're all mad.' Entering the pass and looking back, they had glimpsed Altdorfer clouds, the sun already smearing itself the colour of carnations behind the church-topped hill at Mottram. Further west, orange light flared off an office block miles away in Stockport. 'It was lovely,' she said. 'It really was.' She had enjoyed the drive, too. 'I felt safe.' The big sides of the moor had closed in over her; a stoat had looped across the road on a tight curve in the twilight. 'We were all laughing and singing. We had the stereo on as loud as it would go.' Between the trees she had glimpsed the grey water of the Etherow reservoirs racing along beside them.

'It was almost dark when they parked the car,' she told me, 'but they still thought we would have time to walk up to the quarry and back. It's steep, but it's not far. There are so many little paths up there, all going in different directions.'

She thought about this.

'Somehow I got separated,' she said. 'They didn't notice and they drove back without me.'

'Nice friends,' I said.

'It wasn't their fault. It's very steep up there in the dark. I'd really been enjoying it until then.'

'This woman who found you the next morning – you remember her.'

'Not really. I was so tired. I'd been walking about all night. Up there it's all lumps of grass and mud. At first I could see the road but I could never get down to it. Later, just as I was completely lost, I seemed to be with someone.' She looked at me as if I could help her understand this. 'At first I thought it was Mum,' she appealed. 'The way someone you know is with you in a dream. But it couldn't have been, could it? And anyway, this woman was too young.'

'After you had got down to the village,' I asked, 'what happened?'

'We talked,' was all she would say.

'What about?'

'Miss McGrath asked me all this.'

'Annie,' I said.

'Annie asked me all this. I've told her all this before.'

She moved her hands in her lap. Something she remembered caused her to smile down at them. 'It was the most beautiful morning,' she said. 'I was really tired, but I had a feeling of being *inside* it. We talked about that.' She had walked round the old moorside village of Tintwhistle with the woman whose face she was not yet ready to recall, and that was what they had talked about. 'How sometimes you're so happy everything seems to take you into itself.' A Burmese cat, she remembered, had run up to them along a stone wall, purring to be let into its house. 'No one was awake yet. The valley was full of mist. Then, as we were looking, the sun came up and it all poured away.' The whole valley had emptied itself like a jug of milk, westward towards Manchester. 'She didn't know the

names of any of the hills you can see from there: so I told her. Then
we went into a little graveyard.'

After a time I managed to ask:

'Which of you suggested going into the graveyard?'

She didn't remember.

'It could be important,' I said.

'I can't remember now. She said she had once lived near the
Danube. She was beautiful. She was too tall to be my mother; and
too sad. Anyway, Mum was down here all the time.'

'For God's sake!' I heard myself shout. 'You were with her all
that day and most of the next! Where did she take you?' The girl
shrugged and winced. I knew she couldn't answer: I knew I ought
to stop trying to make her. 'Did she show you anything in the
graveyard? What did she say? Tell me again what she said!'

Suddenly I remembered the weather.

'Two inches of snow fell up there and then melted again. Where
on earth did you go during that?'

'I didn't see any snow,' she said. 'It was beautiful and sunny. It
was warm.'

She looked stubbornly away from me, blinking.

'There's no need to shout,' she said.

'I'm sorry,' I said.

'Miss McGrath didn't shout.'

'Annie,' I said.

'Annie didn't shout.'

I let a minute go by, then asked as lightly as I could:

'And it was this woman who told you the moors are a sea?'

She surprised me by laughing suddenly.

'The river that came out here was bigger than the Danube,' she
said. 'You can say you knew that but you can't prove it!' She sniffed.
She pushed her hair out of her eyes and deftly wiped them with the
back of her wrist. 'Every pebble ever washed down that river to the
sea is embedded somewhere in these moors. I understood that when
I was up there. Even when I was in black mud to my knees, I could
feel the currents and the tides.'

She thought for a moment.

She said: 'Everything is so old.'

Then she said: 'The moors *are* the sea.'

I tried for half an hour to get further, then gave up and left. 'The moors are the sea.' This image of a fixed landscape as being comprised of movement – the flux of suspended sand, the quartz pebbles sucked along by plaited streams of water – was the very last thing I had come for. As I was going she said, 'Wait a minute,' and ran back into the house. After a moment she returned, with some of the orange lilies wrapped in green tissue paper. 'I know you liked these,' she said gravely. 'And I've got far too many.'

I was so surprised I took them.

'Thank you.'

There was still plenty of daylight, so I put the flowers carefully on the back seat of the car and went to look at the graveyard.

I couldn't think where else to start.

Wishart. My mother often pronounced it 'wish hard'. 'Wish hard, Wishart!' she would encourage me, when I was little. Wish hard for what? To stay four years old, and have her attention forever, and not end up in the ground the way she did when I was eleven?

Effectively there were two graveyards at Tintwhistle, one a little higher than the other on the steep hillside above the A628, with thirteen stone steps to connect them. It was like deep winter up there that afternoon. I had no idea what I had come for, but I knew I wasn't tempted to look for it in the upper cemetery. The graves were old and unkempt, dead leaves frozen on to the narrow gravel paths between them. In more than one place a good-sized young tree had broken the stones, or pushed them aside. The flower vases were full of ice. There was a bitter rime on everything, and a rusty iron angel on a plinth to watch over all of it. At least below the steps the living were still making an effort. Someone was keeping the bramble suckers cut back, and I could have had my choice of mixed bouquets in cellophane and yellow ribbon. I left the car blocking the lane outside and wandered from stone to stone, blowing into my hands, reading off the epitaphs as if all that marble were a database whose organisational principle I didn't yet understand.

'Passed into the Higher Life.' 'Faithful Unto Death.' (A line of music was inscribed underneath, with the words 'Come unto me all ye that labour.') 'Fell asleep aged 63 years.' And finally:

'They died that we might live in peace.'

I could hear the heavy traffic grinding past down on the Woodhead Road; the empty bleat of the sheep on the moors above. Light began to go out of the air. It wasn't the approach of evening: just that sudden flattening or greying of the light you sometimes see in the late afternoon. When I looked up again, there was a woman in the upper graveyard, toiling between the stones in silence, just like me.

Later, when Ann McGrath asked me, 'So what was she doing?' I would answer:

'Moving something from one grave to another.'

But at the time who could be certain? Thirty yards away in that illusive light I wasn't entirely sure I could see her anyway. Bundled up in a peach-coloured raincoat and a headscarf, she looked old. Yet when she turned round I saw that she was younger than me, with a sallow Italianate face too broad and heavy in the bones, distorted further by some birth defect which dragged the mouth down in a permanent sneer. Her eyes were dark and beautiful. They winced away from the rest of her face. They repudiated it, moment to moment. I don't believe she saw me there. At the same time I'm convinced she was perfectly aware of me. Can you understand that? Slowly, she turned away again and went back to the graves. One hip was higher than the other, and she walked with an odd painful roll.

'She must have been doing something.'

'She was taking flowers off one grave and putting them on another. That's what I thought. But there weren't any flowers up there. OK?'

'Don't shout, Jake.'

What happened next – why I did what I did – is hard to explain. There was never any reason to mistake this woman for the one the girl had seen. She wasn't tall. She wasn't beautiful. Her gait was so distinctive the girl couldn't have failed to mention it. But when she left the graveyard I turned up my coat collar and followed her: back down the hill, across the Etherow and into Hadfield, where she waited for five or ten minutes at the unmanned rail halt for a stopping train to Manchester Piccadilly. I got on the train behind her and put two or three rows of seats between us.

It was an odd journey. The wide shallow cuttings streamed past us. She stared at a magazine. I stared at her. Every time the train approached a station she got up impatiently and waited for it to stop, only to change her mind as soon as the doors opened. Back in her seat, riffling energetically through the pages of the magazine, she shook her head as if somebody had said something she didn't want to hear. Up and down, up and down: but then when her station turned up at last she seemed to vanish without preamble, as if all that had been designed to confuse or hypnotise me. I woke up and rushed to the open doors. There she was, waiting calmly on the platform for me. We looked each other full in the face. Across her upper lip was a distinct black moustache; her enlarged pores seemed to exude some clumsy power – pheromonal, speechless, very direct. Her raincoat had fallen open. Under it she was wearing a red velvet evening dress, gathered into pleats and pipes and volutes at the shoulders and round the big, awkward-looking breasts. I was still in the train. I waited a moment for something to happen, I didn't know what. I felt my mouth open to speak, but something made me turn my head as quickly as I could and stare away from her until I heard the doors wheeze shut between us. I stared up at the station signboard in astonishment.

Hyde.

The train had begun to move again.

At the other end it was getting dark; lights were coming on in the shops and cafés around Piccadilly. I went back to my hotel room and sat on the bed. When I next looked at my watch it was half past seven. I felt too tired and too puzzled to go and fetch my car from

Tintwhistle. And anyway, it was time to make my report to Annie McGrath.

Annie, a tall girl who had sweated out the Thatcher years in Aids counselling in West London, still wore 501s and a black leather jacket to work. In those old days we had had something going, but I caught her too many times staring out on to the traffic on the Fulham Palace Road at lunchtime, stooped over her own folded arms, her kind, damp, slightly protruberant eyes full of some sense of inadequacy and professional frustration I didn't want to share. How either of us ended up in that sort of work I don't know. She was too easily hurt and I was too impatient. When I stared out of the window, it was to try and catch sight of the hot German saloon cars heading across the flyover for a weekend in the country. I wanted one of my own. 'At least if we'd gone into the media,' I once said to her, 'we'd still be together, living in North London with the rest of our generation, stuffing down the lamb passanda at the Anglo Asian on Stoke Newington Church Street and saying, "There's someone over there I know, but I'm not sure he'll remember me. Nick Hornby, you know, he wrote *Fever Pitch* . . ."'

Now, a decade or more later, we found ourselves in a wine bar in an alley just off St Anne's Square. For some reason they had called it Ganders Go South. You went down a flight of steps, past the bouncer, and inside was a small dance floor, really just a space cleared among the tables in front of the jazz band on its pokey dais in the corner. Ann liked Ganders Go South because they would still serve you garlic mushrooms there at half past eleven at night. Sometimes she didn't get finished until then. We sat down near the bar. Ann ordered the vegetarian lasagne, but I didn't feel like eating, so I had a couple of San Miguel beers instead.

'I went to Hyde,' I said.

'So tell me.'

I gave her a version of my interview with the girl, concentrating on the end-of-term party, the drive up to the moor, the girl becoming separated from her friends.

'They were having so much fun they drove home without her.'

'I already know how she got lost,' Ann said. 'I want to know how she was found.'

I told her. I said:

'If you can make anything of that you're welcome to it.'

I went to the toilet.

'You should have been more persistent,' Ann said when I came back.

'Look,' I warned her, 'I'm not a policeman. This is enough of a nightmare already. This woman, whoever she was, enticed the girl into Tintwhistle graveyard. Then they wandered about in the sunshine all day, while the world you and I live in got two inches of snow. How do you want to explain that?'

' I can't.'

'Can the police?'

'Oh come on, Jake.'

'I might talk to them,' I said.

She laughed.

'They won't talk to you,' she warned me.

'Why?'

'Have you seen yourself today?'

'These are my work clothes.'

She looked round the bar. 'I wonder they let you in here at all, Jake,' she said. Then she added: 'Do you know what's wrong with men like you? You force the rest of us to live in the real world so you don't have to. It's quite clever what you do.'

I kept things light. I said:

'That sounds like the politics of envy to me.'

'I wash my hands of you, Jake.'

People were drifting in from the square with its dark bookshops and trembling rainy light. A couple had begun to dance. The girl was only a secretary, approaching thirty but still pretty in a nervous way, and she was only going to take the man home and fuck him until he passed out, if he didn't pass out before. It couldn't lead to anything but emptiness, misunderstood intentions, and a bad head, and it had happened before in the history of the world. But I suddenly felt fiercely protective of her. I loved the delight on her face, the way her arms laced round his neck, the way she kept on dancing when the music stopped, her delicate, attractive greed.

I heard myself say to Annie:

'Do you want to come back to the hotel with me?'

'No.'

'The police, then. Give me a name.'

'I know a DS at Hyde,' she said. 'His name is Booth. You could talk to him. He always gets missing children because he was a minor player in the old Hindley and Brady investigation. Remember Hindley and Brady, Jake? All those kids tortured in a council house in Hattersley, then dumped on the moors—?'

I remembered them.

'Brady played "The Little Drummer Boy" while Myra Hindley forced a ten-year-old girl to suck him off. They taped it all, and took bad black and white photos.'

'I remember, Annie.'

Later, unable to sleep, I booted up the Dell and plodded aimlessly through my database. Children's names and ages: nothing but children's names and ages. I wouldn't find the girl in there, I knew. I would have trouble finding her in herself. Her adult calm, her care with me and all the others, the sense that she knew – somehow without knowing that she knew – something I would never know, could only leave me puzzled, unassuaged. Among the other rubbish I had brought with me was something to make me sleep: a Sony Discman. I lay on the bed, put the earphones in my ears and switched on. Warren Zevon, *Lawyers Guns and Money*. Nothing the kids would listen to, but not the music of a grown-up either. I wondered vaguely what would happen if I put this burn-out music in the sound system of the car and then drove very fast until I failed to make some tight little curve on a moorland road. I wondered why I hadn't told Ann McGrath anything about my experience in the graveyard. Then I closed my eyes and switched off and spent the rest of the night listening to the aircraft come in at Manchester airport over to the west, each one rumbling its way down some long spiral gradient of dissatisfaction.

When I woke up on Sunday morning I found that the flowers the girl had given me had dropped pollen on to the black plastic casing of the computer. It was light and gritty, a burnt orange colour.

Still unwilling to believe she had spent her missing days on the moor, I wasted three hours touting a Polaroid of the girl around central Manchester, asking people if they'd seen her. Bouncers, dealers, sixteen-year-old Indie clubbers trudging home in the cold with eyes like the bottoms of rivers, old women who lived in doorways off Piccadilly: the girl smiled out of the picture at them, and they all said how pretty she was. Everyone I spoke to wanted to help, but no one could say they had seen her. She looked too much like all the others. At noon I packed it in and caught a bus to Hyde, where I met Detective Sergeant Booth outside the Onward Street police station in the rain. 'Cheerio, then,' he was saying to someone as he came out. He was eating from a paper bag printed with the words FRESH BAKERY TAKEAWAY in red block letters.

Booth and I were much of an age, but thinning hair and a kind of sad disaffection with the realities of his trade made me think he was a lot older. He must have concluded the same, because he gave me a straight, kindly look and called me 'lad'. I was obscurely comforted. He had come west across the Pennines in 1963, an eighteen-year-old PC who raced a Dawes touring bike on his weekends off, supported Sheffield Wednesday, and idolised the young Geoffrey Boycott. Yorkshiremen are easily exiled. Proud to have kept his accent, he still thought of Rotherham as a world away from Greater Manchester. He told me this in the first few minutes of conversation, as if putting his cards on the table. He had, he added, three children, including a teenage daughter, of his own.

'Good fun, kiddies,' he maintained. 'But they'll wear you out if you let 'em.'

'I've been careful not to have any.'

He waited politely in case I wanted to develop the argument. Then he said:

'Aye. Well. Sensible enough.

'Look, about this girl you're interested in. There's not a deal more I can add to what Annie already knows.' He studied his watch. ''Ave yer got a minute?'

I said I had.

'Then I'll show you why.'

We got into his car, an old red Vauxhall Astra which smelled faintly of his wife's running shoes, and he drove up through all the decaying mill towns on to the moor. Stalybridge, Mossley, Greenfield: I soon felt lost. 'Aren't we going to Tintwhistle?' I asked, but he didn't answer. Every house looked like every other house. They could have been killing children at every curve of the A635 where it coiled up through the Chew Valley, beneath thousand-foot slopes chaotic with the spoil from old quarries, and out on to the watershed. Booth stopped at the boundary of his jurisdiction, where decent men like him toggle endlessly and amiably between the emotional states 'Yorkshire' and 'Lancashire', and the peat rolls away north and south, apparently forever, like the landscape of some unimaginable nuclear disaster.

'Look over there, lad,' he invited me. 'That's Wessenden Head, where we dug up what were left of Leslie Anne Downey. A month, we'd bin looking. We were freezing cold and piss-wet through. No one's sure how many kiddies Brady and Hindley buried in this area alone. There were more towards Huddersfield. No one's dared dig yet over at Crowden rifle range.'

He stared at me hard.

'Do you see what I'm suggesting? It's a big moor, this, and your missing lass is home and well.'

'Still,' I said. '*Something* happened to her.'

'She's home and well, lad.'

'Don't you want to know the truth?'

'I crossed her off the books in less than forty-eight hours,' he said stubbornly. 'She turned up alive and well.'

Without warning, black rain swung in across the moor towards us from the direction of Marsden. Booth started the windscreen wipers, then as an afterthought, the engine. 'Aye up,' he said. 'We're in for it now.' Water blurred the windows. It hammered on the roof. A gust of wind rocked the Astra sideways on its suspension. The world became vague and smeary, shrinking to a few clumps of bog-cotton, a bank of peat, a shallow pool pocked with raindrops and full of discarded household rubbish. Booth sat there calm and unmoved. The inside of his car seemed like an enclave of life in a lot of mud and wind.

'It took years to find some of the poor little fuckers,' he remembered. 'When we did, they were nowt but bones and clothes.'

He thought for a moment.

'Bones and clothes,' he repeated.

I couldn't argue with that. We sat without speaking for a moment. The rain turned to sleet, then passed away quickly towards Stockport, as if it had something else to do. Booth watched it go, then he said:

'I'll tek you to Tintwhistle to pick up your car, then.' He grinned. 'Dark blue F-registered Mercedes 190E, was it? We had it reported as blocking a road there.'

'Ah,' I said.

'Bit daft to leave a nice car like that all night unattended.'

'I suppose it was,' I said.

'No suppose about it, lad.'

When he let me out twenty minutes later it was raining again. Tintwhistle looked sodden and dark. The graveyard was empty. When I started the Mercedes, the sound system came alive too. I had had them fit a 120-watt Alpine RDS CD tuner with a six-disc changer in the boot. Music tumbled out of it into the wet air like blocks of concrete into a skip, John Mellencamp's 'Jack & Diane', with its mournful injunction, 'Hold on to sixteen as long as you can.' As if attracted by the noise, Booth, who had been about to drive off, got out of his Astra and wandered over. He listened to the music for a moment, then leaned in through the open driver's window and made turning motions with his right hand to indicate that I should drop the volume. As soon as he thought I could hear him he said:

'Try and see it this way. Truth is just something that's 'appened. You may find it out, you may not. It's a policeman's job to keep folks safe. Home and well, lad, or bones and clothes? I know which I prefer.'

He nodded briefly.

'Say hello to Annie for me,' he said.

'Ay,' I whispered to myself as I watched him drive off towards Hyde. 'I will that, lad. Mind how you go.'

I never saw him again. It was nearly dark, and there was only one place I hadn't been yet: so I went there.

I started from Ashton, just the way the girl had done. Water glittered like strips of silver paper as I dropped into Longdendale. Oak trees green with lichen seemed to hang motionless at each blind curve: dip towards me like Oriental dancers: pivot away suddenly. In the driving mirror I could see last year's dead leaves panicking about in my wake. Above that, Bramah Edge, and the extraordinary peach-coloured remains of the sunset. 'Wow,' I said. I turned the music up. Then the hillside at Crowden reared over me like a black wave, my nerve went, and I let the car coast to a halt. An hour later I was stumbling into Crowden Great Quarry in the dark.

Civil engineers had sliced the top off the hill in the 1800s, using high explosives which left the rock shattered to its heart, a permanently unstable frieze of hanging ribs and collapsing pillars a hundred feet high and three hundred yards long, over which gusts of wind now ruffled and boomed. The floor beneath was hummocky, furrowed, strewn with bits of rusty angle-iron and fallen rocks the size of front room furniture. I entered this landscape with sore ankles and wet feet – nervous, out of breath, cold despite my felt-lined Afghan jacket. I had no idea why I had come. For twenty or thirty minutes I poked about – picking up a Coke can whitened by the weather, examining a name scratched on a stone – as if the quarry itself might be a clue. I trod in sheep shit; talked to myself for company.

I said: ' "Loz woz ere." '

I said: 'Jesus, it's fucking cold in the natural world.'

I said: 'Wish hard, Wishart.'

As if that had been the key, the air filled itself with brightness like a glass filling itself with water.

A dawn evolves, colour to colour, tone to tone, changing all the time. We expect that. We welcome it. But from the outset this was the light of a sunny August morning. Night to day, winter to summer, like theatre lights coming up: and when the transition was complete I stood knee-deep in bilberry and heather. Foxgloves grew on the ledges above me, ferns in the shadows, and bright green moss where water trickled down the rock. Bees zoomed across the open spaces in long flat trajectories. There were sheep cropping unconcernedly at the top of the spoil heaps; sheep bleating distantly from the valley. I could smell the strange, spicy smell of the gritstone itself. I could see the hills in the distance, sleeping like animals, brassy with sunlight, huge with the shadows of clouds, patched with little fields and hanging woods. Beyond all that I thought I could make out the Cheshire Plain, the misty hook of Frodsham Edge on a long grey layered horizon. Closer to, oak trees clung to the slopes, there were holly trees in the curves and braids of the old river bed, little collapsed stone walls half-hidden in the bracken. Up from Crowden, with its shining slate roofs and smoky chimneys, its bright green pocket handkerchief campsite full of blue and orange tents, came the smell of food.

'It was beautiful and sunny,' I heard the girl whisper. 'We walked about all day.'

Another voice added firmly:

'No death.'

I had time to look at the clouds white and grey in a very blue sky, at the dark, fluted combe of Torside Clough, at the vast scoops and salients on the edge of Bleaklow, where the moors were chamfered-off as if someone had sandpapered them long ago. Then it all darkened to night again.

'Come back!' I shouted. 'I'm sorry!'

The quarry walls hung like the volutes of a rotten curtain. Two or three pieces of waste paper blew round my ankles. Then there seemed to be somebody standing behind me. The air was filled with a vile smell, which I thought for a moment was my own blood (so that I couldn't stop my hand flying up to my mouth to stem some silent painless haemorrhage), and I stumbled away between the spoil heaps until I felt it was safe to look back. After a moment I saw the woman in the red velvet evening dress moving off towards the mouth of the quarry. At first she seemed to be floating. Then I heard her picking her way carefully over the broken stones in her high heels, and after that smell faded. The worst thing was that I wanted her to come back. She had put everything equally out of reach to me, the ordinary world as far away as that endless August day. 'Fuck you!' I shouted. And then quieter: 'Just fuck you.' I wiped my nose on the back of my hand and plunged directly down the waiting hillside in the dark.

Back at the Britannia I tried to phone Annie McGrath: no answer. Never any answer.

God save us from the half-abandoned breakfast room of a provincial hotel on a grey morning after dreams of some faded old sexual jealousy whose object we can barely recall. Where they play 'Petite Fleur' and other ballroom favourites at 9.30 in the morning. Where the head waiter follows newcomers helplessly around saying, 'Ah, you're going to sit down there are you sir?' then gives two people the same table. Where you suddenly hear someone say triumphantly, 'The – answer – isn't – zero!', separating the words exactly to give them full value in the empty room. Where the only normal people have already had breakfast and gone. I drank half a cup of coffee and then tried to ring Booth from a payphone in the lobby. He wasn't in his office. Annie was just leaving hers.

She said: 'This is a bad time, Jake.'

'I know,' I said. 'It's the hotel phone.'

'A bad *time*.'

'Look Annie, I'm coming apart here. I need to talk.'

'I can spare you five minutes.'

'No you can't,' I said. 'You can fuck off.' I put the phone down.

It took her ten minutes to ring back.

'This had better be worth it, Jake. Save your tantrums for someone else.'

I considered hanging up again. Instead I told her about Tintwhistle graveyard, the woman in the velvet dress, and what I thought might have happened to the girl. 'Something happened to me up there, too,' I tried to explain. 'It wasn't the same thing. It wasn't so complete. At the time I wanted it to be, that's the horror of it.' I said I knew that this didn't help, but I didn't care. 'Places like that—' I said. And: 'We met something up there.' I said I was going back to London.

Annie was silent for a moment, then she laughed bitterly.

'I'm not paying you for this, Jake.'

'I know,' I said.

She cut the connection without saying goodbye. I went to my room and packed. On the way out I caught a glimpse of myself in the long mirror by the door. I was wearing a plaid workshirt, grey Levis dutifully out at the knee, old-fashioned industrial boots, unravelling fingerless gloves. My hair was going grey, and everything I valued except my German car was stuffed into a bicycle courier's shoulderbag with the Marin logo on the flap.

I asked myself aloud:

'Why the fuck can't you grow up, Jacob?'

No answer.

I thought of all the hotels I'd ever been in, and Annie McGrath saying, 'I wash my hands of you.' I washed my hands of myself. After I check out, I thought, I'll go and see the girl again. I would go and see her once more, just in case I could make head or tail of her.

*

It was Monday market in Hyde town centre. From stalls outside the Clarendon mall, people were trying to sell one another the most broken or pointless things they could find: secondhand shoes, rusty tools, 'Wooden handles, 50p'. Rain lashed the suburbs, to which an easterly wind had brought the smell of sulphur dioxide from factories in Sheffield and Rotherham. Rain dripped steadily down the fronts of the houses into the flower beds. Rain beaded the mahogany-look window frames, darkened the stone beneath the eaves. What I had expected was this: that the girl would greet me at her door, smiling gravely, a pair of scissors and some flower stalks held in one hand so that with the other she could brush her hair out of her eyes in a gesture so uncomplicated I would understand everything. That we would both be survivors of an experience no one else could share. But she wasn't there. The door hung open.

'Hello?' I called.

I knocked. I had learned in the social services that if you knock on an open door, people will give you their hearts.

'Hello?'

No one answered.

'Just a few more questions,' I called.

Then:

'It's Jacob Wishart.'

The hall floor had been polished that morning. In the dining room a watery light fell on brown and gold picture frames. I looked in on the kitchen, which smelled of Kenco coffee and Dettox Creamy Jel. I went up the stairs.

'Hello?'

I found her parents in the bathroom. They were about my own age, perhaps a little younger, but having children had tired them. Someone had thrown them into the bath, where they lay higgledy-piggledy, like cast-off shop dummies, the woman's arms across her husband's face. They were naked, marble-white, and covered all over with small puncture wounds, as if a table fork had been stuck into them repeatedly. Around each group of punctures the flesh was lightly bruised. There was no blood, anywhere. Their eyes were closed, and I thought they were dead. Perhaps they were: but they were still talking to one another.

'We had such hopes for her.'

'We had no hopes at all for the boy.'

'Oh dear no, the boy was all compewter games and daft shoes.'

'No hope for him at all.'

I made some sort of noise from the doorway. The woman's eyes sprang open.

'Oh dear,' she said. 'Wake up, Stan.'

'Gah!' he said, very loudly. His eyes opened too, but he couldn't seem to turn his head to look fully at me. He waved his arms for a moment and became still. He asked his wife: 'Has he come to see the house? Because they never told us to expect him. Will he want showing round?'

'Oh aye, he'll want showing round, love.'

'It's an Italian boiler,' he said. 'Very reliable. Gas, but electrically controlled.'

'After all, why would he come if he didn't want showing round?' She gave me an embarrassed smile. 'We never liked this suite,' she said. 'I wanted Autumn Claret, and a bidet, but they hadn't one in Denton for love or money.'

'He doesn't care about the colour, Linda. It's his wife who'll care about that.'

'Were we here the first time you called?'

'Would you like a cup of tea?'

All this time, they had been trying to stand up and get out of the bath, scuffling with their thin red hands at its rounded edges, trying to pull up on each other's shoulders, fingers leaving in the pale flesh slowly filling indentations, the yellowish soles of their feet skating about on the non-slip surface. The woman would crouch, get both feet under her, and begin to straighten her legs, only to fall backwards into the taps, legs splayed in the air to reveal through a greyish tuft the sore-looking lips of her sex. Her husband pawed at the tiled surround. They made shallow panting sounds, like

children with catarrh. Their knees and elbows bumped hollowly on
the sides of the bath.

'Nice cup of tea,' the mother repeated.

' 'Ave you *cleaned* this bath, Linda?'

I slammed the door on them and ran. Forty-five minutes later I
put the Mercedes through a stone wall somewhere between
Penistone and Barnsley. At the time I had no idea that was where
I was. Evidence suggests I was doing eighty-five miles an hour in a
built-up area. I walked away from it. Would you call that lucky?

'Wish hard, Wishart!'

Age calms you down, they say: but it's only ever made me
anxious. I'm fifty now.

A month or two after I wrote off the Mercedes, a letter arrived for
me at King's Cross. It was from Annie McGrath.

Whatever had happened in Hyde, the girl's parents were still in
their house every day, eating frozen food from Waitrose and doing
the ironing. The 'For Sale' board was still up. Perhaps that's just
what happens to you when the vampire has emptied you out: Bird's
Eye Lean Cuisine and a slow property market, more of the same
things you had all your life. You recover, you beat the clock.
Nobody but me ever saw their wounds, anyway. Their daughter had
gone, this time for good, or so DS Booth thought. He was still
patiently covering the ground. Her parents had wanted her to do
law, at the University of Liverpool. She had a place: but she never
enrolled there. Through Annie, Booth sent a message: Would I keep
an eye open for the girl? I knew I would, but not because he asked.
The thought of her made me shudder. I don't think she's in the
cardboard cities yet. I'd know. If I ever so much as sensed her there,
I'd sell the database and sublease the office and never go back or
follow that trade again.

The rest of Annie's letter was personal. She seemed down. She
was sick of the north, she said. She was sick of the amiable way her
clients accommodated themselves to a life blurred by drink,
handicapped by debt, 'Pissed away,' as she put it, 'among rusty gas

stoves and bits of broken furniture. And I hate the fucking rain,' she added.

'Take care of yourself, Jake,' she advised me. 'No one else will.'

And then:

'I wonder if we could have tried a bit harder, you and me.'

Everyone says that when they're lonely. Next day they wake up and remember you're just something they used to want. After we broke up, Annie went through a lot of boyfriends. She chose probation officers, teachers she met on summer courses, people in the social services generally. They all had lives as ramshackle as hers. After a while she would push her hand through her black leather belt whenever she was talking to a man: cup them over her lower belly. 'Keep Out.' I don't think she was aware of doing it. One of her favourite phrases was 'a haystack of last straws.'

Seven Guesses of the Heart

Falkender the magician lived on an island called Ys, a little way off the coast of mainland Autotelia.

Ys, nine miles long and perhaps four across, lay like a great ship across the Autotelian approaches, to which it presented tall granite cliffs, lashed by wind and rain all winter, tawny with sunlight in the summer dawns. Sea-pinks, saxifrage and rock-rose grew on the cliffs in profusion. The sandy clifftop soil was thick with yellow gorse, the spicy smell of which carried far out to sea, causing sailors suddenly to lift their heads and look for land. Coves and re-entrants dissected the granite, their steep banks on fire with montbretia and sol d'or. Inland, the long shallow bracken-filled valleys turned into dense thickets of elder, briar and holly. Ivy clasped the trees. Push your way through, and you came out suddenly into the fields and orchards and villages of Ys.

Ivy Thorne, Wroe, Natrass Giles, names for places in a dream! Fields tiny and eccentrically shaped. Old man's beard matting the hedges. Sturdy little whitewashed houses tucked away in hollows at the junction of a lane and a stream, or planted on the brow of a hill against a stormy blue sky. Gardens full of clematis and foxgloves. A magic agriculture, which burst the churns and made the granaries creak like ships in a storm. Early potatoes, much in demand in Autotelia. Flowers less forced than persuaded under glass. Whole shoals of fish spilling like polished coins from curious tubby single-masters on to the pink stone quays on the oceanward side of the island. All this produce, Ys sold to the mainland. And though Ysians thought themselves shrewder, happier and more fertile than mainlanders, they kept an eye on Autotelia and Autotelian policy, because that was where their living lay.

Falkender lived in a village called Onvoy, in the parish of Ender Voe. His house was a great foursquare thick-walled thing of honey-coloured granite, like a manse. Its rooms were tall, its wooden floors polished to a buttery sheen, its windows deeply recessed. But you could tell immediately it had seen better days. Look in through a ground-floor window and you saw how dust had dulled the broad-striped orange and ochre rugs. How a chipped enamel teapot, pale blue, stood empty on the kitchen table. Only one live-in servant, a woman called Totty, remained. Salt sea winds had stripped the outside paintwork. The garden was out of hand: indeed there were places in it now where even Falkender didn't like to go.

Despite this – the evidence or symbol, perhaps, of a discontent he had buried as deeply as he was able – Falkender would not have lived anywhere else. Neither the magician nor his wife had been much to Autotelia, although both had relatives there. In forty years together, they had made first a romantic, then a successful, then an acceptable life on Ys: they intended to live it out.

Then their daughter Rosamund died at the end of one winter, and everything changed.

One night some weeks after Rosamund's death, Falkender had an extraordinary dream. In it, he was trying to make his way across some waste ground in a country he didn't recognise. The sea was close. He could hear the tide. He thought he might be on a headland above a shingle beach. The air was salty, and full of a dusty, aromatic smell. The dry vegetation underfoot – heather, bilberry, myrtle – was so dense he could not walk on the ground itself, but was suspended on a kind of springy intractable mat which caught at his feet and ankles. Often he had to force his way through much taller growth, while trying to maintain his balance on a surface he couldn't really see. Panic urged him on, but the reason for it escaped him. He wasn't, for instance, being pursued. He had no idea where he was, or why. He wasn't sure if it was night or day. When he was able to look up for a moment, all he could make out ahead of him was a horizon, and a yellowish, tarry sky. The whole scene was charged with fear: but that sky had more dread in it than he had ever felt in his life before.

'A sky charged with fear!' he told himself the next morning. He laughed. 'What can you possibly mean when you say that?'

He managed to hide the dream from his wife, although it woke him three or four times that week alone. She found out in the end when, trudging along under the charged and mysterious sky, Falkender missed his footing and went down. The world turned instantly to brackish water beneath him. He was drowning before he could catch himself. He woke up thinking he had heard someone scream.

'Did I scream?' he asked his wife.

She was up on one elbow, staring down at him.

'It was more like a croak,' she said.

'I'm all right now.'

'Go back to sleep then.'

'I feel a fool,' he said. 'I must have woken the whole house. The world turned to water under me.'

'Go to sleep now.'

He shivered.

'Right to water under me,' he said.

Something else occurred to him.

'Didn't I wake you?' he asked her anxiously. 'Were you already awake?'

'You go to sleep now,' said his wife.

He turned over.

'I will,' he promised, though he didn't think he would. 'I'll be all right now.'

He hated to disturb his wife. They had lived together for twenty-three years before he discovered she found it hard to sleep. 'Once I've woken up,' she had admitted, 'there's no going back on it.' Then, laughing at his expression: 'Really, don't look so horrified. As a child I never slept. The world was too exciting, especially in the summer. I hardly closed my eyes at all until I was ten.'

'But I *slept* all those years,' Falkender had said: 'while you lay awake.'

'And you'll sleep again, if I know you.'

This time, though, he couldn't sleep. He lay looking at the ceiling for some time, trying to remember what had been happening in the dream to make him wake up screaming. Then he said emptily:

'It was my fault Rosamund died.'

He felt tears spring into his eyes.

'Hush now,' his wife said. 'Hush now, Falkender.'

'I kept her from what she wanted.'

What Rosamund had wanted was to do magic, and he had kept her successfully from that for perhaps fifteen years. Magic had done him no good: no good at all. 'Look around you,' he had told her when she was twelve years old, and full of the despair of it, full of its mad invitation, and desperately angry with him. 'Do you see how well we live? Do you see what comfort we live in? Magic got us all this,' he said bitterly. 'It's a great trade for making money.'

'There's nothing wrong with the way we live!' his daughter shouted. 'I love this house!' She pushed past him and ran out into the garden. 'You're just bitter because it stopped working for you.'

She turned back and added: 'You're just a bitter old man!'

He wasn't used to being shouted at. It made him blink. He had kept her from magic anyway, or so he thought, until inevitably he found her kneeling in the garden one summer night, her arms spread wide and some kind of white, shining frothy substance pouring down towards her and out of the warm moonlit sky. She was catching it and rubbing it over her breasts. She was nineteen years old. Her face was upturned and illuminated, her eyes wide and empty. What shocked him was not her ecstasy. Nor was it his immediate sense that the rite was more difficult, more risky, more productive than anything he had ever tried. It was her nakedness. And not even so much that, as his own intense sexual reaction to it.

'It's not as if she was right, anyway,' he told his wife after the funeral.

Soft rain dripped through the great yew trees and on to the pleasant shadowy pathways beneath, where in the worn wet stone there sometimes floated an image of the sky. The departing mourners talked in low voices. Falkender watched them thoughtfully. Throughout the ceremony, he had stared off between the more distant gravestones in the rainy light, his eyes hurt, hungry, expectant. As if, his wife thought suddenly, he might see Rosamund among them and not be surprised. Who knows what magicians see? Despite his age, his eyes had the intensity of a young man's. They were a startling green, a very bright green. She touched his upper arm gently.

'Hush now,' she said.

'It never stopped working for me.'

He cupped his hands and gazed into them intently.

'Look!' he ordered his wife.

Between his hands, he had inflated a small bubble with a strange viscous surface the gelid blue colour of water from some icy stream. It swelled quickly to the size of an apple. It quivered for a moment as if something was imprisoned there, or as if it was struggling to become something else. Then it grew still. A very faint impression of his daughter's face was caught in it. 'Look!' he urged his wife, as the image began to fade: 'She may even speak to us!' But his wife wasn't quick enough. When the ball had vanished again she advised him:

'Don't tire yourself like this.'

'See!' said Falkender. 'She was wrong about that. It never stopped working for me.'

He saw that his wife was crying.

'I think I just lost faith,' he said.

Every year of his life as a successful magician, and even in the years afterwards, the month of May had been like a door thrown down between Falkender and the truth of things. During the endless winter months he had laid the charge and lighted the fuse. In May he had seen the great green flare and soundless flash of the detonation, through which it was possible to glimpse for an instant the world that lies behind the world we know. (A world, he believed, which in some sense makes – or authorises – our own.) In May, his magic had engaged the magic of the universe itself. In May, even now, every garden in Ys had some invention of Falkender's growing in it. A lawn like a mysterious green pool at twilight. Mists of bluebells beneath the trees. Roses with names as exotic as the flowers he had given them rioting in the sunshine on every rustic trellis. Here a yellow laburnum, there an ornamental rowan with a smell like coconut ice. Great fleshy mallows with blooms the size of a child's face. And above all, hawthorn.

Hawthorn was Falkender's mark. It was his signature. He called it 'The White Tree'; children called him 'the May blossom man'. Everywhere in Ys in May the fields and gardens were full of Falkender's hawthorn, swagged in blossom so heavy it bore the boughs down to the ground; hawthorn which looked like white cloud in a perfect sky, or clipper ships on a green sea, or great women sailing to a wedding swathed in green satin and white lace.

But the last generation to call him 'the May blossom man', Rosamund's generation, were grown up with young children of their own. He had made nothing new for a decade. The White Tree was his professional gift to Ys: but with Rosamund dead, Falkender found himself empty even of pride in that. Long unable to make useful magic for others, he now found himself unable to make it for himself.

Instead, he walked the island, puzzled and tired, in search of the place in his dream.

He could not get rid of the feeling that the dream hid a message – although from whom, or what, he would not have dared admit. He interrogated it nightly, as he might a messenger, using techniques he had learned when he was apprentice to the extraordinary mainland magician Thierry Voulay. 'Every dream,' Voulay had taught, 'is a locked cave. The paradox of dreams – indeed of magic – is that to find the key you must already be inside.' When that failed, Falkender simply memorised each element of the dream landscape, so he could compare them, singly or in combination, with the cliffs and headlands that he knew. The dream became a map. In this way, he learned not to fear it. As a result, perhaps, it went away.

At first he was pleased. Then, after a fortnight undistracted by it, he saw the full misery of his own condition. All along he had hoped for a message from his daughter. The dream had turned out to be only a message from himself, a way of buffering himself against his loss, a kind of senseless puzzle set by his soul to occupy his mind. Grief welled up to replace it, less like water in a spring than blood in a wound. He saw his daughter everywhere, in the condition he had last discovered her. In his memory she rebuked him: 'You're just a bitter old man.' He could not bear to be in Ys in May.

'I'd like to get away for a while,' he told his wife one night.

'That's a good idea.'

'I think I'll go to the mainland.'

She stared at him angrily.

'There's grief and grief, Maklo Falkender,' she said. 'Have you lost your mind?'

He blinked. He touched her hand. He wanted her to stop being angry with him: but before that he had to make her understand his emptiness, his terror. 'I never minded losing the magic,' he said. 'But there's nothing left in me at all now. I feel my age for the first time.'

'Then act it, Maklo. Act your age.'

She thought for a moment.

'That would be the first time, too,' she said.

Unable to answer this old complaint, Falkender was silent. Then he said:

'I thought I would go and visit the mountains.'

No image whatsoever came to mind when he spoke the word *mountains*, and he might as well have been talking about the far side of the moon, somewhere else he had never visited. Sensing this, his wife turned away from him with an exasperated sigh. He waited for a moment, but she was pretending to be asleep. They lay there in the dark and he tried to think of an argument to persuade her. In the end he could only repeat:

'There's nothing left in me since all this.'

And then:

'I'd like to see some mountains.'

After a long time his wife said: 'They'll never let you go, anyway.'

The next afternoon, wandering the almost deserted corridors of the Ysian civil service, he was gripped by the fear that he would be prevented from leaving the island because he was *too old*. He rubbed his face. He sat on a bench near a window and watched a line of watery sunshine pivot across the polished floor, until the feeling went away.

In the end he got most of his travel papers quite easily. When he met resistance, he persisted. If he was forced to, he made things up.

'My health is bad.'

'You need time in a warmer climate?'

'Exactly.'

And in the next department:

'They have new hybrids on the mainland. Tomatoes, cooking apples, whole new *kinds* of potatoes. It's time someone from Ys went to study them.'

'We mustn't let them get ahead!'

'Exactly.'

This feast of invention tired him, but it produced an exit permit and a three-month visa. The actual authorisation to travel in Autotelia, without which he could not buy tickets, was harder to come by.

'You seem to be unsure why you're going,' the official said. She was a tall woman, ten or fifteen years younger than Falkender. Her heavily embroidered bodice, handsome cheekbones and practical manner disconcerted him deeply. 'I would be happy to write you an authorisation otherwise.' She held up the exit permit and visa in front of her and frowned slightly, as if her eyes would focus on one or the other but not both at the same time.

'I'm an old man,' Falkender told her.

She smiled.

'Nevertheless, I would prefer you to make up a coherent story before you leave.'

That evening he went up to his daughter's room and looked out of the window. The weather had taken a turn for the worse. There were high winds, sudden squalls of rain. Nevertheless, warm gleams of setting sunlight came and went unexpectedly in the garden below. He could see something moving in the wild part of the garden, where dense mutated rose briars, subject of an experiment he could never find the energy to finish, had colonised the pathways. For a moment his eyes narrowed angrily, and it looked as though he would go down there to investigate. Then he shook his head and sighed and turned back to the room instead.

It was cold. Cold seemed to seep from the huge old beams and unplastered walls, the cast-iron fireplace. Patches of light fell unevenly across some brocade cushions and a pile of Rosamund's clothes on the fabric-covered sofa. The dull blues and reds of the brocades were picked up in some grey wool-mix skirts, and a striped cotton jacket. A silk sash stood out, thick egg-yolk yellow. Everything else seemed to soak up the light. Falkender sighed again. Nothing of Rosamund's could explain what had happened to her, not even the diary which lay open on a little intricately carved round table by the bed. In it, she had written, on the sixth of May—

'When the rose water in this sealed bottle has finally evaporated, my love for everything will be over.'

Falkender looked for the bottle, but he could find nothing like it. Rose water! What could she have expected from magic anyway? Some stoppered but still unstable mix of opposites? Annihilation and safety? Rapture without pain, always passing yet captured forever? Sometimes he felt as if Rosamund was still in that room, occupying it as if nothing had changed. At the same time, her continued presence made it a different kind of space, faulted and unnatural: suspended, pending, as conditional as his travel warrant. What would she see if she were there? What would be worth her attention?

One of her cats – a young, sweet-natured silvertip with long legs and fur like thick cream, named by Rosamund after the magical ideogram 'Seven Guesses of the Heart' — had come into the room behind him. Since her death this cat had followed Falkender about the house every long afternoon. It would roll on its back in each empty room, leap to its feet at the sound of rain on the window sill. Now it rubbed its head against his leg. It sniffed daringly at a cupboard. It hung for an instant from the lip of an open drawer; slipped off, scattering small items – a scarf, some beads, a very small grimoire bound in wood and velvet.

'You foul demon,' Falkender said absently.

The cat purred loudly. He picked it up and left the room. He stood for a moment on the landing outside, unable to manage both the cat and the door.

'Hold still.'

The heat which has built up in a stone house retreats on cooler days into the stairwell. Leaving the upstairs rooms, you walk into a warm twilight. Falkender was reminded, for no reason he could understand, of a summer evening he had once spent in a garden in the south of Ys. That evening was a long way away now, with its scent of laburnum, its voices from the lawn, a laugh and the clink of a glass. Looking up from – what? A book? The face of a seated woman? – from something, anyway – he had seen his daughter running to him across the lawn. In her hands she held a tiny yellow rose. She was shouting, 'Daddy! It smells of *almonds*!' It had been a tranquil, almost hypnotic moment: the child, the flower, the sound of laughter. Now, as he put the cat down gently, and looked up at nothing, he found himself calmed a second time, by memory. He was falling, further and further into himself.

The next day he went back to the Bureau of Travel. He said:

'Kittens have such sweet breath.'

He raised his arms helplessly.

'Then something happens. After that, nothing you can do will bring back what they were. Do you see what I mean?'

The tall woman stared at him.

'My daughter is dead. I loved her. I don't think I can live here without her. For a while I don't think I can even bear to remember her. Will you give me the permit on those grounds?'

After a long empty moment she began to write.

Some days later, at the beginning of June, Falkender stood with his wife on the worn granite setts of Limport dock, looking out over the harbour towards the Great Bay. Behind him, cottages limewashed pink and white climbed the hill in the bright cool sunshine. Clean washing cracked and flapped gaily on the washing lines. The steep little streets of shops and cafés were bustling with new arrivals – goods, animals, people dressed in the peculiar fashions of the mainland. In front of him, fifteen or twenty sails clustered together on the sheltered water, orange and blue and lime green, like butterflies with folded wings drinking from some pool in an exotic country. Eight o'clock, and the morning tide was up, though not yet full. The air smelled of tar, salt, mud. Falkender breathed it with excitement, anxiety, a curious sense of relief. He had slept badly, exhausted first by dreams of his daughter – who stared at him with a compassion bordering on contempt – and then of that haunted headland above the sea.

This time the headland vegetation was baked and dusty, the sky like a dark blue ceramic. The air seemed to vibrate with heat. Falkender toiled forward. The world went to liquid beneath him. He fell. He drowned. In this version of the dream, though, he fell not into the water but through it, *and into the same landscape again.* There, he struggled towards the sound of the tide, one foot in front of the other in the dry hot smell of heath. Only to have the world turn to water once more, so that he drowned and fell back through, into the dream again and again until he woke up. This time he was screaming out loud. His wife, who had been reading a book, stared down at him helplessly. He clutched at her. He had never felt such terror and despair.

'Help me, help me.'

'Maklo, what is happening to you?'

There was no answer to this, so they had clung together all

night in the dark, numbly facing the monumental changes in their lives.

Now she said:

'We could walk a little. They won't board yet.'

He took her arm.

'I think I'd better wait here.'

She stared away from him. 'If that's what you want,' she said. After a moment or two she made herself laugh. 'Look! My mother used to say, "You can always tell the direction of the wind by the way the gulls face." She was right! See? They're all pointing at the lifeboat station like wooden toys someone has arranged on the beach.'

'Pardon?' said Falkender.

'Have you gone away already?' his wife asked him bitterly. Later, as he picked up his bag and waited his turn to board the boat, she said: 'Why do you have to do this? I don't know what will happen to us.'

Thirty or forty people were ahead of him in the queue, mostly younger people going to the mainland to find work. One or two couples had their children with them. A gull planed steeply over their heads, a precarious flash of white against the windy blue sky. The short, hacking cry of a baby seemed to merge seamlessly for a moment with the gull's repetitive wail, as if they were one species. One species, Falkender thought, raucous and scavenging; one species calling out in pain. To be human is to be mixed and miscegenated like this. To be lost.

'I look ahead,' Falkender's wife said, 'and I don't know what will happen to us.'

'Don't worry,' Falkender begged. 'Please.'

But she wouldn't reply to him until his foot was on the gangplank. Then it was only to repeat, 'Why do you have to do this?' She clung to his arm. Her face trembled. It collapsed finally into tears. 'I don't know what will happen to us.'

Falkender stood on the deck among the other passengers, looking out into the great estuary. He imagined the lines already cast off, the sailors in the bows, the boat bobbing its way out, past little green islands where tangled woods and low hills came right down to tidal water. Disembark on one of those islands, he thought, and you would find a naked boy sitting on a stone, playing the syrinx to a pure white goat. Such a boy might be part of you. You might recognise that boy as yourself, with the thin brown shoulders and black hair of long ago. Admit that, and the things which happened to you thereafter in that place would be both constructive and destructive of the spirit: things fundamentally and irreversibly transforming. You would go willingly, though in horror; return ecstatic but ruined. Magic! Suddenly, he walked across the deck, down the gangplank, and pushed his way back through the crowds on the quay. His wife had already begun to walk away, up the hill into Limport. He caught up with her and took her arm.

'Let's go home,' he said.

'You're a puzzle, Maklo Falkender.'

'I'm an old man.'

'Rubbish.'

The dead Rosamund stood listlessly in her room, looking out into the garden below.

In death she was much as she had been in life: a tall young woman, with her mother's big smooth shoulders and white skin, whose hair had turned an uncompromising red the day she began to do magic.

She often found herself standing at the window, although how she got there, or where she had been before she entered the room, she was always unable to recall. There wasn't much point in it anyway. Just to look at things is never enough. She could no longer handle her favourite objects. She could no longer leaf through the grimoires. She couldn't pick up her favourite cat, or count for him the guesses of his strong, affectionate little heart – *Where will I go now? Who will go with me? What must I do there? What can I be? Who shall I love there? Who will love me?* And the seventh only a repetition of the sixth: *Who will love me?*

'I still love these curtains,' Rosamund said, and was answered promptly:

'If only the room were not so small.'

Was that her own spoiled voice, seven years old and never satisfied? Oh Rosamund, Rosamund! she chided herself. She was at a loss to describe her present state, but she no longer regretted it. Her last act of magic, she knew, had ended her. It had closed her off from the world. But she was no longer sure that this was to describe the operation as *failed*. It was just one unlooked-for consequence. If she cared about anything from her old life – from her life – it was that her father did not seem to be able to make this distinction. She would have liked to tell him, in the voice she imagined adults to reserve for advising other adults, 'You studied under Thierry Voulay, the greatest magician who ever lived. Yet you have forgotten his most basic advice!'

It would be fatal to assume that magic enables us to see through an appearance or shadow to a reality. Magic is only a language. It speaks to us out of the duality of things. Here is the world we are born into. There is the world we sometimes glimpse behind it. Never assume that this world-behind-the-world is in any way prior to our own! It is neither more nor less. It does not generate our world. They generate each other.

Rosamund would have liked to touch her father's arm and add: 'Change is not bad. It is only change. Magic is about change.'

In the end, she whispered that aloud.

'Magic is about change.'

Just then, her mother came into the room, and joined her at the window. Together, at first without speaking, the two women looked down into the garden below. The long, uninterrupted summer days of Ys had warmed the twilight, into which glimmered sweet william like flowers embroidered on a cushion, montbretia spears which seemed to glow pale green from within. Honeysuckle rioted over the sagging old wooden trellises, tangled amiably with the long, elegantly winding runners of an albertine rose, whose petals were a kind of deep salmon pink at the base, fading almost to white at their tips. Drugged by its heavy scent, a few late bees flew in and out of the honeysuckle then away, in low arcs over the grass, where the cat Seven Guesses of the Heart stalked and startled them with sudden leaps and twists and darts.

Further away, in the more formal gardens, a mist the colour of milk, which for an hour had waited among the great dark trunks of the cedar trees, now breathed about the sunken lawns and white stone balustrades. It lay more thickly in the wild part of the garden where, in the theatre of Maklo Falkender's failure, among the mutating roses, the dense thickets of brambles, the bindweed and nettles the height of a man, something seemed to move when you watched.

After a moment, Falkender himself came into view. Mist lapped about his feet as he crossed the lawns. He was wearing a long robe of grey silk and carrying a rosewood staff.

The dead girl watched. The dead girl sighed. The dead girl tapped upon the window pane. For the hundredth time she failed to attract the magician's attention. For the hundredth time she asked her mother: 'When will he let himself see me again? He passes me on the landings, he crosses me on the stairs. He comes into this room every afternoon and allows himself to pretend I am not in it.'

And the mother, who heard her daughter's voice sometimes as the whisper of a leaf on an unswept stair, sometimes like the clear voice of any other young woman, advised:

'Hush now.'

'When will he acknowledge me?'

The mother put her arm round her daughter's shoulders and pulled her close, so that their hips touched warmly in the cold room.

'Give him time,' she said.

She laughed softly.

'Look!' she said.

Down in the unruly garden, the magician had raised his staff. Magic began to flow from him into the darkening air, delicate and hesitant as soap bubbles from a ring. 'Look! Look!' Hip to hip, mother to daughter in the empty room, the women watched Maklo Falkender confront in the only way he could the tangled foliage and unkempt pathways of his own heart.

I Did It

You know how it is. Chelsea lose two nil at home to Portsmouth, and you want to go home and bury an axe in your face. You want to do it, there and then, bury it in your face. You tell your friends, they never believe you. Normally, you'd think twice. What sort of *sound* would it make? That puts you off. But this time, 'Two nil,' you think. 'Christ, that's it, I'm doing it. This time I really am. Chunk. Axe in the face.'

It's easily done. Some people do that and it isn't even football.

Alex did it.

Alex did it and then phoned Nicola.

He said: 'I did it. I said I would, and I have.'

'Is that you, Alex?' she said.

'Don't you even recognise my voice any more?'

'I haven't got time for this,' she said.

She rang off.

Alex rang back. He said: 'You never believed I'd do it.'

'Wrong, Alex,' she said. 'I wished you would.'

'I'm coming to see you.'

'No you're not.'

'I'm coming for lunch,' he said. 'One o'clock.'

He got himself into the Audi and drove from Islington to Soho, where he waited outside her building. There was a sweet April wind. Alex breathed it deeply, feeling nothing he had expected to, only a delighted tranquillity. He did notice that he had quite an appetite. When Nicola came out of the building she stopped and stared at him.

'Still as beautiful as ever,' said Alex, though privately he thought she had put on weight.

'Christ, Alex, you sick fuck.'

'Good, isn't it?' said Alex. 'I hit myself in the face with it until it stuck. It was quite hard to do that.'

'Christ.'

'I had to use a mirror. I kept swinging it in the wrong direction.' He laughed rather wildly. 'And they call it the easy way out!'

'Well I'm not coming to lunch with you like that,' she said.

Later, Alex saw her in a West London restaurant with Chris. They looked happy. Alex, who was less happy, had to turn his face sideways before he could press it up against the glass. Nicola and Chris, he saw, were eating respectively a layered sandwich of hand-rolled buffalo mozzarella with chargrilled vegetables; and bruschetta of seared baby squid. They were drinking red, but Alex couldn't make out the label. It was probably house red. Chris wiped his mouth on a napkin. He smiled. He leaned forward to lightly touch the inside of Nicola's arm above the wrist. Alex waited until they came out of the restaurant and then jumped in front of Nicola waving his arms.

'Like it? It's *your fault.*'

'It's a very female thing,' Nicola was explaining to Chris, 'like giving birth with wolves.'

She said: 'Alex, I'm not having this.'

Chris looked embarrassed.

'Lost your tongue, Chris?' Alex asked him. 'I've lost mine.'

Alex wasn't one hundred per cent certain Chris's name was Chris. Everyone who lived in West London was called Chris, and that was the name he thought he remembered: but he did admit it could easily have been Sam, or Ben. He phoned Nicola up at one o'clock in the morning. 'Chris there with you?'

'Alex, leave me alone.'

'Is it Chris? I had the idea it might be Sam.'

'Alex, I'm getting an injunction.'

'I've had some photographs taken,' Alex said. 'Give one to Chris. It's his fault too.'

'Alex—'

'Is it Chris? They all have the kinds of names you give Border collies. Sam. Mick. Bill. Ben.'

'— for God's sake leave me alone.'

Alex said: 'Bill and Ben, eh?'

He said: 'I did it for you, Nicola.'

And he burst into tears.

Nicola did it next.

'You'll be pleased to know I've done it too,' she said. 'You made me, Alex. Chris couldn't bear you following us about.' It was her turn to burst into tears. 'Alex, he left me for some scrawny little twenty-year-old, and it's your fault. How does that make you feel, Alex?'

It made Alex feel annoyed.

'You've got no imagination of your own,' he said. 'Women never have.'

Nicola laughed nastily.

'I'm coming round to show you, Alex.'

'Show Chris,' said Alex, and hung up.

People all over London are walking about with axes buried in their faces. You see them on tubes and buses, you never know why they did it. It might be that their whole family died in a nuclear incident on a visit to Poland. But it's more likely that they have recently been stood up, or that last night they had to talk to Yuri the comics expert at the Academy Club:

'Nobody would ban *Lady Chatterley's Lover* these days. They just don't have time to read it. Visual images are a different thing.'

Chunk. Axe in the face.

*

The moment Nicola started following Chris, Alex stopped following Nicola.

It happened this way:

One morning he woke with a terrific headache. In the bathroom he was surprised by the thought: Is it a *good* axe? He also thought: Is an axe too much of a statement? Finally he thought: I'm not sure I ever liked this anyway. He examined his face, turning it right and then left, careful to stand back from the mirror. The axe was off-centre, and twisted a bit where it had bounced off his top gum. That had always spoilt it for him, as had the effect it gave of a harelip. He shaved round the axe and looked at it again.

'No. No good.'

Midday, he phoned Nicola.

'I've had it out,' he said.

'Why should I care?'

'They have to lever quite hard,' Alex told her, 'when they're loosening it. It's a very male, a very physical experience. How would I describe it?'

'I didn't ask.'

Alex thought for a minute.

'It's a bit like having your wisdom tooth done,' he explained. 'You know?'

He said: 'Now it's out, I feel great!'

Nicola put the phone down.

Chris told Nicola, as kindly as he could:

'Nicola, you need counselling.'

The very next time she phoned him, he hung up, although not before she had heard her replacement in the background, calling:

'Chris, is that the Mad Bitch? Come and fuck me afterwards! Chris? Chris?'

She phoned Alex.

'Alex, I'm so miserable.'

'Get a life,' advised Alex.

He said: 'I have.'

That was the low point, they now agree. Shortly afterwards they were accepted for joint counselling at Islington Relate. As soon as they felt able to talk over their differences without the help of a third party, they arranged to meet in the Bar Italia on Frith Street. It was a Saturday evening at the beginning of September. Nicola wore her long silver one-sleeved dress from Amanda Wakeley on Fulham Road, and carried an Anya Hindmarch bag with a diamanté clasp. She was a little late. She found Alex watching Italian football on the Bar Italia TV: Juventus v AC Milan.

'Aren't you cold in that?' he asked Nicola. He said: 'You look very nice.'

The counselling service had persuaded Nicola to have her axe out. She felt a little nervous, a little exposed, without it; and she was shocked and upset to see that Alex's was back. He had planted it squarely in the middle of his face. This time he had thought about it properly and gone for a good practical Stanley with a black rubber grip. He looked tired.

'Alex! *Who is it?*'

'What?'

'Alex, *that!*'

'This? Oh, this is just Manchester United losing to City,' laughed Alex. 'I'll get over it.'

The East

I lived for some time in central London. My work kept me busy in the evenings. But during the day, especially the early afternoon, I had nothing better to do than sit in Soho cafés. I liked Soho. I can't remember now if the Bar Italia was open in those days. I know the Living Room wasn't. Anyway, I tended to frequent old-fashioned places with a mixed clientele. Places like Presto's where you could still meet someone over thirty, someone who wasn't in films, advertising or comics: someone with – or more likely without – a real job.

In late 1989, at about the time of the opening-up of East Berlin, I used to see around the streets and parks an old man, a bit frail, strangely dressed, clearly a foreigner in a world where there are few clear foreigners any more. He was reluctant to talk. Sometimes he seemed reluctant even to stop walking. After some effort I cornered him one day in Soho Square. He was sitting on a bench with some pigeons round his feet. He wasn't feeding them. They seemed agitated with pleasure anyway, bobbing and dipping and walking up and down in the sunshine.

'You're reluctant to talk,' I said.

He smiled.

'You would be too,' he said. 'If you were me.'

When I say that he was old I am using the word in a special sense. At first I put his age at sixty or seventy. Later I realised that time had less to do with it than use. I began to think of him not so much as an old man as a young one who had been used up or tired out by some enormous effort of will.

The way he dressed was in itself odd. He always wore a long, very dark gaberdine, unbelted and buttoned from the neck right down to

189

his knees with large buttons of the same colour. It was tight at the shoulders and loose at the hem. The cloth was dusty and had faded unevenly – as if at some time in his life he had stood still for very long periods in strong sunlight – so that it looked grey in one light, purple in another. He also wore a stiff black hat with a round crown and a wide round brim. Both of these items had a strikingly foreign, old-fashioned air.

All the time I knew him he never seemed to shave. Despite that his beard was rarely more than a white stubble. Strong curly white hairs sprouted out of his nose, from deep in his nostrils. Also from the edges of his ears. His eyes, pink-rimmed, with irises of a very pale blue, were always watering. One day they gave him a look of intelligence, and you thought he might be an academic of some kind; the next, a look of cheerful cunning and you didn't know what to think. Every so often he would take out an enormous cotton handkerchief – white with a border of blue and brown lines of different thicknesses – and blow his nose loudly on it. This never failed to attract attention, especially in the crowded Pâtisserie Valerie.

He reminded me of someone but I could never think who. He claimed to have come from the East.

'So. What do you do?' he said.

'I'm an entertainer,' I said. 'Conjuror. Look.'

'Very impressive,' he said.

'What do you do?'

He indicated Soho Square, the pigeons, the young women in the windy sunshine.

'I do nothing, as you see.'

Drawn to one another the way a young man and an old man often are, we began to meet frequently. It was always in Soho. I introduced him to caffè latte and zabaglione. I found, too, that he would eat anything baked with crushed almonds. Confectionery like that reminded him of something eaten daily in the East. He couldn't successfully explain what, and I was left feeling that if I didn't understand him the fault was mine. It was a small thing.

After a while, he began to tell me the story of his escape. He always began the same way, by giving me this advice:

'Michael, never be a refugee.'

'Will I have a choice?'

'A clever answer. Someone as clever as you doesn't need to hear my story.'

'I'm sorry. Go on.'

'I mean this: never try to shove your life into a cheap suitcase at the last moment. Never try to save your books. Never wear your best overcoat. Have a light rucksack ready-packed. Take it with you to the office. Take it to the homes of your lovers. Always wear tough outdoor clothes and boots. Never try to save your family—'

There he broke off, breathing hard and staring at me intently. One side of his lower lip trembled.

'Promise me that, Michael.'

And before he would carry on I had to promise.

'Your English is good,' I said one day.

He smiled.

'Why shouldn't it be?'

'You're a linguist then,' I said.

'We're all linguists in the heart,' said the old man. And his blue eyes glittered like water seen from far off on a good day.

His English was very good indeed. There was never any doubt about his English. But the story he told had such a skewed feel it was like a bad translation, full of innuendos just where you wanted clarity. The language he couched it in was good, it was more than good. The story itself was what needed translating. This he failed to do.

'Every spring, the thaw leaves black mud eighteen inches deep on top of the permanent ice. The day we came west from Zoostry, we were up to our knees in it. People from further back kept catching us. We stumbled along as best we could. They drove past in everything from post vans to horse-drawn sleds. Then, on the outskirts of Avigdor: a child run down ten minutes before we arrived! Stolen military vehicle. Her little white leg was like a stick someone had driven into the mud until it broke. She looked up at us with such dumb surprise.'

He put his face in his hands.

'What could we do? Menkorad, Zentny Norosh, the Triangle: we'd come three hundred miles. We had no morphine, no blankets. No supplies of any kind. The Vorslatt people hadn't eaten for days. You could see them in the evening, trying to cook their shoes.'

We were conscious of our roles. I was young, he was old. I would listen while he spoke. Each time we met the old man had a new story for the young one. But he was careful not to monopolise our conversations. He drew a history from me, too. Who was I? How had I come to be what I was? He listened to my drab little tales – Northern colleges, Northern towns, Hell, Hull and Halifax – with as much interest as I had in his exotic ones.

'What I hate is the women with faces like buns,' I tried to explain. 'Every one of them carrying this plastic bag with a Pierrot printed on it. Do you know what I mean?' Or: 'Up there it still smells of the coking plant. The buses are always late. And there's always this fucking sign on the baker's van: "REAL" BREAD. I mean,' I asked the old man, 'what's that? Inverted fucking commas! Even the fucking bread calls its own existence into question?'

I don't know what he made of Britain through my eyes. But each of his stories further wrenched my idea of Eastern Europe. It dawned on me one day that he wasn't describing any Europe, any East, I knew. Was he using some abandoned nomenclature? For instance, when he spoke of 'Autotelia' perhaps he only meant Bulgaria. Just as when you say 'Bohemia' you are essentially talking about the place we know today – well anyway, the place we used to know – as Czechoslovakia. Encyclopaedias and atlases could tell me nothing. The tiny nation-states he described had gone unrecorded. They lay curled up inside his memory, but nowhere else: bereft of landscape or tradition, cultural heritage or political and economic history.

'The Triangle,' I tried one day: 'I'm not sure I understand you when you say that.'

We were upstairs at Maison Bertaux. Despite that, the old man looked off into the distance, as if the walls were no impediment.

'You said,' he reminded me, 'that my English was perfect.'

'Oh it is. It is.'

His escape, the old man often said, had exhausted his reserves not just of physical but psychic energy: imagination, hope, his whole sense of himself. But in the end I had to ask myself this. If he had come from the East, why should he have had to escape? Wasn't that the whole point? No one had to escape from there any more. I stopped believing him. Slowly he assumed 'a new definition. Just another old man, I told my friends, who had gone mad in a bedsitter in North London. This didn't make his stories any less entertaining (if entertaining is the proper word to use here). Neither did it prevent me from following him around London to see if I could discover more.

At the British Museum he studied trays of broken artefacts from vanished Polynesian cultures. At the Science Museum he was afforded some amusement by an exhibit meant to deconstruct the phlogiston theory of burning. At the Imperial War Museum he stood for almost an hour in front of a diorama of Mons. His face was illuminated by nostalgia. I kept a list. I still have it, though it grows more meaningless to me every year. He visited more than forty sites of this type, including the incomplete buildings of the new British Library. He attended an opera scored by Philip Glass, during which he slept; and the Man Ray exhibition at the Serpentine Gallery. There he smiled sadly over an amazing photograph entitled Rrose Selavy, 1924, as if he had once known its subject.

(Was 'Rrose' the proper spelling here, or a mistake of the Serpentine's? Was the whole name perhaps only an alias or Surrealist nom de guerre, 'Selavy' code for 'C'est la vie'? How would one ever find out? I still puzzle over this. Had Man Ray somehow managed to reach out over the years and counter the old man's mystery with a mystery of his own?)

Museums, art galleries, exhibitions.

These are not inexplicable locations. But how to describe the others? Abandoned cinemas in Haringey and East Finchley. The filled-in dock network between Surrey Quays and the river. Railway arches in Forest Hill and Putney. He visited them all. Even less explicable were the deserted intersections of arterial roads, viewed at midnight; the rainswept forecourts of Ikea, Wickes, Do It All, entered after closing time. At these venues he met other displaced people. They were men or women with white faces, often well dressed but bothered by two or three winter flies. I never heard them speak. They stood in groups of two or three, apparently studying the entrance arch of the Blackwall Tunnel or the north-west corner of the Tottenham Hale one-way system.

I don't know why I say 'apparently' here. But it seems apt enough. I shadowed him for a month. Nothing was revealed. Did he know I was there? Was the very meaninglessness of his itinerary a way of telling me how little I could learn?

Eventually, irritable and determined, I followed him all the way home.

Well, in fact I didn't.

He lived on Anson Road, one of the wide, endless, tree-lined streets that connect Tufnell Park and Holloway. An entire generation disappeared into those streets and never came out again. They came to attend the polytechnic and ended up staring at the peeling wallpaper above the Ascot. They put money in the gas meters and payphones. They paid or were unable to pay the rent. Answering the doorbell, they left a trail of wet footprints on the stairs from the bathroom – it was for someone else. They arrived young and quickly became middle-aged – in the end they owned a shelf of outdated sociology texts and some albums on the verge of collectibility. They had become bald men in black leather jackets, women like fat pigeons with woollen coats and very red lipstick.

Motionless in the pouring rain, I watched him move to and fro behind an uncurtained third-floor window. It was three o'clock in the afternoon. Light from the bare bulb above his head gleamed dully on the yellowed wallpaper. He still had his hat on. If you had asked me then, I would have identified him as the perfect inhabitant of the vanished '60s bedsitterland I have just described. It was the last time I could have claimed that. I was wrong about the old man. Perhaps I was wrong about Tufnell Park, too.

About an hour later he left the house and went off towards Holloway. I watched him out of sight then hurried up the cracked stone steps and rang doorbells until someone buzzed me in. The lino on the stairs was grey-green, the fire-retardant door of each bedsitter a starved matt white. I let myself into the old man's room – Hey Presto! – and looked around.

It was one of three single rooms partitioned out of the original double, with about twelve feet by seven of floor space. The stuff crowded in there fell into two broad categories, that which had been provided by the landlord and that which belonged to the old man himself. Into the former category fell the single bed (but not its yellow coverlet); the Baby Belling stove (but not the coffee-maker on its blackened front ring); the wardrobe with its peeling veneers, but not the short feathered stick propped up in one corner of it. Into the latter, a random collection of small objects (but not the chipped green chest of drawers he had arranged them on); an oval mirror (but not the stained sink he had positioned it above); and two or three items of clothing hanging on a hook on the back of the door.

I sat on the bed for some time studying these things. I felt only faintly guilty for being in there with them, perhaps because I could make nothing of them or the life they represented. The coffee-maker seemed bulbous and misproportioned. The mirror frame featured in bas-relief what appeared to be a fight between mink. The feathers were dyed fluorescent greens and reds; or were they? One moment the items on the chest of drawers looked like the residue of a hundred days out – trips to the seaside, trips to the country, river trips in hired boats – the next they seemed otherwordly, unreadable, impassive. A brass lizard, part of a triangular candle, a few polished stones, a tiny red tin of ointment, two or three ornamental boxes – all placed carefully around a framed photograph and smelling faintly of incense. As the light went out of the air outside, they seemed to shift a little, to settle towards one another. There was a faint, objective sigh in the air – the sound that inanimate things might make if they relaxed – a smell of dust.

Suddenly I realised what the design on the yellow bedcover was intended to represent. I got to my feet quickly and, blundering out of the room, slammed the door behind me, breathing as if I had run halfway down the Strand after a bus. I was desperate to get out of there. Then something compelled me to go back in and break everything I could find. In the end, I was breaking perfectly ordinary things. They seemed wrong to me. I broke a Birds of the World tea tray; a mug with Ronald McDonald's face.

The old man vanished from Soho. Within a week I missed him. I missed the challenge of him. Also, I remembered his watery blue eyes and his trembling lip, and wondered if I had gone too far. About a month later he walked into Presto's and sat down opposite me. His coat was glazed with dirt, as if he had been living in the street. He looked ill. His face was emaciated, his movements stiff; his hands had a continual slight tremor. When he spoke, I could hear his breath going effortfully in and out in the pauses between sentences.

'You don't look too well,' I said. 'Can I get you something?'

When the waitress came he ordered zabaglione but had trouble with the spoon. 'I can't eat this,' he said helplessly. To start with it was hard to get him to say anything else. He kept looking at me out of the side of his eye, like a nervous horse. If he wasn't watching me, he was watching the pedestrians entering Old Compton Street.

'No different here,' he said.

Suddenly, he laid his hand over mine.

'Michael, these people are animals! You must be so careful with them!' He stared hard at me. 'Michael, promise me you'll be careful!'

'I promise,' I said.

This seemed to relax him. He began spooning up the zabaglione very fast and noisily.

'I haven't eaten!' he said. 'I haven't dared eat!' He said: 'Someone broke into my room. My things. I—'

He looked out of the window.

'Look, that man!'

'It's just a man,' I said.

'No. He—'

He stopped.

'I haven't been back there,' he said.

'You feel violated,' I said.

'It's not that,' he said. He took his hat off and looked inside it. 'It's the terror of the return journey. You know?'

I didn't know.

'Despite that,' he told me, 'I'm determined to go back.'

'Do you mean the bedsit?' I asked.

He stared at me.

'Home,' he said. 'The terror of the journey home.'

'Ah.'

He said that he could no longer get on with the Western life. That was what he called it: the Western life. He shrugged, wiped around the inside of the hat with his handkerchief.

'I'm going back to the East.'

By then, I suppose, every journey had become a terror for him. As soon as he finished eating, I offered to help him along Charing Cross Road to the tube station and put him on a train. He eyed me uncertainly. I saw that he was frightened of me now, whatever he might say. Not because I had wrecked his room. He couldn't know I had done that. It was because I was human.

He thought. Then he said:

'Very well. Thank you. At least someone has been kind to me.'

It was the early evening rush hour. We walked slowly. He leaned on my arm. Despite it all, he was still interested in the West. The newest Japanese sports car or motorcycle, parked at the kerb like a halogen-lit sculpture, would stop him dead. A bookshop window would draw him across the pavement against the grain of the crowds. Paperbacks and maps, cheap souvenir T-shirts: he winced away from secretaries, but he wouldn't be put off the things that attracted him.

Leicester Square station was a nightmare. Tourists and school-children marbled a solid pack of commuters like the fat in beef. He clung to the escalator rail. When he found his platform at last, he wavered near the edge of it, nodding morosely as the older kids kicked the younger ones and tried to push them on to the rails. 'I suppose the train will be crowded,' he said. It was. 'I don't think I can get on,' he said; but he did. Before it pulled away, there was one of those empty moments typical to the Underground. (The carriage doors remain open. Apart from some faint ticking noises the train is silent and goes nowhere. People begin to look at one another.) For perhaps a minute the old man stared out at me from between two women in business suits and heavy eye make-up, terror in his eyes. I stared back uncomfortably, aware that everyone was watching us. He fumbled suddenly in his coat.

'Take this, Michael. Please take it.'

He pressed into my hand something small and angular, folding my fingers round it gently with his own.

At that the doors banged shut and the train drew away from the platform.

That was the last I saw of him.

When I looked down I saw that he had given me the little framed photograph which had stood on the chest of drawers in his room, surrounded like an icon by the votive objects of his exile. Something I had failed to break.

I found it difficult to pick up my existence where it had left off.

At night I worked, drawing dyed feathers out of a top hat. Hey Presto. By day I could not get the old man out of my head. I was bitterly sorry to have been the cause of his despair. But how could I help that now? In addition, Soho seemed empty to me without his ironies. I missed the sound of him snorting into his large hand-kerchief. I was bored.

To get away – and perhaps as a kind of penance too – I revisited many of the sites I had followed him to, haunting a street of deserted factories here, the strip of derelict land behind a Sainsbury's there. I was attracted to Hackney and Wanstead, the bleak parks, the chains of reservoirs which lay like mirrors discarded northward along the Lea Valley. Winter turned to Spring. In Clissold Park the wind tore the petals off the crocuses and blew them about. Male pigeons fluttered down to the paths, inflating themselves to bob and dip. The females looked up in faux surprise and walked in rather aimless arcs. It was Spring, and suddenly the streets were full of haggard young men and women from Stoke Newington, made tired and anxious by their success at marriage, culture journalism and modern parenting. They looked so awkward somehow, so uncomfortable with their lot. I stared at them puzzledly all one afternoon. They gave me an idea. I went back to the old man's bedsitter.

It was empty.

Even the carpet had gone. All I could find of him was a diagram drawn on the floor in chalk; a permanent sense that the room had only just been vacated.

I sat there in the silence.

I thought to myself:

So. The world is now full of people like him. People who have taken advantage of political change to infiltrate a society in which they would otherwise be easily discovered. Every lonely Soviet businessman we overhear discussing kilos of this, kilos of that in a pub in Cosmo Place. Every white-faced fifteen-year-old girl in a belted black PVC jacket, being sick on the Central Line platform at Tottenham Court Road. Kazakhstanis with cowed mothers, Kurds with political magazines, Estonians who run literary agencies from rather nice houses in Camberwell – they are all less from the East than the 'East'.

Is it possible to believe that?

The photograph he had given me was no help.

It had been taken in a garden darkened with laurel and close-set silver birch – a family picture centred on a very attractive black-haired woman in her mid-thirties. She wore a long jumper over jeans. Her brown eyes had the round, frank, slightly protrusive look and nervous vivacity associated with thyroid disorder. Her smile was delighted and ironic at once – the smile of a lively art student rather surprised to find herself a matron. In front of her stood two boys five and ten years old, resembling her closely about the mouth and eyes. And there, behind the three of them, with his hand on her shoulder and his face slightly out of focus, stood the old man: younger-looking but clearly himself. Was he her father? Or were they a marriage? It was hard to say. I inclined to the former. I found myself staring as deeply into the photograph as he had stared into my face when he said:

'Michael, never become a refugee!'

I placed it on the floor in front of me.

Towards dark, the world spun briefly. Vertigo! I thought. I thought I heard a bird call sweetly from one of the laurel bushes in the picture. I felt myself falling in towards it. I thought I heard a woman's voice exclaim—

'Aren't we lucky to have this? Aren't we?'

I stopped myself in time.

Those were the words I used to myself, 'in time'; although what I meant by them I wasn't then entirely sure. I went out of the bedsit and locked the door behind me. I went down into the quiet street.

The room is mine now. I don't live in it. I keep it locked when I'm not there. I bought a small chest of drawers and painted it green. On it I put a few of the things that have had meaning in my life so far. A ceramic rose brooch bought from a stall in Camden in 1986. A box of Norwegian matches. Some shells which, if you put your nose close to them, still give off the faint smell of the East Anglian coast. One or two things like that, set in front of the old man's photograph. Once a week I go there and stare into his daughter's eyes until I begin to feel myself falling.

'In time,' I tell myself. 'In time.'

Suicide Coast

Four thirty in the afternoon in a converted warehouse near Mile End underground station. Heavy, persistent summer rain was falling on the roof. Inside, the air was still and humid, dark despite the fluorescent lights. It smelled of sweat, dust, gymnasts' chalk. Twenty-five feet above the thick blue crash-mats, a boy with dreadlocks and baggy knee-length shorts was supporting his entire weight on two fingers of his right hand. The muscles of his upper back, black and shiny with sweat, fanned out exotically with the effort, like the hood of a cobra or the shell of a crab. One leg trailed behind him for balance. He had raised the other so that the knee was almost touching his chin. For two or three minutes he had been trying to get the ball of his foot in the same place as his fingers. Each time he moved his centre of gravity shifted and he had to go back to a resting position. Eventually he said quietly:

'I'm coming off.'

We all looked up. It was a slow afternoon in Mile End. Nobody bothers much with training in the middle of summer. Some teenagers were in from the local schools and colleges. A couple of men in their late thirties had sneaked out of a civil engineering contract near Cannon Street. Everyone was tired. Humidity had made the handholds slippery. Despite that, a serious atmosphere prevailed.

'Go on,' we encouraged him. 'You can do it.'

We didn't know him, or one another, from Adam.

'Go on!'

The boy on the wall laughed. He was good but not that good. He didn't want to fall off in front of everyone. An intention tremor moved through his bent leg. Losing patience with himself he scraped at the foothold with the toe of his boot. He lunged upwards. His body pivoted away from the wall and dropped on to the mats, which, absorbing the energy of the fall, made a sound like a badly winded heavyweight boxer. Chalk and dust billowed up. He got to his feet, laughing and shaking his dreadlocks.

'I can never do that.'

'You'll get it in the end,' I told him. 'Me, I'm going to fall off this roof once more then fuck off home. It's too hot in here.'

'See you, man.'

I had spent most of that winter in London, assembling copy for MAX, a Web-site that fronted the adventure sports software industry. They were always interested in stuff about cave diving, BASE jumping, snowboarding, hang gliding, ATB and so on: but they didn't want to know about rock climbing.

'Not enough to buy,' my editor said succinctly. 'And too obviously skill-based.' He leafed through my samples. 'The punter needs equipment to invest in. It strengthens his self-image. With the machine parked in his hall, he believes he could disconnect from the software and still do the sport.' He tapped a shot of Isobelle Patissier seven hundred feet up some knife-edge arête in Colorado. 'Where's the hardware? These are just bodies.'

'The boots are pretty high tech.'

'Yeah? And how much a pair? Fifty, a hundred and fifty? Mick, we can get them to lay out three grand for the *frame* of an ATB.'

He thought for a moment. Then he said: 'We might do something with the women.'

'The good ones are French.'

'Even better.'

I gathered the stuff together and put it away.

'I'm off then,' I said.

'You still got the 190?'

I nodded.

'Take care in that thing,' he said.

'I will.'

'Focke Wolf 190,' he said. 'Hey.'

'It's a Mercedes,' I said.

He laughed. He shook his head.

'Focke Wolf, Mercedes, no one drives themselves any more,' he said. 'You mad fucker.'

He looked round his office – a dusty metal desk, a couple of posters with the MAX logo, a couple of PCs. He said: 'No one comes in here in person any more. You ever hear of the modem?'

'Once or twice,' I said.

'Well they've invented it now.'

I looked around too.

'One day,' I said, 'the poor wankers are going to want back what you stole from them.'

'Come on. They pissed it all away long before we arrived.'

As I left the office he advised:

'Keep walking the walk, Mick.'

I looked at my watch. It was late and the MAX premises were in EC1. But I thought that if I got a move on and cut up through Tottenham, I could go and see a friend of mine. His name was Ed and I had known him since the 1980s.

Back then, I was trying to write a book about people like him. Ed Johnson sounded interesting. He had done everything from roped-access engineering in Telford to harvesting birds' nests for soup in South-East Asia. But he was hard to pin down. If I was in Birmingham he was in Exeter. If we were both in London he had something else to do. In the end it was Moscow Davis who made the introduction.

Moscow was a short, hard, cheerful girl with big feet and bedraggled hair. She was barely out of her teens. She had come from Oldham, I think, originally, and she had an indescribably snuffling accent. She and Ed had worked as steeplejacks together before they both moved down from the North in search of work. They had once been around a lot together. She thought Johnson would enjoy talking to me if I was still interested. I was. The arrangement we made was to be on the lookout for him in one of the Suicide Coast pubs, the Harbour Lights, that Sunday afternoon.

'Sunday afternoons are quiet, so we can have a chat,' said Moscow. 'Everyone's eating their dinner then.'

We had been in the pub for half an hour when Johnson arrived, wearing patched 501s and a dirty T-shirt with a picture of a mole on the front of it. He came over to our table and began kicking morosely at the legs of Moscow's chair. The little finger of his left hand was splinted and wrapped in a wad of bandage.

'This is Ed,' Moscow told me, not looking at him.

'Fuck off, Moscow,' Ed told her, not looking at me. He scratched his armpit and stared vaguely into the air above Moscow's head. 'I want my money back,' he said. Neither of them could think of anything to add to this, and after a pause he wandered off.

'He's always like that,' Moscow said. 'You don't want to pay any attention.' Later in the afternoon she said: 'You'll get on well with Ed, though. You'll like him. He's a mad bastard.'

'You say that about all the boys,' I said.

In this case Moscow was right, because I had heard it not just from her, and later I would get proof of it anyway – if you can ever get proof of anything. Everyone said that Ed should be in a straitjacket. In the end, nothing could be arranged. Johnson was in a bad mood, and Moscow had to be up the Coast that week, on Canvey Island, to do some work on one of the cracking-plants there. There was always a lot of that kind of work, oil work, chemical work, on Canvey Island. 'I haven't time for him,' Moscow explained as she got up to go. 'I'll see you later, anyway,' she promised.

As soon as she was gone, Ed Johnson came back and sat down in front of me. He grinned. 'Ever done anything worth doing in your whole life?' he asked me. 'Anything real?'

The MAX editor was right: since coring got popular, the roads had been deserted. I left EC1 and whacked the 190 up through Hackney until I got the Lea Valley reservoirs on my right like a splatter of moonlit verglas. On empty roads the only mistakes that need concern you are your own; every bend becomes a dreamy interrogation of your own technique. Life should be more like that. I made good time. Ed lived just back from Montagu Road, in a quiet street behind the Jewish Cemetery. He shared his flat with a woman in her early thirties whose name was Caitlin. Caitlin had black hair and soft, honest brown eyes. She and I were old friends. We hugged briefly on the doorstep. She looked up and down the street and shivered.

'Come in,' she said. 'It's cold.'

'You should wear a jumper.'

'I'll tell him you're here,' she said. 'Do you want some coffee?'

Caitlin had softened the edges of Ed's life, but less perhaps than either of them had hoped. His taste was still very minimal – white paint, ash floors, one or two items of furniture from Heal's. And there was still a competition Klein mounted on the living room wall, its polished aerospace alloys glittering in the halogen lights.

'Espresso,' I said.

'I'm not giving you espresso at this time of night. You'll explode.'

'It was worth a try.'

'Ed!' she called. 'Ed! Mick's here!'

He didn't answer.

She shrugged at me, as if to say, 'What can I do?' and went into the back room. I heard their voices but not what they were saying. After that she went upstairs. 'Go in and see him,' she suggested when she came down again three or four minutes later. 'I told him you were here.' She had pulled a Jigsaw sweater on over her Racing Green shirt and Levis; and fastened her hair back hastily with a dark brown velvet scrunchy.

'That looks nice,' I said. 'Do you want me to fetch him out?'

'I doubt he'll come.'

The back room was down a narrow corridor. Ed had turned it into a bleak combination of office and storage. The walls were done with one coat of what builders call 'obliterating emulsion' and covered with metal shelves. Chipped diving tanks hollow with the ghosts of exotic gases were stacked by the filing cabinet. His BASE chute spilled half out of its pack, yards of cold nylon a vile but exciting rose colour – a colour which made you want to be hurtling downwards face-first screaming with fear until you heard the canopy bang out behind you and you knew you weren't going to die that day (although you might still break both legs). The cheap beige carpet was strewn with high-access mess – hanks of greying static rope; a yellow bucket stuffed with tools; Ed's Petzl stop, harness and knocked-about CPTs. Everything was layered with dust. The radiators were turned off. There was a bed made up in one corner. Deep in the clutter on the cheap white desk stood a 5-gig Mac with a screen to design-industry specs. It was spraying Ed's face with icy blue light.

'Hi Ed.'

'Hi Mick.'

There was a long silence after that. Ed stared at the screen. I stared at his back. Just when I thought he had forgotten I was there, he said:

'Fuck off and talk to Caitlin a moment.'

'I brought us some beer.'

'That's great.'

'What are you running here?'

'It's a game. I'm running a game, Mick.'

Ed had lost weight since I last saw him. Though they retained their distinctive cabled structure, his forearms were a lot thinner. Without releasing him from anything it represented, the yoke of muscle had lifted from his shoulders. I had expected that. But I was surprised by how much flesh had melted off his face, leaving long vertical lines of sinew, fins of bone above the cheeks and at the corners of the jaw. His eyes were a long way back in his head. In a way it suited him. He would have seemed OK – a little tired perhaps; a little burned down, like someone who was working too hard – if it hadn't been for the light from the display. Hunched in his chair with that splashing off him, he looked like a vampire. He looked like a junkie.

I peered over his shoulder.

'You were never into this shit,' I said.

He grinned.

'Everyone's into it now. Why not me? Wanking away and pretending it's sex.'

'Oh come on.'

He looked down at himself.

'It's better than living,' he said.

There was no answer to that.

I went and asked Caitlin, 'Has he been doing this long?'

'Not long,' she said. 'Have some coffee.'

We sat in the L-shaped living area drinking decaffeinated Java. The sofa was big enough for Caitlin to curl up in a corner of it like a cat. She had turned the overhead lights off, tucked her bare feet up under her. She was smoking a cigarette. 'It's been a bloody awful day,' she warned me. 'So don't say a word.' She grinned wryly, then we both looked up at the Klein for a minute or two. Some kind of ambient music was issuing faintly from the stereo speakers, full of South American bird calls and bouts of muted drumming. 'Is he winning?' she asked.

'He didn't tell me.'

'You're lucky. It's all he ever tells me.'

'Aren't you worried?' I said.

She smiled.

'He's still using a screen,' she said. 'He's not plugging in.'

'Yet,' I said.

'Yet,' she agreed equably. 'Want more coffee? Or will you do me a favour?'

I put my empty cup on the floor.

'Do you a favour,' I said.

'Cut my hair.'

I got up and went to her end of the sofa. She turned away from me so I could release her hair from the scrunchy. 'Shake it,' I said. She shook it. She ran her hands through it. Perfume came up; something I didn't recognise. 'It doesn't need much,' I said. I switched the overhead light back on and fetched a kitchen chair. 'Sit here. No, right in the light. You'll have to take your jumper off.'

'The good scissors are in the bathroom,' she said.

Cut my hair. She had asked me that before, two or three days after she decided we should split up. I remembered the calm that came over me at the gentle, careful sound of the scissors, the way her hair felt as I lifted it away from the nape of her neck, the tenderness and fear because everything was changing around the two of us forever and somehow this quiet action signalised and blessed that. The shock of these memories made me ask:

'How are you two getting on?'

She lowered her head to help me cut. I felt her smile.

'You and Ed always liked the same kind of girls,' she said.

'Yes,' I said.

I finished the cut, then lightly kissed the nape of her neck. 'There,' I said. Beneath the perfume she smelled faintly of hypo-allergenic soap and unscented deodorants. 'No, Mick,' she said softly. 'Please.' I adjusted the collar of her shirt, let her hair fall back round it. My hand was still on her shoulder. She had to turn her head at an awkward angle to look up at me. Her eyes were wide and full of pain. 'Mick.' I kissed her mouth and brushed the side of her face with my fingertips. Her arms went round my neck, I felt her settle in the chair. I touched her breasts. They were warm, the cotton shirt was clean and cool. She made a small noise and pulled me closer. Just then, in the back room among the dusty air tanks and disused parachutes, Ed Johnson fell out of his chair and began to thrash about, the back of his head thudding rhythmically on the floor.

Caitlin pushed me away.

'Ed?' she called, from the passage door.

'Help!' cried Ed.

'I'll go,' I said.

Caitlin put her arm across the doorway and stared up at me calmly.

'No,' she said.

'How can you lift him on your own?'

'This is me and Ed,' she said.

'For God's sake!'

'It's late, Mick. I'll let you out, then I'll go and help him.'

At the front door I said:

'I think you're mad. Is this happening a lot? You're a fool to let him do this.'

'It's his life.'

I looked at her. She shrugged.

'Will you be all right?' I said.

When I offered to kiss her goodbye, she turned her face away.

'Fuck off then, both of you,' I said.

I knew which game Ed was playing, because I had seen the software wrapper discarded on the desk near his Mac. Its visuals were cheap and schematic, its values self-consciously retro. It was nothing like the stuff we sold off the MAX site, which was quite literally the experience itself, stripped of its consequences. You had to plug in for that: you had to be cored. This was just a game; less a game, even, than a trip. You flew a silvery V-shaped graphic down an endless V-shaped corridor, a notional perspective sometimes bounded by lines of objects, sometimes just by lines, sometimes bounded only by your memory of boundaries. Sometimes the graphic floated and mushed like a moth. Sometimes it travelled in flat vicious arcs at an apparent Mach 5. There were no guns, no opponent. There was no competition. You flew. Sometimes the horizon tilted one way, sometimes the other. You could choose your own music. It was a bleakly minimal experience. But after a minute or two, five at the most, you felt as if you could fly your icon down the perspective forever, to the soundtrack of your own life.

It was quite popular.

It was called *Out There*.

'Rock climbing is theatre,' I once wrote.

It had all the qualities of theatre, I went on, but a theatre-in-reverse:

'In obedience to some devious vanished script, the actors abandon the stage and begin to scale the seating arrangements, the balconies and hanging boxes now occupied only by cleaning-women.'

'Oh, very deep,' said Ed Johnson when he read this. 'Shall I tell you what's wrong here? Eh? Shall I tell you?'

'Piss off, Ed.'

'If you fall on your face from a hundred feet up, it comes off the front of your head *and you don't get a second go.* Next to that, theatre is wank. Theatre is flat. Theatre is *Suicide Coast.*'

Ed hated anywhere flat. 'Welcome to the Suicide Coast,' he used to say when I first knew him. To start with, that had been because he lived in Canterbury. But it had quickly become his way of describing most places, most experiences. You didn't actually have to be near the sea. Suicide Coast syndrome had caused Ed to do some stupid things in his time. One day, when he and Moscow still worked in roped-access engineering together, they were going up in the lift to the top of some shitty council highrise in Birmingham or Bristol, when suddenly Ed said:

'Do you bet me I can keep the doors open with my head?'

'What?'

'Next floor! When the doors start to close, do you bet me I can stop them with my head?'

It was Monday morning. The lift smelled of piss. They had been hand-ripping mastic out of expansion joints for two weeks, using Stanley knives. Moscow was tired, hung over, weighed-down by a collection of CPTs, mastic guns and hundred-foot coils of rope. Her right arm was numb from repeating the same action hour after hour, day after day.

'Fuck off, Ed,' she said.

But she knew Ed would do it whether she took the bet or not.

Two or three days after she first introduced me to Ed, Moscow telephoned me. She had got herself a couple of weeks cutting out on Thamesmead Estate. 'They don't half work hard, these fuckers,' she said. We talked about that for a minute or two then she asked:

'Well?'

'Well what, Moscow?'

'Ed. Was he what you were looking for, then? Or what?'

I said that though I was impressed I didn't think I would be able to write anything about Ed.

'He's a mad fucker, though, isn't he?'

'Oh he is,' I said. 'He certainly is.'

The way Moscow said 'isn't he' made it sound like 'innie'.

Another thing I once wrote:

'Climbing takes place in a special kind of space, the rules of which are simple. You must be able to see immediately what you have to lose; and you must choose the risk you take.'

What do I know?

I know that a life without consequences isn't a life at all. Also, if you want to do something difficult, something real, you can't shirk the pain. What I learned in the old days, from Ed and Moscow, from Gabe King, Justine Townsend and all the others who taught me to climb rock or jump off buildings or stay the right way up in a tube of pitch dark water two degrees off freezing and two hundred feet under the ground, was that you can't just plug in and be a star: you have to practise. You have to keep loading your fingers until the tendons swell.

So it's back to the Mile End wall, with its few thousand square feet of board and bolt-on holds, its few thousand cubic metres of emphysemic air through which one very bright ray of sun sometimes falls in the middle of the afternoon, illuminating nothing much at all. Back to the sound of the fan heater, the dust-filled Akai radio playing some mournful aggressive thing, and every so often a boy's voice saying softly, 'Oh shit,' as some sequence or other fails to work out. You go back there, and if you have to fall off the same ceiling move thirty times in an afternoon, that's what you do. The mats give their gusty wheeze, chalk dust flies up, the fan heater

213

above the Monkey House door rattles and chokes and flatlines briefly before puttering on.

'Jesus Christ. I don't know why I do this.'

Caitlin telephoned me.

'Come to supper,' she said.

'No,' I said.

'Mick, why?'

'Because I'm sick of it.'

'Sick of what?'

'You. Me. Him. Everything.'

'Look,' she said, 'he's sorry about what happened last time.'

'Oh, *he*'s sorry.'

'We're both sorry, Mick.'

'All right, then: I'm sorry, too.'

There was a gentle laugh at the other end.

'So you should be.'

I went along all the deserted roads and got there at about eight, to find a brand new motorcycle parked on the pavement outside the house. It was a Kawasaki *Ninja*. Its fairing had been removed, to give it the look of a '60s café racer, but no one was fooled. Even at a glance it appeared too hunched, too short-coupled: too knowing. The remaining plastics shone with their own harsh inner light.

Caitlin met me on the doorstep. She put her hands on my shoulders and kissed me. 'Mm,' she said. She was wearing white tennis shorts and a soft dark blue sweatshirt.

'We've got to stop meeting like this,' I said.

She smiled and pushed me away.

'My hands smell of garlic,' she said.

Just as we were going inside, she turned back and nodded at the Kawa.

'That thing,' she said.

'It's a motorcycle, Caitlin.'

'It's his.'

I stared at her.

'Be enthusiastic,' she said. 'Please.'

'But—'

'Please?'

The main course was penne with mushrooms in an olive and tomato sauce. Ed had cooked it, Caitlin said, but she served. Ed pushed his chair over to the table and rubbed his hands. He picked his plate up and passed it under his nose. 'Wow!' he said. As we ate, we talked about this and that. The Kawa was behind everything we said, but Ed wouldn't mention it until I did. Caitlin smiled at us both. She shook her head as if to say: 'Children! You children!' It was like Christmas, and she was the parent. The three of us could feel Ed's excitement and impatience. He grinned secretively. He glanced up from his food at one or both of us; quickly back down again. Finally, he couldn't hold back any longer.

'What do you think, then?' he said. 'What do you think, Mick?'

'I think this is good pasta,' I said. 'For a cripple.'

He grinned and wiped his mouth.

'It's not bad,' he said, 'is it?'

'I think what I like best is the way you've let the mushrooms take up a touch of sesame oil.'

'Have some more. There's plenty.'

'That's new to me in Italian food,' I said. 'Sesame oil.'

Ed drank some more beer.

'It was just an idea,' he said.

'You children,' said Caitlin. She shook her head. She got up and took the plates away. 'There's ice cream for pudding,' she said over her shoulder just before she disappeared. When I was sure she was occupied in the kitchen I said:

'Nice idea, Ed: a *motor*cycle. What are you going to do with it? Hang it on the wall with the Klein?'

He drank the rest of his beer, opened a new one and poured it thoughtfully into his glass. He watched the bubbles rising through it, then grinned at me as if he had made a decision. He had. In that moment I saw that he was lost, but not what I could do about it.

'Isn't it brilliant? Isn't it just a *fucker*, that bike? I haven't had a bike since I was seventeen. There's a story attached to that.'

'Ed—'

'Do you want to hear it or not?'

Caitlin came back in with the ice cream and served it out to us and sat down.

'Tell us, Ed,' she said tiredly. 'Tell us the story about that.'

Ed held on to his glass hard with both hands and stared into it for a long time as if he was trying to see the past there. 'I had some ace times on bikes when I was a kid,' he said finally: 'but they were always someone else's. My old dear – she really hated bikes, my old dear. You know: they were dirty, they were dangerous, she wasn't going to have one in the house. Did that stop me? It did not. I bought one of the first good Ducatti 125s in Britain, *but I had to keep it in a coal cellar down the road.*'

'That's really funny, Ed.'

'Fuck off, Mick. I'm seventeen, I'm still at school, and I've got this fucking *projectile* stashed in someone's coal cellar. The whole time I had it, the old dear never knew. I'm walking three miles in the piss-wet rain every night, dressed to go to the library, then unlocking this thing and *stuffing* it round the back lanes with my best white shortie raincoat ballooning up like a fucking tent.'

He looked puzzledly down at his plate.

'What's this? Oh. Ice cream. Ever ridden a bike in a raincoat?' he asked Caitlin.

Caitlin shook her head. She was staring at him with a hypnotised expression; she was breaking wafers into her ice cream.

'Well they were all the rage then,' he said.

He added: 'The drag's enormous.'

'Eat your pudding, Ed,' I said. 'And stop boasting. How fast would a 125 go in those days? Eighty miles an hour? Eighty-five?'

'They went faster if you ground your teeth, Mick,' Ed said. 'Do you want to hear the rest?'

'Of course I want to hear it, Ed.'

'Walk three miles in the piss-wet rain,' said Ed, 'to go for a ride on a motorbike, what a joke. But the real joke is this: the fucker had an alloy crank-case. That was a big deal in those days, an alloy crank-case. The first time I dropped it on a bend, it cracked. Oil everywhere. I pushed it back to the coal-house and left it there. You couldn't weld an alloy crank-case worth shit in those days. I had three years' payments left to make on a bunch of scrap.'

He grinned at us triumphantly.

'Ask me how long I'd had it,' he ordered.

'How long, Mick?'

'Three weeks. I'd had the fucker three weeks.'

He began to laugh. Suddenly, his face went so white it looked green. He looked rapidly from side to side, like someone who can't understand where he is. At the same time, he pushed himself up out of the wheelchair until his arms wouldn't straighten any further and he was almost standing up. He tilted his head back until the tendons in his neck stood out. He shouted, 'I want to get out of here! Caitlin, I want to get out!' Then his arms buckled and he let his weight go on to his feet and his legs folded up like putty and he fell forward with a gasp, his face in the ice cream and his hands smashing and clutching and scraping at anything they touched on the dinner table until he had bunched the cloth up under him and everything was a sodden mess of food and broken dishes, and he had slipped out of the chair and on to the floor. Then he let himself slump and go quite still.

'Help me,' said Caitlin.

We couldn't get him back into the chair. As we tried, his head flopped forward, and I could see quite clearly the bruises and deep, half-healed scabs at the base of his skull, where they had cored his cervical spine for the computer connection. When he initialised *Out There* now, the graphics came up live in his head. No more screen. Only the endless V of the perspective. The endless, effortless dip-and-bank of the viewpoint. What did he see out there? Did he see himself, hunched up on the Kawasaki *Ninja*? Did he see highways, bridges, tunnels, weird motorcycle flights through endless space?

*

217

Halfway along the passage, he woke up.

'Caitlin!' he shouted.

'I'm here.'

'Caitlin!'

'I'm here, Ed.'

'Caitlin, I never did any of that.'

'Hush, Ed. Let's get you to bed.'

'Listen!' he shouted. '*Listen.*'

He started to thrash about and we had to lay him down where he was. The passage was so narrow his head hit one wall then the other, with a solid noise. He stared desperately at Caitlin, his face smeared with Ben & Jerry's. 'I never could ride a bike,' he admitted. 'I made all that up.'

She bent down and put her arms round his neck.

'I know,' she said.

'I made all that up!' he shouted.

'It's all right. It's all right.'

We got him into bed in the back room. She wiped the ice cream off his face with a Kleenex. He stared over her shoulder at the wall, rigid with fear and self-loathing. 'Hush,' she said. 'You're all right.' That made him cry; him crying made her cry. I didn't know whether to cry or laugh. I sat down and watched them for a moment, then got to my feet. I felt tired.

'It's late,' I said. 'I think I'll go.'

Caitlin followed me out on to the doorstep. It was another cold night. Condensation had beaded on the fuel tank of the Kawasaki, so that it looked like some sort of frosted confection in the streetlight.

'Look,' she said, 'can you do anything with that?'

I shrugged.

'It's all brand new,' I said. I drew a line in the condensation, along the curve of the tank; then another, at an angle to it.

'I could see if the dealer would take it back.'

'Thanks.'

I laughed.

'Go in now,' I advised her. 'It's cold.'

'Thanks, Mick. Really.'

'That's what you always say.'

The way Ed got his paraplegia was this. It was a miserable January about four months after Caitlin left me to go and live with him. He was working over in mid-Wales with Moscow Davis. They had landed the inspection contract for three point-blocks owned by the local council; penalty clauses meant they had to complete that month. They lived in a bed-and-breakfast place a mile from the job, coming back so tired in the evening that they just about had time to eat fish and chips and watch *Coronation Street* before they fell asleep with their mouths open. 'We were too fucked even to take drugs,' Ed admitted afterwards, in a kind of wonder. 'Can you imagine that?' Their hands were bashed and bleeding from hitting themselves with sample hammers in the freezing rain. At the end of every afternoon the sunset light caught a thin, delicate layer of water-ice that had welded Moscow's hair to her cheek. Ed wasn't just tired, he was missing Caitlin. One Friday he said, 'I'm fucked off with this, let's have a weekend at home.'

'We agreed we'd have to work weekends,' Moscow reminded him. She watched a long string of snot leave her nose, stretch out like spider-silk, then snap and vanish on the wind. 'To finish in time,' she said.

'Come on, you wanker,' Ed said. 'Do something real in your life.'

'I never wank,' said Moscow. 'I can't fancy myself.'

They got in her 1984 320i with the M-Technic pack, Garrett turbo and extra wide wheels, and while the light died out of a bad afternoon she pushed it eastward through the Cambrians, letting the rear end hang out on corners. She had Lou Reed *Retro* on the CD and her plan was to draw a line straight across the map and connect with the M4 at the Severn Bridge. It was ghostly and fog all the way out of Wales that night, lost sheep coming at you from groups of wet trees and folds in the hills.

'Tregaron to Abergwesyn. One of the great back roads!' Moscow shouted over the music, as they passed a single lonely house in the rain, miles away from anywhere, facing south into the rolling moors of mid-Wales.

Ed shouted back: 'They can go faster than this, these 320s.' So on the next bend she let the rear end hang out an inch too far and they surfed five hundred feet into a ravine below Cefn Coch, with the BMW crumpled up round them like a chocolate wrapper. Just before they went over, the tape had got to 'Sweet Jane' – the live version with the applause welling up across the opening chords as if God himself was stepping out on stage. In the bottom of the ravine a shallow stream ran through pressure-metamorphosed Ordovician shale. Ed sat until daylight the next morning, conscious but unable to move, watching the water hurry towards him and listening to Moscow die of a punctured lung in the heavy smell of fuel. It was a long wait. Once or twice she regained consciousness and said: 'I'm sorry, Ed.'

Once or twice he heard himself reassure her, 'No, it was my fault.'

At Southwestern Orthopaedic a consultant told him that key motor nerves had been ripped out of his spine.

'Stuff the fuckers back in again then!' he said, in an attempt to impress her.

She smiled.

'That's exactly what we're going to try,' she replied. 'We'll do a tuck-and-glue and encourage the spinal cord to send new filaments into the old cable channel.'

She thought for a moment.

'We'll be working very close to the cord itself,' she warned him.

Ed stared at her.

'It was a joke,' he said.

For a while it seemed to work. Two months later he could flex the muscles in his upper legs. But nothing more happened; and, worried that a second try would only make the damage worse, they had to leave it.

Mile End Monkey House. Hanging upside down from a painful foot-hook, you chalk your hands meditatively, staring at the sweaty triangular mark your back left on the blue plastic cover of the mat last time you fell on it. Then, reluctantly, feeling your stomach muscles grind as they curl you upright again, you clutch the starting holds and go for the move: reach up: lock out on two fingers: let your left leg swing out to rebalance: strain upwards with your right fingertips, and just as you brush the crucial hold, fall off again.

'Jesus Christ. I don't know why I come here.'

You come so that next weekend you can get into a Cosworth-engined Merc 190E and drive very fast down the M4 ('No one drives themselves any more!') to a limestone outcrop high above the Wye Valley. Let go here and you will not land on a blue safety mat in a puff of chalk dust. Instead you will plummet eighty feet straight down until you hit a small ledge, catapult out into the trees, and land a little later face-first among moss-grown boulders flecked with sunshine. Now all the practice is over. Now you are on the route. Your friends look up, shading their eyes against the white glare of the rock. They are wondering if you can make the move. So are you. The only exit from shit creek is to put two fingers of your left hand into a razor-sharp solution pocket, lean away from it to the full extent of your arm, run your feet up in front of you, and, just as you are about to fall off, lunge with your right hand for the good hold above.

At the top of the cliff grows a large yew tree. You can see it very clearly. It has a short horizontal trunk, and contorted limbs perhaps eighteen inches thick curving out over the drop as if they had just that moment stopped moving. When you reach it you will be safe. But at this stage on a climb, the top of anything is an empty hypothesis. You look up: it might as well be the other side of the Atlantic. All that air is burning away below you like a fuse. Suddenly you're moving anyway. Excitement has short-circuited the normal connections between intention and action. Where you look, you go. No effort seems to be involved. It's like falling upwards. It's like that moment when you first understood how to swim, or ride a bike. Height and fear have returned you to your childhood. Just as it was then, your duty is only to yourself. Until you get safely down again, contracts, business meetings, household bills, emotional problems, will mean nothing.

When you finally reach that yew tree at the top of the climb, you find it full of grown men and women wearing faded shorts and T-shirts. They are all in their forties and fifties. They have all escaped. With their bare brown arms, their hair bleached out by weeks of sunshine, they sit at every fork or junction, legs dangling in the dusty air, like child-pirates out of some storybook of the '20s: an investment banker from Greenwich, an Aids counsellor from Bow; a designer of French Connection clothes; a publisher's editor. There is a comfortable silence broken by the odd friendly murmur as you arrive, but their eyes are inturned and they would prefer to be alone, staring dreamily out over the valley, the curve of the river, the woods which seem to stretch away to Tintern Abbey and then Wales. This is the other side of excitement, the other pleasure of height: the space without anxiety. The space without anxiety. The space without anxiety. The space without anxiety. The space without anxiety. The space without anxiety. The space without anxiety. The space with—

You are left with this familiar glitch or loop in the MAX ware. *Suicide Coast* won't play any further. Reluctantly, you abandon Mick to his world of sad acts, his faith that reality can be relied upon to scaffold his perceptions. To run him again from the beginning would only make the frailty of that faith more obvious. So you wait until everything has gone black, unplug yourself from the machine, and walk away, unconsciously rolling your shoulders to ease the stiffness, massaging the sore place at the back of your neck. What will you do next? Everything is flat out here. No one drives themselves any more.

The Neon Heart Murders

All down the west coast of the island at night glitter the lights of a city five miles long, its towers like black and gold cigarette packs standing on end. In the malls fluorescent light skids off the surfaces of hard and soft designer goods: matte plastics, foams of lace and oyster satin, the precise curves of cars and shoes and shoulder pads. This city is well-known for the scent of Anaïs-Anaïs in its streets; stacked video screens in the cocktail lounges; and, down by the ocean front – where men push past you smelling of sweat and seafood, and you can hear the soundtrack of your own life playing from the dashboard of a white car – neon of green, red or frosty blue. Music pulses from the amusement arcades, clears its throat in the night clubs. In the jazz bars they serve only Black Heart rum, and you can hear the intricate bass lines twenty miles out to sea.

The best of the bars is the Long Bar at the Café Surf, with its décor of strained contrasts. Marble pillars and designer blinds with thin aerodynamic slats. Cane tables and salt-blistered chrome bar taps. Forgotten movie stars crowd the walls in brushed aluminium frames. Exotic beers glitter from the shelves of the cooler. While under the red neon sign 'Live Music Nightly', the Café Surf two-piece – piano and tenor saxophone – ambles its way through the evening's middle set.

The pianist, a young man with a mobile mouth, plays the house Kawai with one hand while with the other he coaxes from a piano-top synthesiser the sound of a deceptively relaxed bass. Just now he is Relaxin' in Camarillo. He picked this tune up from a Spanish bootleg CD so cheap its cover showed not Charlie Parker but Johnny Hodges. The rhythms flick and rip across one another, tangle and separate.

The saxophonist is an older man. White face, black rollneck, white hands. Years of music have tightened the muscles round his mouth into two deep grooves. Every so often he stops to watch the pianist take a solo. At these times his expression is one of puzzled admiration, as if he heard someone this good once before but – because he has played so much music since – now forgets who or where. (It was in a bar much like this one, somewhere less relaxed, on some bigger mass of land perhaps. Perhaps it wasn't in a bar at all.) This is the sole acknowledgement the old can give the young. Anything more would be too bitter; but so would anything less. He nods his head in time, pulls sharply on his cigarette, glances down at the saxophone in front of him.

Possibilities cascade.

A middle-aged man who looked like Albert Einstein used to come in during the middle set and buy a drink. He would stare round helplessly for a moment then smile and light his pipe. He would sit down in a corner in his raincoat; get up again to put a match carefully into an ashtray on the corner of the bar; sit down again. He used to do all this with a kind of meticulous politeness, as if he was in someone's front room; or as if, at home, his wife required of him an unflagging formal acknowledgement of her efforts. He would stare at his pipe. He would start a conversation with a girl old enough to be his granddaughter, getting out his wallet to show her – and her friend, who wore torn black net tights and industrial shoes – something which looked in the undependable Long Bar light like a business card; which they would admire.

In fact he was not as old as he looked; he and his wife lived apart; and he was a detective.

His name was Aschemann.

Though he loved the city Aschemann often complained to himself:

'Phony music, cheap neon, streets which reek of bad money. Hands which make a big gun look small. All the burned-down rooms and lists of suspects. Crimes you might commit yourself, after a late night call. Those suburbs, you have to solve them like a labyrinth. And always some half empty hotel! Always someone luring the innocent down the curve of the street, but before you can investigate, before you can earn a blind dime, you have to find out what's behind that door.

'The true detective,' he used to warn his assistants (mainly local young men and women on one-month trials from the uniformed branch, neat and ambitious, fluent in three Pacific Rim languages), 'starts in the centre of the maze. Crimes make their way through to him. Never forget: you uncover your own heart at the heart of it.'

His original visits to the Long Bar were made during the investigation of a series of crimes against women. First on the scene of the original killing, he had discovered two lines of a poem tattooed in the shaven armpit of the victim:

Send me a neon heart
Unarmed with a walk like a girl

She was a fourteen-year-old prostitute from the Rim – a grown-up girl in box-fresh Minnie Mouse shoes. Forensic investigation proved the tattoo to have been made after the heart stopped beating, in the style of a Carmody tattooist now dead but popular a year or two before.

'Find out how this is possible,' he told his assistant.

When Aschemann first walked through the door of the Café Surf, it was not night: it was late morning. The bar was full of sunlight and bright air. Taupe sand blew across the floor tiles, and a toddler was crawling about between the cane tables, wearing only a T-shirt with the legend SURF NOIR. Meanings – all incongruous – splashed off this like drops of water, as the dead metaphors trapped inside the live one collided and reverberated endlessly and elastically, taking up new positions relative to one another. SURF NOIR, which is a whole new existence; which is a 'world' implied in two words, dispelled in an instant; which is foam on the appalling multitextual sea we drift on.

'Which is probably,' Aschemann noted, 'the name of an after-shave.'

In his search for the tattoo murderer, Aschemann had himself driven about the city in an unmarked car. He sat alertly in the front passenger seat as the rose-red Cadillac descended each steep dogleg curve of Maricachel Hill, down through the Moneytown palms and white designer duplexes to the Corniche. He stood trying to light his pipe in the strong salt winds which scraped the harbour mole in the middle of the day. He watched from Suicide Point the late-afternoon sunbathers on Three Mile Beach, the evening windsurfers in the bay.

Less in a search for clues than a search for himself – for a detective capable of understanding the crime – he visited his estranged wife, a thirty-six-year-old agoraphobe living in squalor in the 'suicide suburbs' up the coast. When he arrived, boys in long grey shorts and singlets were skateboarding the concrete service road between her house and the beach. They looked tired and blank. Sand blew into Aschemann's face as he raised his hand to knock at the door. Before she could answer, he went back and sat in the car on the passenger side of the front bench-seat and explained to his driver:

'There are kinds of agoraphobes to whom even the arrival of a letter or a telephone call is too much of the outside world. Someone else has to answer it for them. Yet as soon as you step into their houses they become monsters. It is less that they are uncomfortable in public than that they only feel in control on their own ground. Agoraphobia can be a very aggressive territorial strategy: refusal to go out is a way of forcing the outside to come in to where it is manageable. On the agoraphobe's home ground you must walk through the agoraphobe's maze.'

In his wife's rooms every inch of floor and furniture space was filled up, so that you didn't quite know how to get from the door to the sofa; and once you had got there you couldn't get up and move about except with extreme caution. All quick movement was damped by this labyrinth, where there was even a code – three or four quick pulls on the cord – to get the lavatory light to go on. Therapy only confused her, her friends no longer came to see her, and she had retreated into a further labyrinth, of drink, fuddled political principles and old emotional entanglements. At Christmas he bought her a perfume she liked called Ashes of Roses. The rest of the time he tried to stay away.

'Come over,' she would encourage him. 'I'll get the Black Heart Rum you like so much.' She phoned him two or three times a week to talk about their lives together, to find out what the weather was like where he was, discuss the view from her window. 'You see that boat out in the Bay? Do you see it too? The blue one? What sort of boat is that?' But when he visited he rarely had the courage or energy to make himself go in, because if he did she would soon sigh and say, 'We had such times together, before you took up with that whore from Carmody.'

'Even though it is over between us,' Aschemann told his driver as the Cadillac slipped away between the rag-mop palms and peeling pastel-coloured beach houses either side of Suntory Boulevard, 'I sometimes seem to be the person who cares most about her. I am no longer in a position to look after her, yet no one else will. Because of this I feel not only guilt but an increasing sense of irritation with people I once thought of as "more her friends than mine". They have abandoned her as completely as I have. This makes them no better than me.' Thinking he heard the rumble of skateboard wheels on concrete, he turned to look out the rear window. Sand was blowing across the road in the purple light. 'Go back,' he said.

The murders took him all over the island. The first evening he walked into the Café Surf and sat down, Aschemann noticed this—

The band was placed at the end of the Long Bar, near the lavatory door. People kept coming out of the lavatory while the band was playing, pushing between the piano and the bar. There were very fat women in jeans, very tall men wearing raincoats, thin boys like camp inmates with shaven heads, people crippled in small and grotesque ways. For a moment, as each of these figures appeared in the weird orange light, it seemed as if the music was squeezing them into existence; as if there was some sort of unformed darkness out there at the back of the Café Surf, and the band was squashing it like a fistful of wet mud into these shapes. It was that sort of music.

While Aschemann was drinking his first glass of rum, the band squeezed out two or three thin boys in singlets, earrings and studded leather belts. As he ordered his second, and drank that more slowly, in little sips that coated his mouth with the taste of burnt sugar, it squeezed out some boots with pointed steel tips, and an old lady in a print dress; it squeezed out a suede cowboy hat. It began squeezing out people young and old, and people middle-aged. Surprisingly few of them were middle-aged.

'Get back,' whispered the saxophone, 'get back. Get back to where you once belonged.'

But they never did. They bought drinks at the bar and then, laughing and shouting, wandered out into the lighted street. Were they in themselves a kind of surf or spray, brought into being where the powerful tidal forces of the music came into rhythmic contact with the fixed land of the Long Bar? Thoughtfully, the man who looked like Einstein watched them go.

Other crimes came and went, but the murders continued, each one publishing new lines of the verse. There was nothing to connect the victims but their shaven armpit and Carmody-style tattoo. 'And, of course,' as Aschemann would remind his latest assistant, 'the investigation itself.' Aschemann had forbidden the detective branch to work the case. Track record as well as seniority allowed him to do that, sheer weight of cases solved, paperwork successfully filed. Word went out that it was his crime. 'He can keep it,' was most people's opinion.

After perhaps six months, his own wife became a victim.

Alerted by a neighbour, they found her sprawled among the broken furniture, boxes of clothes, the piles of local ad-sheets, fashion magazines and old record albums, which had divided the floor of the room into the narrow waist-high alleys of the maze. It was hot in there. Up from all the yellowed pages, stronger than the smell of the body, came a stifling odour of dust and salt. It got in your mouth as well as your nose. A rich yellow light filtered through the wafer-thin slats of the wooden blinds. She had fallen awkwardly, wedged sideways with one arm trapped beneath her and the other draped across a copy of *Harpers & Queen*, her left hand clutching an empty tumbler, her cheap sun-faded print dress disarranged to show a yellow thigh: but not one of those piles of stuff, the uniformed men remarked, had been disturbed by her fall. There were no signs of a struggle. It was as if her murderer had been as constrained in here as anyone else. Tattooed in her armpit were the lines:

Send me a neon heart
  Send it with love
Seek me inside

When they turned her over, they found her other hand clutching a letter Aschemann had sent her when they were still young. Called to the scene by a reluctant junior investigator, Aschemann examined this letter for a moment – giving less attention, it seemed to what he had written than to the cheap airmail-quality paper he had written it on all those years ago – then went and stood puzzledly in the centre of the maze. The assembled police, sweating into their uniforms, spoke in low voices and avoided his eyes. He understood all this – the coming and going, the flickering glare of the forensic cameras – but it was as if he was seeing it for the first time. Outside, the afternoon skateboarders in their SURF NOIR shirts rumbled to and fro on the corrugated concrete of the beach road. If he peered between the slats of the blind, he knew, he would be able to see Carmody, Moneytown, the Harbour Mole, the whole city tattooed stark and clear in strong violet light into the armpit of the Bay. After a moment or two, he said, 'Bring me the details in my office later.'

He said: 'Do a good job here.'

Later, he found himself looking out from Suicide Point in the twilight. Behind him, a new driver sat in the rose-coloured Cadillac, talking quietly into the dash radio. There was a tender hazy light, a warm wind at the edge of the cliff, the whisper of the tide below. A few eroded bristle-cone pines, a patch of red earth bared and compacted by tourists' feet. An extraordinary sense of freedom. He walked back to the car in the soft wind.

'I was only in their way there,' he said. 'Tell them I know they'll do a good job.'

That evening he visited the Surf again.

He sat at the Long Bar and watched the band stroll through their second set of the evening. They were as amused, as meditative – as guilty, Aschemann thought – as ever.

The pianist must always be setting one thing against another. Every piece he played was a turn against – a joke upon – some other piece, some other pianist, some other instrument. He cloaked this obsession with a cleverness which made it amusing. But even his generously cut summer suit, which sometimes hung from its own massive shoulder pads as if it was empty, was a joke on the old jazz-men; and you could tell that when he was alone in his room at night he was compelled to play one hand against the other. If no one else was there, he would play against himself, and then against the self thus created, and then against the next: until all fixed notion of self had leaked away into this infinite slippage and he could relax for a second in the sharp light and cigarette smoke, like someone caught fleetingly in a black and white photograph by Herman Leonard.

The saxophonist, meanwhile, nodded his head in time, pulled sharply on his cigarette, glanced down at the saxophone in front of him. Possibilities cascaded: the saxophonist entertained each one with an almost Oriental patience. Long ago he came to some understanding of things incommunicable to the young, the obsessed, the energetic, because to them it would seem bland and seamlessly self-evident: 'That which is the most complex is the most simple,' perhaps; or 'It is only because no music is possible that any music at all is possible'. The universe now remade itself for him continually, out of a metaphor, two or three invariable rules, and a musical instrument called – for some reason known only to God – the saxophone.

That night the band squeezed out two dock-boys with dyed brushcuts, arm in arm with an emaciated blonde who kept wiping her nose on her pliable white forearm. Bebop golems, Aschemann thought, as he followed them along the Corniche in the soft warm scented darkness, then up Moneytown into Carmody: bebop golems. In Carmody, he lost them among the bars and transsexual brothels, the streets that stank of perspiration, oil products and lemon grass. One minute they were still distinguishable, the next they had merged with the life around them. They were gone, and all he could see was life. He could not really take in his wife's death, because all he could see around him was life.

Every evening after that he visited the Long Bar. The band squeezed out its golems. After his second glass of rum Aschemann shadowed them into the warm air and black heart of the city. He could smell the guilt and excitement that came up out of the gratings to meet them. He could smell their excitement at being newly alive there, in Carmody among the sights! One night, standing momentarily thoughtful at 9th and Hennepin, he was picked up by a Marilyn Monroe lookalike in a white wrap-bodice evening dress and tomato red stilt-heel shoes. She was thirty, beautiful. She only needed a brushed aluminium frame. She took him to her room in a fourth-floor walk up behind the bottled-milk dairy at Tiger Shore.

It was bare: grey board floor, bare bulb, a single bentwood chair. On the wall opposite the window, the shadow of the slatted blind falling across a poster. SURF NOIR. 'Hey,' she said. 'Why don't you sit here—?' When she bent forward from the waist to undo his raincoat, the white dress presented her breasts to him in a flickering light. She knelt, and he could hear her breathing. It was placid, rather catarrhal. Later she lifted the hem of the dress and positioned herself astride him. So close, he saw that her gait, the shadows round her eyes, the foundation caked in the downy hairs by the corners of her mouth, had conspired beneath the undependable Carmody neon to make her seem older than she was. She whispered when he came: 'There. There now.' She was young enough for that act of generosity. She was a victim. With or without costume, she was one of the city's highwire artistes. He had no idea what she was. He paid her. He returned to the Long Bar, and, resting in the music and light as he drank a third glass of rum, he thought:

Does it matter who she is, when every night here the world is somehow touched?

Eventually, Aschemann too was murdered.

No one knew what happened. Two of his staff, called to the Café Surf at three o'clock in the morning, found him not inside but out at the back on the wet sand beneath the pier. The air was warm and soft. Aschemann had squeezed some of the wet sand up into a kind of fist near his face. Had he been close to a killer? Or had he simply come down to look at the shallow water lapping almost tentatively at the base of each rusty pillar, the water a tepid purple colour fluorescing suddenly in little flickers and glimmers as a response to the headlights sweeping along the Corniche above?

When they found him, Aschemann was alive but unspeaking. Unsure about procedure, his latest driver had alerted the uniform police. They walked about on the beach with torches. They called an ambulance and tried to make him comfortable while they waited for it to arrive. But the ambulance was held up on 14th and warbled its way down through Moneytown too late. Aschemann raised himself suddenly and said, 'Someone must tell my wife.' After that, he was silent again. The detective branch arrived.

'Can you hear us?' they asked, 'Can you tell us who did this?'

They advised one another tiredly, 'Forget it, Jack.'

In fact he was conscious until he died. He listened to all their soft talk. He smelled the smell of their cigarette smoke. But he made no attempt to impart the secret he knew. Instead, he thought about the band at the Café Surf. He thought about the black surf along the island's beaches at night, black surf with an oily violet sheen on the swell as it mounts. Wave after wave of new inhabitants. 'Life in the breaks,' he thought of saying to the assembled detectives. 'That's what surfers call them. Look there, in the breaks.' He thought of the poem. He thought about his crime. He thought about his wife waiting for everyone to come to her in her minotaur's cave; and the Carmody whore, who went out along the highwire from her room to everyone.

'We can never see the truth,' he thought: 'But does that matter at this level of things, when all that counts is sight itself?' Even though he was dying and could barely lift his head, he looked out across the bay at the lights on the other side and thought, 'For instance: I've been here and seen this.'

What if the city is itself a surf, of buildings and people and consumer goods? What if the motives that power it are tidal? What if unpredictable winds play against masses of water, currents too complex to understand? What if crimes are whipped off the crest of events like spray, with no more cause than that?

At this time of night, halfway through the middle set, the lights of the Café Surf go dim. There is a smell of food and, between numbers, laughter and shouting. But the tables closest to the musicians are empty, as if an arc of fallout has cleared them. These tables are cluttered with empty Giraffe Beer bottles and crumpled serviettes. At the Long Bar they serve a cocktail called 'Ninety Per Cent Neon'. Marilyn Monroe leans out of a brushed aluminium frame, upper body bent forward a little from the waist, head tilted back to laugh, so that her breasts are offered to the paying customers wrapped in silk, jazz, red light from the neon sign. It's a life, the saxophonist often thinks, with a sagging twist of lemon left at the bottom, like an empty glass.

But what does he know?

Black Houses

I was introduced to Elaine on the pavement outside Black's club one winter in the early '90s. She was wearing a belted PVC jacket over a Lycra skirt. She had bobbed hair and bright red lipstick, and as I began to say hello she was already turning away to laugh at something someone else had said.

I can't imagine her in Black's. She was less Dean Street than Princelet Street: the ICA was more her line. Originally she had been some kind of performance artist: now, slowed down by years of drugs and touring, she was running for cover, becoming one of those academics who think of themselves as writers. She talked a lot about creative space, which is as much a giveaway as having the words Subsidised Arts tattooed on your forehead. The first time we fucked she called out, 'I can't control this. I can't work out what kind of man you are.' No one had ever said anything like that to me in bed before. Not while they were coming, anyway. I was impressed.

It was a one-night stand that got loose in both our lives and pushed them out of shape. We had nothing in common but each other. She lived near Ely. I was soon commuting to see her at weekends. It was a winter thing from the start. We went for walks. Cold evenings, we would light a fire and lie on a quilt in front of it, or sit in some old pub whose name I forget. We went somewhere on the coast, so she could pore over the map of a drowned town. We visited churches. She loved places, which she called 'sites'. She loved sites and structures. She had a rusty Ford she drove over kerbs with complete abandon. She drove me out into the hard frost and glittering fenland light to look at black houses. Black houses are vernacular, Jonathan Meades probably once said something about

239

them. You find them all over the fens, east into Suffolk, north up to the Norfolk coast. They confront you eerily from the flat exhausted landscape. Black houses are made of wood. They are either like chicken hutches or big hollow boats, their tarred, closely lapped wooden boards warped with age into the curves of a loaded wherry drifting slowly between reeds against a sky full of thunder. Elaine said that black houses were full of history, death, human stuff. You could imagine it as a sort of smell that filled them, as rich and thick as broccoli and Stilton soup. They made her shiver.

Every time we saw a black house she warned me:

'I'll always be alone. I'm the kind of person who always has a bolt-hole ready. I always have a bag packed.'

I mentioned this in my diary, then went on:

'Despite this, all her old lovers still hang around her house. They rent places in the same street, they drop in for cups of tea. An American, a couple of drama-academics like herself – oh, and a piano tuner called Edward, who always gives me a wan, defeated smile. They're kind and good-humoured, with a reassuring fund of intelligence held in reserve.'

While to her I wrote like this—

Dear Elaine:

I wrote you a letter.

Then I ate it, at Burger King, King's Cross station, the dead dog end of a Sunday night.

I wrote you a letter then sent it to myself instead.

I wrote you a letter, took it out into the street and gave it to the first person I saw. They were very surprised.

It wasn't this letter.

I wrote you a letter and tried to transmit it to you by sheer psychic power.

Did you feel anything?

Now I've been with you in your house I can remember your smell.

But only suddenly, without expecting to.

I loved going to sleep with you in the firelight on the floor. I already miss waking up in the night and feeling your skin on mine, and I love to wake up in my own bed and remember that. Is that wrong? Is it unsuitable? However you answer, I'll miss it. Whatever you say, your skin is so smooth.

I've met people before. But not you. I try to remember most the way you put your head on one side and smile. I try to remember most the things you whisper when I'm fucking you.

I wrote you a letter. I put it in a shoebox and floated it down the Grand Union Canal, past timber yards, gasometers and sleeping swans. It went past Mile End. It went past Islington. It went past Regent's Park Zoo, sinking imperceptibly all the way.

I wrote you a letter, it spoke to the water.

Let's not think.

Let's be happy instead.

Walk my feet off. 'Seal me with a kiss.' Let's not think. Show me your underwear. Draw me into you and I'll fuck you until we know exactly what to do. It's this: I've met people before. But not you.

Not you.

I rarely posted these efforts. I preferred to give them to her in person. I liked to watch her read them, though I can see now how tiring this must have been.

Twelve months on, near the end of the relationship, we were living together in East Dulwich, which Elaine called 'Dull Eastwich'. We had a four-bedroomed house like a great hollow box, and a forsythia, which flowered in the first week of March. Elaine bumped the Ford up and down the kerb, or drove it to part-time creative writing jobs in Liverpool and Birmingham. I stayed in all day working on my theory that everyone is a vampire; or watched the comings and goings of Lord Arquiss, some Lucanesque family catastrophe of whose had condemned him to live at number 31 across the road.

Lord Arquiss was seventy-seven. He kept a Volvo the colour of a cheap brogue, and a fifty-year-old ex-ballerina who claimed to be his wife. From the disaster they had salvaged an amazing 3rd Reich-style bed, the elongated black wooden posts of which were capped with vast polished eagles like lecterns. Every night you could see the two of them sitting up in this thing like bull terriers in a pram. They never closed the bedroom curtains. People wondered, but I'm certain he was a proper lord. He came complete with Parkinson's disease, a new hip replacement, and an old tendency to booze. All of this caused him to appear in the street naked but for a maroon silk shortie dressing gown and glove-leather slippers. He would root about in the back of the Volvo for something he never found and then drive slowly away, only to reappear less than five minutes later and spend half an hour trying to repark it in a space that would have been small for a Nissan Micra.

In an attempt to go unrecognised, the ballerina wore dark glasses, a white raincoat, and a Hermès headscarf whatever the season. She too left the house each morning. Eleven sharp, she was hurrying away in the direction of East Dulwich Grove, thin, already arthritic, a parcel of anxieties wrapped up in rain. Her tartan shopping trolley clinked with bottles.

Your turn to send something.

Send me a recipe.

Send ricotta & spinach, send tomato & garlic; send seafood risotto. Send ingredients, weights. Send cooking times. Send warnings.

Send Ascii the cat.

Send me the inner door of your studio. Send me the place it leads to once a year (but only if your second name is Rachel). Send the light outside the window, the light inside the supermarket. Send me a picture, pack it in music. Wrap yourself round it.

Wrap it in the touch of you.

Wrap me in the touch of you.

We know everything now. We know nothing until the next time mouth opens on mouth. In the morning it is rain on the roof, a pale diffused light on walls so like the walls of your studio, nothing but to be warm and to have the pleasure of turning towards you naked even as you turn towards me.

'Hello.'

I can remember being so far inside you! I can remember how you bring my mouth down to yours, and how in that moment I notice the air on both our skins, and then my whole perception is withdrawing itself to be there inside, so that my cock feels heavy and languid and filled with me and with the world and I could be this forever – forever – or only until I withdraw gently, and gently turn you over and in three or four strokes fuck, fuck, fuck you until you cry out for some feeling I can't imagine. You say, 'We can't live together, this won't work,' but you cry out from that feeling.

I can remember it.

Soon after we moved into the Dulwich house, we were called over to number 31 at one in the morning to help pick Lord Arquiss up.

His wife ran about in the empty street for a while, trying to attract our attention. A light, dry snow was dusting the road, wreathing and twisting along like dust round each quick little step. 'Look at this,' said Elaine, who knew a performance when she saw one. 'Not dancing but waving.' She waved back until the ballerina gave up and rang our bell.

'I wouldn't ask,' the ballerina told us, 'but he's had a little bit much to drink, so we can't really call the ambulance.'

Their front room was full of furniture too big for it, dimly lit by standard lamps with tasselled satin shades. Lord Arquiss lay waiting for us on the carpet at the base of a display cabinet, arranged on the glass shelves of which were hundreds of very small items in a kind of bright blue glass. He was looking up mischievously from the side of his eye. One of his slippers had fallen off. His legs, thick but somehow graceful, poked out of the bottom of the shortie dressing gown, their colour somewhere between white and cream. His skin was very smooth. He had a faint, distinct smell – not unpleasant – which reminded me of babies. We got him up off the floor and back into his chair with difficulty. He was still a heavy man, even in a dressing gown and with naked, biscuit-coloured balls.

He looked unrepentant; the ballerina looked relieved. 'You must have a drink,' they urged; filled two glasses with Famous Grouse; and spent an hour telling us anecdotes of people called Tippy or Ticky – people who were Malcolm Sargent's mistress in some old days even the participants barely now recall – people who had been well used to falling down and being picked up again. They were quite funny stories (the upshot of many of them seemed to be that Ticky had the siffy wiffy), and the two old bores were as grotesque as you'd like. But it was all too good to be true, really, so I didn't feel tempted to go back, even though Lord Arquiss knocked on the door a few afternoons later, stood there shaking for a bit, and finally managed to invite us round for a drink that evening. I had a feeling we had cruised the interview and got the job. Luckily, Elaine was in Liverpool, so I could make our excuses.

If you want a black house, we can live in one—

It is a house that belongs to neither of us. From its windows we can see masts, sails, a strip of pebbles at a steep angle to the estuary. At night we can hear rigging tap and flutter against aluminium spars. We can see the moon in the ruffled surface of tidal water. We can hear ourselves crunching back up the shingle after some long rainy afternoon walk.

You say, 'We're too different, we could never live with one another.'

In the black house we already do.

A short flight of bare wooden steps gives access to the small top room with its sloping ceiling and white wainscotting to catch the light. Up there I keep a brass vase, a brass lizard, a perfect brass aeroplane hardly bigger than a button. On one wall of the bigger room on the landing below, a mirror is so placed that, lying on my bed with the door open, I can see up the steps and into the top room.

The door is open now.

It's April, and the light is very strong.

It is like being in a film.

You are naked, standing on an old blue and white towel, washing yourself with warm water from an enamel bowl, sometimes crouched over it, sometimes almost upright, your thigh muscles strongly delineated. You look down at each shoulder as you wash it. You smile. Warm water pours across your breasts. I see all this in the mirror, but at the same time I imagine it, I make it.

I see this too, I understand this:

If I was to enter the mirror I could be with you in some more acute, more heartbreaking, more real way than if I simply left my room and took the stairs and perhaps clasped you gently from behind and pushed into you standing up so that both our mouths made a surprised O – which in that light and cool air and in that part of the year, would be heartbreaking enough in itself. But just as I am preparing to go up into the mirror, you kneel down to wash between your legs. I see the clear water run through your pubic hair, I see the lips of your cunt silhouetted against the light and the water running off them and back into the bowl. Everything in that moment is held in the light, clarified by it; held in the mirror and intensified by it.

So what if you say we can't live together? We can live separately in this house. Almost anything can happen now. Everything hinges on what happens now.

Nothing need happen now.

All the time I lived in Dulwich I knew what was happening. The house smelled of 3-in-1 at night: it was Elaine, oiling the hinges of the bolt-hole door. Her way of reminding me was to say apropos of nothing: 'We've got so much. Why have we got so many problems?' If I started to answer she would go on quickly, 'I really have to think about things. I don't know what to do.' If I didn't, her face would take on an impatient, pitying look, as if she was trying to deal with a teenager. The only way I could vent my anger at this was to jog through the deep sand of the horse-ride in East Dulwich Park. I would do a mile on and then a mile off, for ten miles or so. Sometimes even that wasn't enough. So I would go up to Dulwich Wood and run about in there until all the little hills and fallen logs had worn me down. I would arrive home, lathered in sweat and still feeling murderous, to find Lord Arquiss had finally finished parking his car and was ready for a chat at the kerb in his leather slippers. He pronounced 'fast' as 'fawst'; and talking of other drivers, said things like: 'I mean really some of them are almost menacing you. They're trying to frighten you into driving fawster.'

Then, in the same conversation—

'Novembah! Ha ha yes, Novembah!'

Even in their class nobody says fawster any more. For Lord Arquiss – and Mrs Lord Arquiss – the good days were all in the past. I couldn't imagine what they might have been like. It's hard to visualise what people like them did back then, although I suppose you could put some sort of picture together from the obvious elements. (Somerset Maugham's memoirs. The fawst goings-on in an early Ian Fleming novel.) On the other hand I could easily imagine some of the things they might still feel for one another: a kind of panicky distaste, a dreary alcoholic senses of dependence, a sudden fear of being alone, some mixture of comfort and horror such as you might experience if you slept night after night in sheets you couldn't be bothered to change.

Clearly, they still could feel. They tried to keep up appearances. They tried to keep alive the memory of Squiffy and Jiffy and Phipps. But were they anything much more than a memory of themselves? For each other, I mean? A kind of tired, escaping memory of themselves?

You sometimes heard her shout, at night. Had he fallen down again?

The last time I had anything to do with Lord Arquiss, he needed his shoes fastened. His wife had gone away the day before, for her mother's funeral somewhere in Scotland. So it fell to me. He made his way across the road four inches at a step – I watched him coming, all the way, wondering how I could refuse – and I knelt in my own doorway with the wet light coming in around his big bulky form and put neat bows in his expensive leather laces.

'I can manage the boots,' he told me, 'and the socks. But somehow not the laces. Can't spend the time down there.' Then he said: 'In the seventh year of Parkinson's you get things like that. It's not bad though is it: seven years?'

'It's not bad at all,' I reassured him, although I really had no way of knowing whether it was bad or not.

Do you like me to say 'cunt'? Do you hate it? It feels dangerous to me, but proper. Male languages are such a threat, even to men. But I love your cunt, and to name it doesn't feel like male language to me.

I can imagine the little room with its sloping ceiling, the bowl of water, the towel, the flicker like a signal between the two poles mirror/world mirror/world mirror/world.

But what we have is to touch. In the end, that's what so extraordinary. To touch, here and now. To feel the water on your skin on my skin. To have your buttocks fit so perfectly into the hollow of my hips that I think I might faint. To feel you slip so wetly on to me that I don't for an instant feel anything at all. To watch you kneel astride me – still a little damp from the water – to have your cunt licked until you can no longer bear it, and you tangle your hands in my hair and press me to you hard and come.

I can imagine the little room, and the stairs, and the bowl of water, and the towel left forgotten to dry on the floor.

I can imagine the house split in two, and hear you talk and watch you in the summer garden. I've known people feel safe in such houses, shiver with safeness when they hear rain on their skylights, turn luxuriously beneath the Delft blue quilt on a cold morning. None of that is so far out of the world. None of that is so hard to have.

So go on then.

Explain to me why yearning is so dangerous and wrong.

Then I can answer:

I know what you mean.

I almost know what you mean.

I think I almost know.

So we live in a house with two houses in it, what's hard about that, perhaps by a tidal river; and are thus enabled to bathe in the same light in different ways; and you come to me; and I come to you; and at the end of it every possible image of both of us is printed imperceptibly on the walls of the house. Whatever else happens, those images are always there, fluorescing; densely imbricated yet always divisible; always lisible. What is so bad about that? What is so bad if only the water, or the light itself, comes to read them?

I know how we could live together now. Make me come into your hand. Use my come to write the alphabet on us in the dark. After that we can start.

We've already started.

A few week's after the ageing ballerina's mother's funeral, the Arquiss house seemed to close up on itself. The lights were off early, the curtains drawn so that you couldn't see into the upper room with that monstrous black bed and its carved wooden eagles. Mrs Lord Arquiss stopped going out. If you saw Mr Lord Arquiss, he was sheepishly allowing himself to be helped into his car by a competent young woman of his own class. She always made sure he was dressed; but she couldn't park the Volvo any better than him.

Soon, you didn't see him at all. I heard that he had died. I never found out how the ballerina got on without him because by then I had moved on too.

I send you a letter.

I say Elaine to myself.

Pale light flickers away at the edge of vision like some sudden opening-out of the inner landscape. In that exact instant the phone rings.

It's you.

I say 'pale light', I say 'inner landscape', but that isn't what I mean.

You say, 'Everything is wrong between us.'

I say, 'Oh. Hello.'

But what I mean to say is this:

Sit up close to the wall here in this near darkness with your legs open and drawn up – so you look like a new letter in the alphabet – some character made of residual light or memory or desire itself – and your smile becomes so hard to see it seems progenitive, the first, most elusive, most amiable and indrawn smile there ever was – and whisper to me, 'Can you fuck me like this, do you think you can fuck me like this, do you want to fuck me like this?'

What I mean is, yes, I think I can.

I think I do.

It's you.

Sit up close, here. Open your legs. Or here. Lie down while I kneel above you. Or here. Can I come on you? It's you. Here. I come on you.

I come on you.

You say, 'There's no need to be so gentle.' You say, 'Oh Martin, Martin, Martin, what are you doing to me?'

You say:

'You don't have to be so gentle.'

I come on your skin and feel an extraordinary release.

I write you like this:

Leaning naked against the white wainscotting in the top room of my part of our house – one leg straight, palms of your hands against the wall – looking down at yourself, very relaxed. I don't know what you are thinking. Pale aerial light fills the room, spraying off the walls and across two or three items of furniture – a table, a chair, perhaps a stripped wooden box. I am trying to describe to myself the strange, orangey-gold colour of the hair between your legs. I hear my own voice say:

'Bend your knees a little more. Now slide down a little. No! Not that far! Just an inch or two.

'Yes. That.'

The phone rings two storeys down, far away, unassuming. I kneel in front of you. 'Don't answer, don't answer!' I have found the perfect distance to measure. You raise your head and look away into some distance of your own.

Two white pebbles on the top of the box. A flint with a hole in it. The phone is still ringing. The phone is still travelling imperceptibly further away, like some complex illustration of a point in General Relativity.

'What shall we do this afternoon?'

The afternoon too is slipping away.

If I can avoid it, I don't think of East Dulwich now: but when I do I think of hailstones – how in March, just before the forsythia flowered, they would begin to fall without warning out of a clear sky, bouncing vigorously off the road like insects. Suddenly, in the abandoned midsection of the day, there would be a movement at the ground floor window facing me. It was Lord Arquiss's ageing ballerina, shifting uneasily behind the net curtain because she had mistaken the sound of the hail for the sound of an approaching car. Once or twice a week she was allowed to care for her grandchildren. They were girls of ten and twelve; their bodies were filled with a kind of brutish energy, their arms with in-line skates. You heard their voices shouting from the house, full of the confidence of their future (or less of their own future, I suspect, than the future of their whole sex). They didn't look as if they had inherited the siffy-wiffy. The ballerina kept them close, surrendering them only to the imperative beep of her daughter's Land Rover Discovery.

The daughter was one of those women made self-important by an unrelenting consciousness of herself as someone able to cope. She bustled in and out of the street, ignoring anyone else who happened to be there, calling peremptorily to children and grand-mother alike, in and out in a moment on her way to the next appointment, the next problem, the next solution. She favoured Sloany tailored jackets with padded shoulders and wore her hair that lank way they had then.

*

I write your name and images of you tumble away, getting smaller.

'Elaine,' I write, and it's you, asleep in the back of the car, then some strange pub in the middle of nowhere. 'Elaine.' There! Behind that fringe of trees! Water. Some houses with big fronts. We turn into the sun and it blinds us.

What sort of images can I send you?

What sort can you send me? We blew it from the start. You started with a bad idea.

You kneel in front of me. I kneel in front of you. Outside it's sleet, wind. It's snow. It's snow all the way to the sea, pasted on to black buildings, small figures. Snow is falling on the pebble beaches: within an hour, twilight will fall on the snow.

We kneel to touch one another, naked in some upstairs room in some old house. Look out the window. No, don't look at me.

Look out the window while I do this.

Images of us go tumbling away across the landscape. We shed images which go tumbling away over the fallen snow. Images while I do this. Now you do this too, and I go tumbling away.

Do this.

Later, setting sun on ice, behind trees.

Black buildings, and a rim of ice at the edge of the sea. (I write 'Elaine—' and we walk out from behind some wooden buildings by the sea.) Black buildings, bare grey boards, a fringe of reeds at the edge of a dyke, a fringe of masts at the edge of an inlet, some shabby old pub in the middle of the snow. Instead of watching TV we should have wrapped up warm, driven away, and faced the new year from somewhere out there in the dark, not even sure where we were. (I write 'Elaine,' and we're in Brown's, watching the wind fan snow-eddies down the road. Student waiters and waitresses turn up the music and dance in the snow, and you make the sign for wankers and finish your drink.)

Kneel here. Face me. Don't look at me. Don't tell me anything.

I'll kneel here if you don't talk. I'll come in your hand. You come in mine, biting your lip, staring out the window at the snow. Let's give up language, make Egon Schiele figures in an upstairs room.

Let's not tell each other anything at all.

Let's be a black house.

Let's be pictures tumbling away across the fens, some forgotten couple walking out from behind wooden buildings – let's be a couple in a shabby old car, making a turn, picking up a hitch-hiker, blinking in the sun.

What sort of images are these?

Elaine?

It's like being in a computer game. One moment you have needs, the next, quite suddenly, they're satisfied or sidelined. The field of vision seems empty. Then you detect this faint serpentine flicker as the fractals grow and boil, and new needs have replaced the old. Desire is desire. You can't talk your way out of it. It ripples off like the pleats of an old accordion from wherever you stand in your life, a kind of dusty but convoluted interior space. I think of that when people recommend, 'Go away and be for a while,' and invite you to come back when you are 'less needy'. They are really saying, 'Go away until you are less difficult to handle.' I'm not willing to be told that. I doubt that Wiffy or Spermy or the ageing ballerina were, either. Not until right up to the end.

Elaine never gave up her own house. About a month after she went back to pick up the threads of the life I had interrupted, I visited Ely. I had understood the escape kit. I had found the key to the bolt-hole: it was those lovers who stayed around. They performed a stabilising function. They were there so she could go off her rails in reasonable comfort. Determining never to be one of them, I made sure she was in Liverpool and spent one Saturday morning painting the front door of her house black. I thought that would do it. Afterwards I wrote to a friend of mine:

'Her life is a performance. You're a support player, an audience, a theatre. She uses you not only on stage but as the stage. You become what she would call the "performance space". She wants you to fill the same role as all the others. Act this: someone who was warned, someone who burned himself on her through no visible fault of hers. Act this: someone who is willing to be reasonable, shelter her from his pain, stay around on reduced terms, claim his place in her story. I was unable to see this at first. My inexperience disoriented me. What made it plain was the note she left – all "I" – and "What I need" – that, and the choice of Elizabeth Taylor novel she made from my shelves the night we first fucked. *Angel.* Of course. Am I slow? I am.'

While to her, in a letter, I wrote:

'I would do anything if you would come back.'

Science & the Arts

Mona was in her late thirties. Two years before we met she spent some months in a psychiatric hospital. By the time it became clear that the constant pain she complained about was not imaginary but the result of a botched operation, her career was ruined and her immune system had broken down. She was anorexic, subject to panic attacks and suffering from depression.

She lived for a while in Stoke Newington, where she had a short affair with a journalist, then moved to Camden, where she took courses in pain management. She enrolled at the Slade. We were introduced about a year after that, and began seeing one another every two weeks or so. She was unhappily involved with a sculptor – a dependent, manipulative man in his fifties. I was unhappily involved with a woman who had turned to novel-writing after a career in TV drama. For a while our mutual friends tried to matchmake us, but they weren't successful.

Mona's flat was in a quiet crescent north of Camden High Street. It comprised three rooms (one of which she used as a studio), kitchen and bathroom. The kitchen was very small. Mona didn't eat much so she lived mainly at the other end of the flat in the room which faced on to the street. There she had a computer, some bookshelves, a sofa, a television and, arranged so she could watch the television from it, her bed.

The bed was a small double, made up with a quilt and a stained white throw. There were two pillows, one old and very yellowed and without a pillowcase. When the pain was bad, or when she was cold, Mona would pull the quilt up to her chin and watch television from the bed while her visitor sat on the sofa. Or halfway through the evening she would get into bed like a child, with all her clothes on.

It was disconcerting. Even though you knew she was dressed, there was always a moment of uncertainty when she threw back the covers to get out again.

A bad day always made Mona feel as if she was on the edge of a relapse. She phoned me at seven o'clock one evening. 'I don't think I've been eating,' she said. The week before, she had finally managed to end her relationship with the sculptor, who had just had major surgery of his own. I went over to Camden to see if I could help. She was glad to have someone look after her for an hour or two, but careful to make it clear that though she was attracted to me, and knew I was attracted to her, she didn't want an affair with anybody at the moment.

I said I hadn't come for that. I didn't expect a return on helping someone.

She asked if she could hug me. I said yes. I was sitting on the sofa. She knelt on the floor in front of me and I put my arms round her. It felt awkward to me but it was what she wanted.

'I'm listening to your heart,' she said at one point. 'It's a great comfort to me.'

'You should cry as much as you want to,' I said.

She knelt on the floor like that for nearly an hour. To someone coming in we would have resembled one of Egon Schiele's relentlessly awkward couples, but without the sex. All I could think was how much her knees must hurt. I hadn't seen her for a month and she was even thinner than I remembered. Eventually she got up and went to bed. As soon as I thought she was feeling better, I cooked her a meal which we ate in front of the television. I made her promise to eat more often and take things easy for a few days. When I stood up to go at half past eleven or a quarter to twelve, she said anxiously, 'Are you sure you can get home at this time of night? If it's difficult you're welcome to stay.'

I would be all right, I told her, home was only a few stops along the Northern line. In fact I was tired out by the effort of cooking.

I wanted to go back so I could think about what any of this meant.

Two days later we were in a Pizza Express. She had asked me to explain the idea of 'quantum memory' to her so she could incorporate it into some work she was doing for the Slade foundation course. I was just saying something like, 'Light can be a wave or a particle according to what the observer expects,' when she interrupted: 'This is very phallic, isn't it? Here you are talking about very small things and look what I'm doing.' She was rubbing her fingers up and down the candle-holder on the table between us. I didn't know what to make of that so I said: 'It is, isn't it? Ha ha,' then I went back to explaining the dual nature of light.

'I've written it all down,' I said.

I walked her home. She went into the bathroom and changed into a pair of cotton pyjamas and a scruffy, homemade-looking grey pullover. 'I took what you said to heart,' she told me. 'I really did. Honestly, I've been eating much more.' She spread a portfolio of her work on the floor so that we could look at it. There were photographs of strange tall constructions she had made using bandages, wire, scraps of paper with quotations about illness on them. She had photographs of her surgery, and of the sculptor's. She was interested in text as object. She said that she used quotes from other people because she found it hard to trust her own opinions. I said that I had got round that in the 1970s by presenting my own opinions as quotations from other people, which seemed to authorise them for me until I had enough confidence to present them as my own. Then I made a cup of tea, watched part of a television programme about risk management, and got up to go at about half past eleven.

'It's quite late,' she said. 'You're welcome to stay if it's too late to get home.'

'The tubes run for another hour,' I said.

Earlier I had signed one of my books to her. Inside it I had written, 'Eat well. Get strong. Take care.' It was a novel about a woman who wanted to fly but the best she could get was a cosmetic treatment that made her look like a bird. I apologised to Mona that all my books seemed to feature women who became very ill after a series of operations.

This is what I had written down for her about quantum memory—

Every particle that has ever been involved with another particle somehow remembers that involvement & takes it forward into the next transaction. Everything that has ever been joined remains joined in some way. This is only at the level of very small things.

Quantum indeterminacy:

(a) If you know where a particle is, you can't know its velocity. If you know its velocity you can't know where it is.

(b) Light can be described as both a wave-form or a particle. It is not 'both at the same time': it is genuinely one or the other according to what kind of machinery you use to observe it.

Quantum particles begin as a potential of the condition we call empty space. They are then 'observed', or locked into place, by the rest of the universe: that is, one of their potential states is contexted by local conditions and 'chosen' to become real. The option the universe didn't take up, however, still continues to exist in some more informal way.

Since each of these options can be spoken of as having a 'memory' of the other, and since every mechanism for human memory proposed so far – from chemical cellular memory to a more broadly distributed holographic memory – has been discounted, some scientists have toyed with the idea that memory may be stored at the quantum level in transactions like those I've described.

As science it is speculative. As a metaphor quite nice. All the rest – quantum indeterminacy, the dual nature of light and so on – is fact, as far as fact can be ascertained using contemporary experimental tools.

It was time I learned to protect women from my enthusiasms: so the ex-scriptwriter had told me, just before she ended our relationship on the grounds that a photograph of me with an old girl-friend had appeared in the pages of *Publishing News*. Women, she believed, saw men's enthusiasm as a form of bullying. She called it 'male energy'. I wasn't protecting Mona from my enthusiasm by sending her confused ideas about quantum physics printed in 18 point Gill Sans Condensed Bold type. Perhaps Mona thought of enthusiasm as male energy too. Perhaps that was why she had found herself giving the candle a hand job in the Pizza Express.

Mona haunted her flat wearing her shabby pullovers with very short skirts and thick tights. She was part of the clutter, an uncompleted gesture, thin as a stick but always elegant. She was so composed I walked past her in the living room without seeing her. When I went back in she was standing by the table with one hand flat on the tabletop, staring down at a page of the newspaper, lifting it but not quite turning it.

'Hi,' I said.

'Oh, hello!' She spoke as if she had forgotten there was anyone else in the flat; or as if I had rung her up after a long absence.

'I thought you were in the other room,' I said.

'No,' she said. 'I was here all the time.'

That evening we went into the West End to see *The English Patient*. Mona walked very slowly along Shaftesbury Avenue to the cinema. We got seats at the end of a row and sat leaning a little away from each other. She had taken the outer seat so that she could stand up in the aisle when she needed to. Standing up was one of the techniques she had been taught to help manage her pain. In one scene in the film a man was supposed to be having his fingers cut off. Or perhaps it was his thumbs. You didn't see anything, but there was a sudden indrawn breath from the audience. All over the cinema people were wincing in case they did see something. Mona gasped and clutched my hand. She pulled me closer to her and we sat like that for a moment or two.

'I'm not sure about that film,' she said on the way out of the cinema. 'Its heart's too far in the right place.'

I asked her what she meant.

'Oh, I don't know,' she said. 'I think I need a cup of tea.'

When we got back to her flat, I went to the kitchen to make it. While I was in there putting teabags in the cups and doing a bit of washing up while I waited for the kettle to boil, I heard her go into the bathroom then come out again. 'I'm getting into bed,' she called. 'It's cold in here. Aren't you cold?' I said I was OK. When I took the tea into the front room, she had the television on. We watched that and drank our tea, and then I got up to go.

'I worry about you leaving so late,' Mona said. 'Are you sure you can get a train this late? It would be so easy for you to stay.'

'No,' I said. 'Honestly, the trains seem to run forever.'

'You could be mugged or anything,' she said.

I laughed.

She had the bedclothes up to her chin. She was just eyes.

'I want you to stay,' she said.

'That's different,' I said.

I took the cups away and switched the TV off. She watched me undress. Then she lifted the edge of the quilt to encourage me to get in with her.

'I thought you'd still have your clothes on,' I said.

She looked up at me anxiously, holding the quilt back so I could see.

'I'm bleeding a bit,' she said. 'You won't mind, will you?'